FRANKIE BEST HATES QUESTS

The accidental adventure of a lifetime

CHRIS SMITH

Illustrated by
KENNETH ANDERSON

PUFFIN

PUFFIN BOOKS
UK | USA | Canada | Ireland | Australia
India | New Zealand | South Africa

Imprint is part of the Penguin Random House group of companies whose addresses can be found at global.penguinrandomhouse.com.

www.penguin.co.uk www.puffin.co.uk www.ladybird.co.uk

First published 2022

001

Text design by Anita Mangan

Printed and bound in Great Britain by Clays Ltd, Elcograf S.p.A.

The authorized representative in the EEA is Penguin Random House Ireland, Morrison Chambers, 32 Nassau Street, Dublin DO2 YH68

A CIP catalogue record for this book is available from the British Library

ISBN: 978-0-241-52211-0

All correspondence to:

Puffin Books, Penguin Random House Children's
One Embassy Gardens, 8 Viaduct Gardens
London SW11 7BW

For my mum

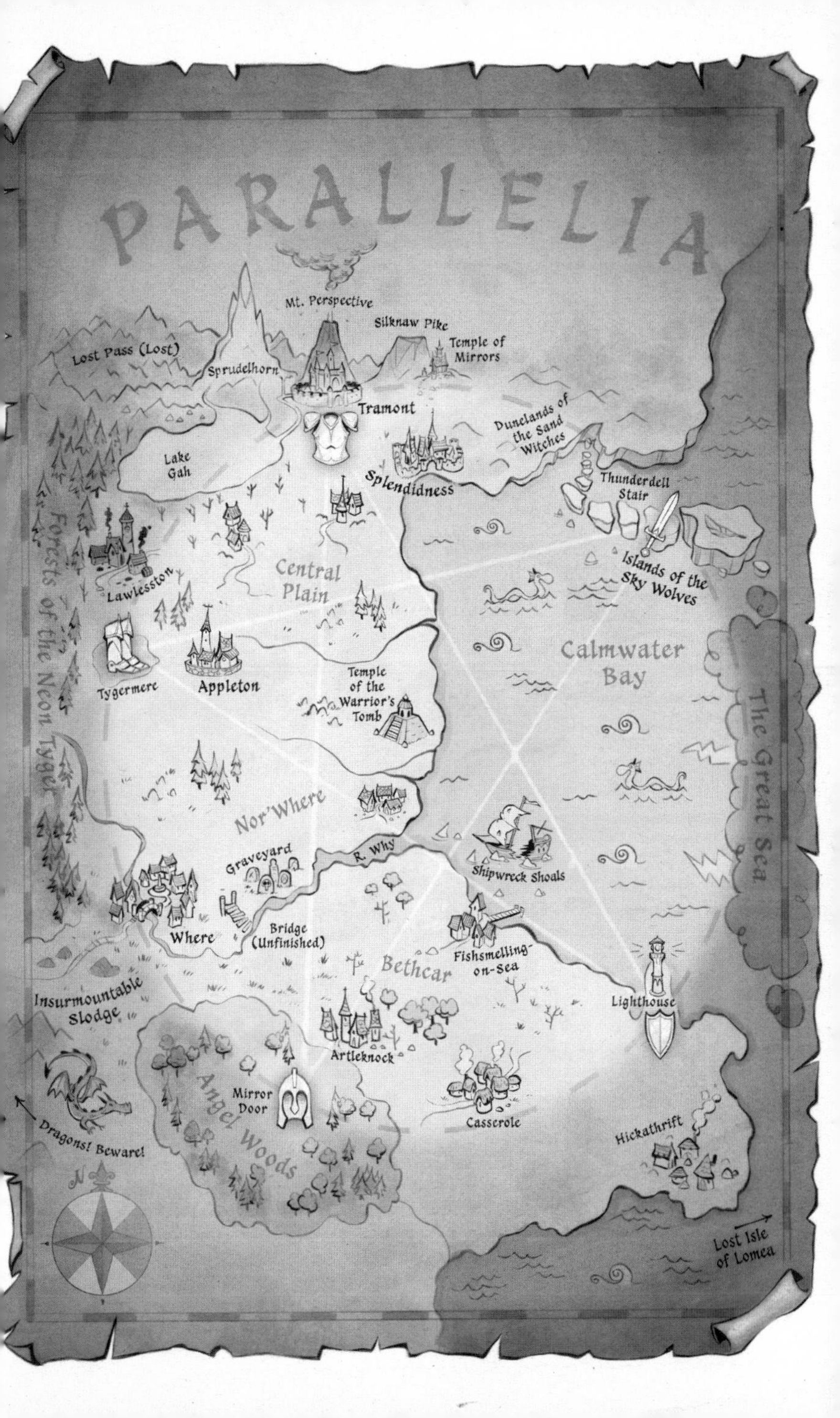
PARALLELIA
Mt. Perspective
Silknaw Pike
Temple of Mirrors
Lost Pass (Lost)
Sprudelhorn
Tramont
Dunelands of the Sand Witches
Lake Gah
Splendidness
Thunderdell Stair
Forests of the Neon Tyger
Lawlesston
Central Plain
Islands of the Sky Wolves
Calmwater Bay
Tygermere
Appleton
Temple of the Warrior's Tomb
The Great Sea
Nor'Where
R. Why
Graveyard
Shipwreck Shoals
Where
Bridge (Unfinished)
Bethcar
Fishsmelling-on-Sea
Lighthouse
Insurmountable Slodge
Artleknock
Mirror Door
Angel Woods
Casserole
Dragons! Beware!
Hickathrift
N
Lost Isle of Lomea

Right, listen.

I just want to make one thing totally clear before we get going, OK?

This is not a story about some mystical quest through a magical land.

It's not a story about fantastical creatures, or elves, or witches, or any of that rubbish.

Just wanted to get that out of the way before Chapter 1, in case you were put off by the title.

And, most of all, it is not a story about a princess.

Even though that's what my dad always calls me – Princess.

And that's what he called me on the day this story begins. The day he said goodbye.

Frankie Best

CHAPTER 1

'OK, Princess?'

In the back seat of the car, Frankie Best scowled so hard that her eyes almost vanished inside a fold of face. '**Don't**,' she growled, '**call me Princess**. You know this. Frankie's fine. Just Frankie.'

Her father took one hand off the steering wheel to hold it up in a gesture of apology. 'Sorry, sorry,' he said over his shoulder. 'Are you OK, Just Frankie?'

She gave a brief scorn-snort that meant *I'm twelve – too old for that lame dad joke*. But somehow a side order of smile squeezed its way in at the same time. 'The answer to your question, Just Dad,' she replied, 'is a giant-sized no. Why did Aunty Fi's appendix have to explode – this week of all weeks?'

Beside her in the back seat, her brother Joel looked up from his book. 'Did it actually explode?' he asked, eyes wide. 'Cool!'

Annoyed, Frankie batted the book from his hands. 'Of course it didn't actually explode,' she told him. 'Body parts don't just explode. Only an eight-year-old would think that.'

'HEY!' protested Joel. '**You lost my place!** I'd just encountered Throm the Barbarian.' He flicked frantically through the pages, muttering to himself. 'I remember battling the Rock Grub at 352 – I'll have to start again from there.'

Frankie rolled her eyes and gave a dramatic *humph*, pushing herself backwards into her seat as if it would slow the car down and delay her exile. She'd been looking forward to spending a week with her aunt while Mum and Dad went off on their latest expedition. Fi was her dad's sister – much younger than him – and she was basically a non-stop spoiling machine. 'Help yourself to anything you want!' was her mantra, and her house was always well stocked with treats.

But there would be no week with Fun Aunt Fi this time. She was in hospital, recovering from an emergency operation, and, after a series of increasingly frantic phone calls, Frankie and Joel were about to be abandoned at their grandad's house. The prospect made Frankie almost yearn for her own bout of appendicitis. It wasn't that she didn't like her grandfather – it was just that she hardly knew him. She had vague memories of playing with him when she'd been tiny, but over the last few years the old man had become a virtual stranger.

As if reading her thoughts, Frankie's mum twisted round in the passenger seat. 'I know Grandad's place isn't exactly kid-friendly,' she said.

'Is that why we never go and visit him, ever?' said Joel, thumb jammed firmly in the middle of his book.

His mother ignored the question. 'But you're old enough to amuse yourselves for a week, right?'

In reply, Frankie waved her phone, which throughout the entire conversation had been clasped firmly in her right hand, and Joel held up his book.

'Well, there you are, then,' their mum said decisively. 'You've both got a good week's worth of entertainment sorted there.'

Automatically, Frankie glanced down at the screen in her hand. No messages had popped up for the last few minutes. With a jolt of shock, she saw the words

NO SIGNAL

across the top and her own startled face reflected back at her from a rectangle of blankness. 'Oh!' she exclaimed. 'There's no service – but we're not there yet, right?'

'Here we are,' sang her dad, pushing the button to put on the handbrake. 'And there's Grandad, all ready to . . . **What on earth is he doing?**'

With difficulty, Frankie tore her eyes away from the horrifying words on her phone to see that they'd parked in front of her grandad's house. It stood in its own large garden overlooking a neatly mown village green, and it was impossible to look at it without the word 'ramshackle' coming to mind.

In fact – Frankie thought to herself as she looked up at the many windows, none of which seemed to be at the same level – *the word 'ramshackle' doesn't quite do it justice. Frankly, it's an insult to rams. And shackles. This place is a dump.*

In the overgrown front garden, wading in waist-high weeds, stood a man in stripy pyjamas and a

purple dressing gown. His long white hair was held back in an untidy ponytail and he was clutching an enormous green net in one hand. He was peering intently through one of the front windows of the house, crouched down slightly and with his other hand held up to the glass to shield his eyes from the bright sunshine.

'Why is Grandad looking in through his own front window?' asked Joel, pressing his face closer for a better view. 'And why is he holding a net? And why isn't he dressed at –' he glanced down at his sister's

phone – 'three twenty-three p.m.?'

'Dad!' shouted their mum sharply, snapping her door open and stepping down into the lane. Grandad turned his face towards them, holding a finger up to his lips. 'Wait in the car for a minute,' Mum told the rest of the family. 'It looks like I need to have a word with him. Several words, in fact.'

Dad frowned. 'I thought you'd made this clear on the phone,' he said, exchanging a look with her. 'I thought he'd promised there wouldn't be any of this . . . this stuff for the week.'

'I thought so, too,' she replied, looking over the car roof at her pyjama-clad parent with an expression that clearly forecast stormy weather ahead. Frankie recognized it from the time she'd spilled a whole can of fizzy orange on a new and very expensive cream-coloured rug. Without further words, Mum slammed the car door and strode into the front garden, grasping the old man firmly by the elbow and leading him inside.

'What stuff did Grandad promise there wouldn't be any of this week?' demanded Joel. 'Why is Mum angry with him? Is it something to do with the same reason we never come to visit Grandad? What does he want to catch in his big net?'

'Oh . . . butterflies, I should think, Joel,' said Dad.

Not especially convincing, thought Frankie. *And why did he only answer the last question?*

'Let's just wait here for a couple of minutes,' her father went on, 'and let Mum and Grandad have a little chat. Then we'll go in and get you settled.' He glanced at his watch. 'Flight leaves in three hours,' he muttered.

In the end, they only lasted five minutes in the car. With the sun beating down on the roof and the engine switched off, it quickly became intolerably hot. Plus, Dad kept glancing nervously at his watch, clearly impatient to get to the airport. Finally, he flung his door open. 'Come on, then,' he told them. 'Get your stuff. I'm sure that's enough time for Mum to tell Grandad not to . . . that is, to have a lovely catch-up with Grandad. Let's go in.'

Frankie grabbed her bag from the boot and trailed after her dad and brother, glancing once again at her phone, which still stubbornly insisted there was

NO SIGNAL.

As they approached the front door, she could hear her mum's voice, raised in full orange-rug-rage mode.

'You're always going on about wanting to see the kids more,' she was saying furiously, 'and I've been very clear about the conditions. For just one week, I ask you to keep that flipping door shut, to try and maintain at least an appearance of being something close to normal . . .'

'It just slipped through, Kate. It's not my fault,' answered Grandad. 'I thought I'd be able to get it back before you arrived, that's all. But the Sentinels can handle it – don't worry. I promise you, I'll take good care of the children. They won't know anything's . . . Oh hello!' He had caught sight of Frankie and Joel, bags in hand, standing uncertainly in the doorway. Grandad and Mum were facing each other angrily in the cluttered hallway, Mum with one pointing finger still raised.

'Did you catch any butterflies, Grandad?' asked Joel innocently. 'I like your house. We haven't been here for years and years and years. It's just like Spingle's Cottage, isn't it?'

'Butterflies?' their grandfather replied, coming over and squatting down with a click of old knees to be at eye level. 'No, not yet. But maybe we can have another go later – how about that? And what about you, Frances? Fancy a spot of butterfly hunting?'

'Frankie's fine, thanks, Grandad,' she told him.

Clearly, there was some fairly hardcore grown-up stuff going on here, but she wanted no part of it. There was only one thing Frankie was bothered about.

'Thanks for having us to stay,' she went on politely. 'Now, if you just want to give me the Wi-Fi code, that'd be great.'

Her grandfather's craggy face creased into a frown. **'The . . . the what? Whose code?'**

'Wi-Fi code,' Frankie repeated briskly. But, as her grandfather continued to look at her blankly, a cold spiral of pure fear wound its way down from her shoulders. Something fluttered inside her chest like a canary that's just about to have a really, really bad day down the mine.

Surely, Frankie thought to herself. *Surely* . . .

'The Wi-Fi code?' she repeated. 'The, you know . . . code. For the Wi-Fi. **WHY . . . FIE . . .**' She enunciated the last two syllables loudly, sounding like one of those annoying people on holiday who don't speak the language and just shout things slowly at the waiter as if they'll learn English through sheer volume.

'I don't know what that is, I'm afraid, petal,' said Grandad. 'Is it something to do with television?'

'Are you actually kidding me?'

'Because I don't have a telly, you see . . .'

By now, the canary inside Frankie was spiralling towards the ground like a downed fighter plane, black smoke belching from its bird bottom. **'WHAT?'** Her voice leaped up several octaves, and even more decibels, and at that moment there was a scuffling and a thump from the living room to her right.

'Dad . . .' said Frankie's mum in a warning tone of voice.

'Oh, don't worry about that,' he soothed. 'It's just, er, the cat. No, not the cat. I haven't got a cat, have I? It's just the, ah, the wind. Yes, terrible wind we get here. Wind central, it is.'

'Mum,' said Frankie pleadingly, 'you are not about to abandon me for a whole week in a house with no functioning internet connection? Right? And no TV even?'

'I've got lots of books,' Grandad protested mildly. 'And I think there's a couple of jigsaws somewhere.'

'I like jigsaws,' said Joel, nodding approvingly. 'Do any of them have dragons on?'

'Of course you like jigsaws,' Frankie told him. 'You're the world's biggest nerd.'

'I'm not actually that big,' he replied. 'I was one hundred and twenty centimetres high three weeks ago, which is below average for my age.'

Frankie released a brief scream of frustration.

Their dad – who throughout this whole exchange had been hovering in the front doorway, looking at his watch approximately every eighteen seconds – broke in at this point. 'Kate,' he said tensely, 'we've really, really got to go.'

'Go, go – we're fine here!' Grandad reassured him, his bright, bird-like eyes twinkling. 'Got everything you need? Long johns, igloo blueprints, reindeer repellant?'

'I can see where Mum gets her comedy talents from,' said Frankie icily. 'And there's no such thing as reindeer repellant.'

'Nonsense,' he said. 'I use it every day.'

'There aren't any reindeer around here.'

'Pre-cisely!' He grinned. 'Strong stuff, isn't it?'

Frankie groaned.

'Right –' her mum pulled her in for a brief hug – 'we're off. See you in a week. Be good!'

'But, Mum!' wailed Frankie. **'The Wi-Fi! And there's no phone signal. How am I supposed to –'**

'Bye!' Already her mother was waving from the garden path.

'Bye, Princess!' her father called cheerily, holding open the car door.

'DON'T CALL ME PRINCESS!' snapped Frankie automatically, but only half-heartedly. Suddenly she had other problems to deal with.

Within seconds, the car had started and roared away, carrying her parents towards their week in the wilderness above the Arctic Circle. But Frankie felt as if she had entered a wasteland far more challenging than the frozen tundra.

'No Wi-Fi at all – seriously?' she repeated weakly to her grandfather, hoping wildly that this had all been some form of elaborate welcoming joke.

'It'll do you good to spend a week without the **prrrrrrecious**,' taunted Joel.

That was his nickname for Frankie's phone – a nickname that she found incredibly infuriating, mostly because it was so accurate. Every time she reached into her pocket, it seemed he was somewhere nearby, croaking, 'The **prrrrrrecious** is calling us. **Yessss, musst** look at the **prrrrrrecious**,' until she chased him away. But now, of course, there was no point looking at it. She did anyway, though:

NO SIGNAL.

'Make yourselves at home, then,' said her grandad, looking slightly awkward and embarrassed now the three of them had been left alone. 'Feel free to, you know, have an explore.' He waved vaguely at the staircase.

'Awesome!' breathed Joel excitedly. 'This house is brilliant! I'm going to check all the wardrobes for fauns!' He pelted away up the stairs, leaving Frankie and her grandad alone in the untidy hall.

'I'm just going to check on the cat,' he told her. 'No, not the cat. Still don't have a cat. I'm going to check on the wind.' He disappeared into the living room, dressing gown billowing out behind him like a wizard's cloak. 'Don't worry!' he called over his shoulder. 'It won't be so bad. You'll see.'

'It's already bad,' moaned Frankie quietly to herself, slumping down on the stairs and closing her eyes. 'Badder than bad. No phone signal. No Wi-Fi. Trapped here for a week. This is worse than actual prison.'

The Journal of Frankie Best

I have decided to start this journal because it now seems inevitable that I

shall die of boredom within the next seven days, and I want to leave a record of my life so far. I've found this old notebook in my bedroom at Grandad's house and, although it feels kind of like school to be writing on actual paper with an actual pen, there is literally no alternative in this house, which appears to come from Victorian times.

My name is Frankie Best and I am twelve years old. I'm staying here at Grandad's house for a week while Mum and Dad go camping in the Arctic. You know, writing that down, it strikes me that's not an entirely normal thing for parents to do. Perhaps a bit of an explanation is in order. Here you go.

You know that mobile game *Spingle's Quest*? The one where you have to manoeuvre the little green elf, Spingle, round a forest, collecting gemstones? Everyone went absolutely mad about it like four years ago? Well, my mum and dad created it. And if *you're* now thinking to yourself: *Wow, cool parents!* well, that's exactly what I thought, too . . . four years ago. But I was eight, to be fair. The same age Joel is now.

When you're eight, having parents who designed the hottest game of the year is amazing. Everyone wanted to ask me questions about how they came up with the idea. Everyone wanted me to explain how to unlock that secret level where you get to play as a baby dragon. (There's a hidden door in the back of a tree trunk in the north-west corner of the forest, if you didn't look it up online already.) And everyone wanted to come back to mine for a play date to try and get secrets out of Mum and Dad about *Spingle's Quest II*,

then *Spingle's Quest III: The Dragon's Secret.*

My innocent little eight-year-old brain thought that *Spingle's Quest* was the most brilliant thing ever. I had posters on my bedroom wall, all the soft toys lined up at the head of my bed . . . the lot.

But last September it all went badly pear-shaped.

Over the summer, between the end of one school and the beginning of another, everything changed – and nobody thought to send me the memo. Loads of the same kids were there when I wandered through the gates on the first day. Sure, the lessons were going to be different, but surely things would be basically the same. How wrong could I have been?

Two of my best friends from my last school, Bernie and Evie, were talking to a crowd of kids I didn't know. I happily marched up to them and said 'hi' . . . little suspecting that I was about to be ambushed.

'Oh, here she is,' said Bernie to one of the boys. 'Hi, Frankie.'

I scattered a general wave round the crowd of newbies, along with what I now realize was my last truly innocent smile. My childhood was about to end with the finality of a crow flying through the rotor blades of a helicopter. And I know that's a troubling image – but I need you to understand just how hideous this was. Listen.

'Is it true then?' asked the boy, smirking.

He had a plump, reddish face and – I'm not just adding this in with hindsight, promise – a mean, smug kind of expression.

'Did your parents build *Spingle's Quest*?'

It's really hard to write down the amount of sarcasm he managed to get into those last two words. He said them in a kind of high-pitched, childish voice, elongating the 'l' sound, and tottering forward on tiptoe in a clumsy imitation of the way Spingle walks in the game. Everybody else in the group broke up laughing – including Evie, who I knew for a fact had been sleeping under an elf-themed duvet cover as recently as mid-July.

I shuffled my feet. Sure, now would have been the perfect time to stand up for my parents and their game. I should have had the strength of character to defend Spingle and all his elfy ways . . . but it was day one. School's a harsh, unforgiving place. So instead I curled my mouth into what I hoped was a cool, cynical sneer.

'Yeah . . . lamest thing ever,' I told him. 'I was hoping nobody would find out.' The laughter grew louder, but at least now we were all laughing together.

Just like that, my parents' job had gone from being the most wonderful thing in the world to a hideous embarrassment.

There seemed to be some unspoken agreement among everybody that now we were at secondary school, *Spingle's Quest* was no longer cool. There were certain things you were allowed to be interested in – phones being the principal one – but elves were definitely not welcome. And you know what? I felt embarrassed and, soon, pretty furious about it. I felt as if Spingle the Elf had let me down and made me look ridiculous in front of everybody.

That very first day I went home and took down the *Spingle's Quest* posters. I bagged up the soft toys – Spingle the Elf, Darzil the Dragon, Wombo the Wise Old Warlock, all of them – and stuffed them under my bed.

'Too grown-up for Spingle now?' said my mum quizzically when she came in to say goodnight. I groaned and pulled the duvet over my head.

'Do me a favour, OK?' I asked her. 'Just don't

mention Spingle the Elf to me ever again.'

There was a pause, then I felt her hand pat my head through the duvet before her footsteps receded and the door closed.

Anyway, look, I got sidetracked here. I was telling *you* where my parents were going for a week and why we were being dumped at my grandad's house, wasn't I? So basically, when they want to come up with new ideas, they take themselves off somewhere. And, as quite a lot of money's started coming in from the games, their expeditions have been getting more and more elaborate. To brainstorm ideas for *Spingle's Quest II*, they camped on some island in a Scottish loch. The third game was dreamed up in the Sahara Desert, would you believe – they spent a week messing about with camels there. And now, to come up with ideas for *Spingle's Quest IV*, they're spending a week trekking through Lapland.

They have two rules for these creative expeditions: it has to be somewhere they've never been before, and they have to be completely out of touch with the rest of the world. No phones, no emails, nothing. And, ironically, that's exactly the situation I now find myself in here at Grandad's house. We're not even supposed to be here – we're meant to be at Aunty Fi's, stuffing ourselves with chocolate in front of a huge TV. Curses upon Aunty Fi's rubbish, low-quality appendix and its ability to ruin my life.

OK – so I'm stuck here for the week. I'm going to make a list of things I want to do to fill the time.

1. Find a phone signal.

Yep, that should just about cover it. Frankie Best, signing off from Day One of the GREAT EXILE. If you find this book next to my wizened, died-of-boredom body, please tell my parents I will NEVER FORGIVE THEM FOR THIS – NO, NOT EVER.

Right, goodnight.

CHAPTER 2

Frankie's quest for a working phone signal began first thing the following morning. And, like all the best quests, it ended with the discovery of something very unexpected. Not that Frankie would have described it as a quest, you understand. Ever since she'd turned her back on all things to do with elves, magical forests and wizards, the word 'quest' had the same effect on her as a medium-sized electric shock. In other words, she didn't like it very much.

Frankie woke early and spent a few minutes looking up at the fluttering cobwebs in the corners of the ceiling, and being annoyed with the birds who seemed to be making a completely unnecessary amount of noise right outside the rickety old sash window. Automatically, she reached out for the phone charging on the bedside table, but the words

NO SIGNAL

were still firmly in place. The green battery icon showing it was a hundred per cent full seemed to be taunting her. *All juiced up*, it seemed to say, *and no messages to show you*.

A faint wisp of panic floated through Frankie's brain. What if someone had sent her a text and was wondering why she hadn't replied? What if her friends had started up a group chat without her? She had to know what was going on. Abruptly pushing herself bolt upright, she nodded to herself. It was time for action.

Grandad was already sitting at the cluttered kitchen table when she stumped downstairs. He was refilling an old-fashioned cup and saucer from a chipped teapot and whistling a little tune to himself, still dressed in his stripy pyjamas and purple dressing gown. This morning though, instead of bare feet, he was sporting a pair of large and very battered black lace-up boots.

'Going to work on the vegetables today,' he

explained, pointing to them out of the window. 'You're welcome to come and help me out with a bit of weeding if you like, Frances.'

'Frankie.' She corrected him automatically, sitting down and sorting through the mini cereal boxes he'd laid out, discounting the boring healthy ones that adults always feel obliged to sneak in. *He's obviously bought these in specially,* she thought to herself, softening slightly for a moment as she looked over at his long, thin face. *That was kind.*

Vague memories kept coming back to her the longer she spent in this rickety old cottage. Memories of playing here when she was a toddler, exploring up and down the wooden staircases. But it was too long ago to bring anything clearly to mind except a general sense of happiness and excitement.

'So – vegetables?' she asked, pouring something sugary into a bowl.

'That's right. Got some lovely marrows coming on.' He gestured out of the back window to a large area of raised vegetable beds partly screened by a tall hedge. They seemed to be the only part of the garden or – indeed – the house that was kept in any kind of order. A pile of plates was stacked beside the sink, and Frankie tried to eat her cereal without wondering too hard whether the bowl was completely clean.

'Happy weeding, Grandad,' she told him, 'but straight after breakfast I'm going to scour the whole region until I find somewhere my phone works.'

She'd spent a large part of the previous evening exploring the entire house, leaning out of windows and perching on chairs, holding her phone aloft like some sacred talisman, but to no effect.

'Well . . . nice day for it, at least,' he replied blandly, gesturing at the sunshine that was already pouring through the dusty windows.

'Morning, Grandad. Morning, Frankie,' came a voice from the hallway, accompanied by the sound of footsteps pelting down the stairs. 'Morning, Frankie's best friend, who is her phone. Did you catch the thing you wanted to catch with your big net, Grandad?'

Joel arrived in the kitchen, red-faced and excited, clutching a large black book in one hand. 'I looked for it all over the house until bedtime. I found this book though, which is amazing. So, did you catch it?'

'Eh, what?' Grandad choked slightly on his tea, looking up guiltily. 'No, no, I told you – it was just butterflies.'

'I know you said that when Mum was here,' said Joel matter-of-factly. 'But it wasn't butterflies. I'm *eight*. I know when grown-ups are lying. And the noise wasn't a cat, because you said you don't have a cat so it can't be. Non-existent cats make no noises. So, did you catch it?'

'Erm, no,' said Grandad reluctantly. 'I, er, think it's gone out of the front window, actually.'

'Aha!' Joel sat down at the table with a look of triumph. 'So it wasn't the wind, either! Because the wind doesn't go out of the front window.'

'Look –' Grandad waggled a teaspoon at him – 'whatever made the noise, it's no concern of yours, all right? Your mum would kill me if . . . What I mean is, it's all under control. It's being sorted. So don't you worry your head about it, young man. Eat your cereal and then you can come and help me thin out my seedlings.'

'Seedlings sound nice,' said Joel, absent-mindedly selecting a small box of something bran-based. 'Seedlings sound like little plant creatures that live in the warm earth with just their heads popping up. I wonder if there's anything about seedlings in this book full of strange creatures. Or maybe you wanted to catch a ping wing in your net.'

This time Grandad actually spurted tea out of his nose in shock.

'PLLLTHHHH!' he spluttered. 'A what? Where did you hear about them?'

He glanced guiltily towards the front door as if their mum was going to march back in and start telling him off. As he did so, a curious pendant slipped out of his pyjama top. It was a metal five-pointed star inside a circle, fastened round his neck on a leather thong. Frankie frowned – once again, a vague memory was being stirred up, like silt at the bottom of a pond.

'Ping wings? I read about them in here.' Joel was waving the black notebook.

'There's three whole pages about them. Look, Frankie!' He smoothed the book out on the table and pushed it towards her. 'It's full of amazing creatures. It's a bestiary!'

His sister peered over the top of her spoon and sighed in irritation. On the page Joel was indicating was a detailed drawing of a small, fat bird with stumpy little wings, carefully picked out in watercolour. The picture was surrounded by densely packed spidery writing in black ink.

'A bestiary,' Joel continued, 'is a book about strange, imaginary creatures.'

'Imaginary!' blurted Grandad. 'That's right! Just a bit of fun. That can't do any harm, can it?' He mopped his face with a tea towel, looking relieved. 'Imaginary,' he said to himself again. 'Yes, that's it.'

'I know what a bestiary is,' Frankie retorted, still gazing at the book. Something about it seemed oddly familiar. Once again, very old memories seemed to swirl and shift deep inside her brain. But before they could fully solidify, her grandfather reached over and slammed the book shut.

'Vegetables!' he declared decisively. 'You can look at the, erm, imaginary beasts later, all right, Joel?'

'OK,' agreed Joel, spooning what looked like milk-moistened hamster bedding into his mouth. 'Frankie, do you want to come and meet the seedlings?'

'That's a hard no from me,' his sister replied. She had, at best, a nodding acquaintance with vegetables. She didn't want to spend her Sunday getting on first-name terms with them – not even the baby ones.

'Is it because you're going to spend all day gazing at the **prrrrrrecious?**' Joel asked, using his cereal milk to gargle the last word irritatingly.

'I just want to catch up with my friends,' she snapped back at him. 'A concept you wouldn't understand as you don't actually *have* any.'

Frankie hated it when people accused her of being addicted to her phone. Her mum was always doing it, which seemed pretty rich coming from an app developer.

'I'm going into the village,' she announced, pointedly not asking if Joel wanted to come too. 'Thanks for breakfast, Grandad.' She left the table and sailed elegantly out of the front door and down the cobbled path, only slightly spoiling her air of cool unconcern by tripping over a pottery gnome.

• • •

The village where Frankie Best was doomed to spend her week of exile was, she had to admit, really quite pretty. A church spire rose above the rooftops of thatched cottages with neat hedges and flower beds. Directly opposite her grandad's front garden was a row of tall horse-chestnut trees and – beyond these – the large triangular village green, sloping gently downwards to a fern-fringed, duck-dotted pond.

Frankie marched across the neatly mown grass of the green, once again holding her phone aloft before her, expecting the screen to flicker into life at any moment. But the black rectangle stayed determinedly blank. The scrubbed stonework of the buildings reflected the sunlight as she sank down on to a bench, still holding up the phone as if the extra metre or so of altitude would actually help. After a while waving it from side to side, she finally gave up and stuck it moodily back in her pocket.

As the sun beat down on the back of Frankie's neck and the pond shimmered in the heat, she realized she'd stomped out of the house without drinking anything that morning, and began to regret her decision really rather a lot. Luckily, on the other side of the pond a sign declared:

in the centre of a row of cottages, and she wandered over with her tongue hanging out. Large windows on either side of the door were filled with posters, and a board of advertisements was covered with small, handwritten cards offering dog-walking services or lawnmowers for sale. An old-fashioned bell set on a long spring tinkled as she pushed inside, grateful to be out of the heat.

There didn't seem to be anybody around. The scrubbed wooden counter with its ancient-looking till was deserted. A beaded curtain that covered a doorway behind it was undulating gently as if someone had recently passed through. Frankie started to wander round the small shop, absent-mindedly picking things up and putting them down as she waited for someone to appear and let her pay for one of the cold drinks she could see stacked in a tall fridge near the door.

She nearly jumped out of her skin a moment later when a voice right behind her suddenly said, **'Oh, those are truly amazing, aren't they?'**

Frankie had been vacantly staring at the latest piece of produce she'd grabbed – one of those instant noodle pots. She was so alarmed she actually threw it high into the air as she spun round to see who had spoken.

A woman in a floral dress had appeared behind her, apparently having moved across the shop completely silently. She had kind, crinkly eyes and cheeks that were deltas of red veins framing a wide smile. But her hat was the thing that really caught Frankie's attention. Despite the hot day, she was wearing one of those large knitted hats with ear flaps – the ones people always buy at festivals and walk around in, looking as if they're off to herd alpacas in the Andes for a year. This one was fashioned from chunky yarn in garish shades of purple and orange.

'I'm so sorry I startled you, dear,' the woman said, reaching out a hand and deftly catching the snack pot as it tumbled earthwards. 'I just think these are absolutely marvellous, though.' She held out the pot for Frankie's inspection.

'Yeah . . .' Frankie wasn't quite sure how to respond to such enthusiasm for what were, after all, just instant noodles. 'They're, um . . . great.'

'Mumbai Madman,' the little woman read from the label 'That's my favourite flavour. It's an entire meal, you know!' She replaced it on the shelf. 'You just add hot water and stir, and within minutes – by total magic – it's become cooked noodles that taste of curry! It's really quite incredible. I don't think I'll ever get over it.'

By now, Frankie had started to think that the shopkeeper must be messing around with her. Nobody, surely, was that enthusiastic about instant pot snacks. 'I just wanted a drink, actually,' she mumbled.

'Oh yes, I've got those!' the woman said, the ear flaps on her hat bobbing as she bustled over to the fridge and gestured proudly as if revealing some priceless hoard of treasure. 'They do them in bottles,' she added, pointing to the bottom shelves, 'or these are made of metal!' She opened the door and brandished a chilled can delightedly. 'You open it at the top and it functions as a handy goblet! No need to pour!'

'Right . . .' Frankie eyed her suspiciously, but she seemed entirely sincere. 'I'll . . . just have one of these then, please,' she said, reaching gingerly past the woman to grab a lemonade.

Two minutes later, having been briefly delayed

while the shopkeeper marvelled at the detailed pictures on the coins she handed over as change, Frankie was sitting back on the bench with her drink, busily wondering whether she'd actually ended up in the country's weirdest village. Net-waving pensioners, mysterious noises, shopkeepers that were really, really strangely excited about noodles . . . She couldn't wait to see what her school friends would make of it when she messaged them.

If I ever can, she thought glumly.

Deciding to have one last try, she pulled out the phone and vainly waved it around in the air again.

'You'll have to get it higher than that,' called a voice from behind and – oddly enough – above her.

Frankie turned her head to see a tall wooden ladder propped against one of the trees at the top of the village green. Partly concealed among the foliage at treetop height was a boy in blue overalls. He was, thought Frankie, about her own age, and when he poked his head out from among the leaves she was puzzled to see that he, too, was wearing a pointy knitted hat with long ear flaps. This one was a shocking shade of bright yellow.

What was going on in this mad village? She

speculated wildly – some secret community of South American llama shepherds who'd decided to relocate to the English countryside because they were getting tired of being constantly spat at?

'No signal anywhere that low down,' said the flap-hatted kid, a hand emerging from the foliage to point at Frankie's phone. 'The only place I can get mine to work is up here!'

'And what, exactly, are you doing up a tree?' Frankie enquired politely.

'Oh, just trying to catch this p– this pigeon,' the boy replied.

At the same moment, there was a shaking and a commotion in the branches to his right. He lunged sideways. 'Got you!' The ladder wobbled crazily as the creature he'd caught struggled violently.

Normally, this would have been Frankie's cue to ask a few questions, beginning with Question One: *Why are you up a tree, catching pigeons?* But she had stopped paying proper attention several seconds ago when she experienced a flash of pure inspiration.

In cartoons, they sometimes draw this moment as a light bulb appearing on top of someone's head, and that was exactly how Frankie felt – as if a bright light had pinged into life right above her. She'd been looking past the boy in the tree towards her grandad's cottage – and she'd suddenly noticed something that made her whole head fizz. There was an entire row of small, crooked windows set into the tiles of the roof. Windows that, during her frantic signal-scouring expedition the night before, she was sure she hadn't looked out of.

Frankie scrambled to her feet. 'Thanks!' she called to the boy in the yellow hat as she sprinted past the bottom of his ladder and across the road to her grandad's house. 'See you later! Enjoy your captive pigeon!' She bundled up the garden path, babbling to herself: **'Attic. Attic, attic, attic. There's an attic. Where's the ladder to the attic?'**

She barged the front door open unthinkingly, upsetting a container of walking sticks that clattered wildly across the tiled hall, and charged up the stairs, still muttering 'attic' to herself like a mantra. On the landing, she scanned the ceiling excitedly, convinced there would be a hatchway she'd missed in the gloom of the previous evening.

At Frankie's parents' house, the area under the roof was what you might describe as a standard-issue loft – a triangular space that you access by pulling down a panel and climbing up a wobbly folding ladder. It was full of suitcases, cardboard boxes stuffed with ancient things like CDs or video cassettes and a persistent dusty, attic-esque smell. But her grandfather's house didn't appear to have hatches in any of the ceilings.

Brow furrowed in confusion, she wandered from room to room. None of them seemed to be on the same level – the wooden floorboards sloped off at strange angles and steps appeared in odd places to trip you up. Frankie crossed the landing, passing a set of shelves cluttered with more books and ornaments, including a large model of an old-fashioned sailing ship. She peered into her grandfather's bedroom, which overlooked the front of the house, but there was no hatchway there, either.

Next to it was a small, bare room that she'd explored briefly the previous evening. It had wood-panelled walls, and some kind of rustic ornament made of long, colourful feathers was suspended from the metal light fitting in the centre. It rotated slowly, catching the light as it turned.

Frankie stopped and sighed; this was the last room

to check, and there didn't seem to be an attic entrance in here, either. As a last resort, she went round, pushing the panels in the walls, smiling to herself at the prospect of one of them suddenly springing open. She wasn't expecting it to happen, of course – it was just a way of passing the time while she thought of other places to search. That being the case, she was more than a little surprised when, at her touch, one of the panels in the wall did spring open.

Frankie was so shocked by this turn of events that she hardly noticed the strange tingling sensation that shot up her arm simultaneously – almost as if it was coming back to life after she'd lain on it and given it pins and needles.

As Frankie's hand touched the wooden panel, it pivoted outwards like a door. At the same time it seemed to emit a slight glow, but her brain dismissed that as a trick of the light or a reflection from the bright feathers. She was much more interested in what was behind it – a narrow staircase. Frankie grinned in triumph. **Stairs = altitude. Altitude = contact with friends.** Without pausing, she levered herself through the narrow opening and began to climb, pulling her phone out of her jeans pocket as she did so and thumbing it into life.

Even if it hadn't been behind a secret panel – which it was – the staircase would still have been a very unusual one. It didn't just curve in one direction – it seemed to double back on itself more than once and change direction unexpectedly. Frankie had the strange feeling she was climbing up through a large snake; the staircase almost gave the impression that it was slowly moving.

But at that point she wasn't paying much attention to anything except the screen in front of her eyes as she desperately hoped for a signal. And sure enough, as she reached the room at the top of the staircase, there was a cacophony of chirrups, bleeps and whistles as all her different message-alert tones started to sing out at once. It was the sweetest sound she had heard in a full twenty-four hours and, without really looking around, she sank on to the edge of an oversized armchair and began to read and reply.

It's a funny thing, but the lives your friends have in your imagination are always way more exciting than they turn out to be in reality. Inside her head, all Frankie's contacts had been swapping jokes, chatting, doing loads of fun stuff, and she'd been missing out.

They'd been gossiping about her, wondering why she wasn't replying, getting all catty behind her back . . . In fact, it turned out nobody had really noticed she wasn't online. Sure, it had only been a day, but she couldn't help feeling a bit deflated.

When she told her Best Friends group she was stuck in her grandad's house with no phone signal, she had expected a tidal wave of outraged sympathy. However, there was nothing except

Oh cool, digital detox!
Enjoy!

from Bernie.

Despite the deluge of notifications that came in, it took Frankie a surprisingly short amount of time to glance through her chats, ignore the memes and reply to the few messages she'd been sent. Less than ten minutes later, she sat back huffily in the armchair – which she now noticed was very well-sat-in and therefore highly comfortable – and finally had a look around.

The room at the top of the house was lined with

bookcases filled with the oldest books Frankie had ever seen. Some had dark brown, cracked spines that looked almost like tree trunks, and a few were sewn together using what looked like pale, ancient leather. They were piled on the shelves untidily, but something about the groupings made her realize there was some kind of order in the chaos. It looked like whoever had put them there – Grandad presumably – knew exactly where each book was.

The windows she'd spotted from the village green – high up and frosted with dust and decades-old dead flies – filtered the late-morning sunlight into a soft-focus golden glow. *Great place to settle down with a book*, Frankie mused, before recoiling from that thought in horror. What was she thinking? She'd be joining arch-nerd Joel at the jigsaw table if she wasn't careful.

Underneath the window was a large, leather-topped desk with a sheet of yellowing paper spread out on top which was held down at the corners with four large purplish pebbles. And on the wall opposite was a large, brass-framed mirror, its ancient surface criss-crossed with cracks and scratches. The mirror, which hung from an odd-looking, elaborate hook, reflected the light in peculiar directions – it made Frankie's eyes feel funny as she stared at it, as though they were somehow trying to focus on something much further away. Slightly reluctantly, she dragged her gaze away from it, pushed herself out of the armchair and went over to the desk, rolling her eyes as she realized what was spread out beneath the makeshift paperweights.

It was a map – but not just any map. Not a normal map that tells you the way to actual places. This was the kind of map that Joel loved to draw – the kind her mum and dad spent hours putting together when they were designing their games. The kind (she pushed this thought away as soon as it surfaced) that until quite recently Frankie had loved to make herself.

It was a map of nowhere – a map of some weird, imaginary kingdom. There were several clues.

Firstly, the paper was thick and parchmenty – yellow and brown in places and frayed around the edges.

Secondly, it was drawn in ink, with forests and mountains shown as miniature pictures of trees and summits. Tiny images of what looked like swimming horses sported in the wide bay that filled the right-hand side of the map.

Thirdly, the names were a massive giveaway:

Fishsmelling-on-Sea,

Frankie read with another eye roll at the lameness of it all.

Splendidness,
River Why,
Lawlesston . . .

And the final sign that this wasn't a map to anywhere in the real world was the strange, starlike pattern that was traced over the surface in different-coloured inks. The lines joined different places on the map, creating the shape of a five-pointed star within a circle – one line was in faded red, another yellow, and one in some kind of glittery silvery ink.

Frankie traced the star with a finger. It seemed oddly familiar somehow. She had the strangest feeling she'd seen this exact shape very recently.

'Whoa . . . what is **that?**' gasped an excited voice behind her. She'd been so engrossed in the map and its strange pattern that she hadn't heard Joel climbing the stairs. 'How did you get up here?' he asked breathlessly, picking his way through the soft, dusty light of the attic room towards the table.

'Duh . . . up the stairs?' his sister replied.

'Yes, but how did you even discover the stairs? There isn't a door leading to them. How did you find the secret entrance? Have you been especially chosen by some mystical force? Why did it choose you and not me? You hate this kind of . . . **Wow! Look at this!**' His hand joined hers in tracing the odd pattern across the yellowed map.

'Why aren't you in the garden doing weeding?' she demanded.

'Seedlings,' said Joel sadly, 'are not as exciting as they sound. But this is **amazing!**'

'It's, like, the lamest thing ever.' Frankie was slightly needled that she'd been interrupted, but also determined to continue in her role of cool, fantasy-hating big sister. 'It looks like something you'd make up for one of your crazy stories about . . . What's the guy called?' Joel was always asking her to listen to tales he'd made up about his character in the role-playing game *Wyverns and Warlocks*, and she loved teasing him about the ridiculous name he'd given his fictional hero.

'Laideraan Ardvok is his name, as you very well know,' huffed Joel. 'Adventurer for hire and level-nine Ranger.'

'Looks like the sort of place he'd be right at home,' she said sarcastically, nodding at the map. Her tone seemed to be lost on Joel, though.

'Yeah,' he said excitedly. 'It's fantastic, isn't it? Do you think Grandad came up with all this stuff? Look at this.' He jabbed a finger at the top of the map where a smoking mountain loomed over numerous pictures of houses. 'Why do they all live so close to the volcano, do you think?'

His sister shrugged. 'I dunno. They probably have, like, magical heatproof hats or something.'

She was fully expecting him to realize she was teasing him, but he was too enthralled with the map.

'Look here,' he whispered, fascinated, running his hand down to the south, where several of the coloured lines intersected in the middle of what was apparently a large forest. 'This is written in different pen.'

In spite of herself, Frankie leaned in close to see what he was talking about. Sure enough, among all the other writing in old-fashioned ink were two words in what looked suspiciously like modern-day biro.

'"Mirror Door",' read Joel. 'What's a Mirror Door?'

'Who knows? Who cares?' she said grumpily. 'Door made of mirrors? Mirror made of doors? What does it matter? It's just made up. Grandad must be writing some geeky fantasy story. Maybe that's where you get it from. You two should collaborate. Together . . . Grandad and Joel –' she adopted a deep, wizardy voice – 'open the Mirror Door!'

There was a deep click from across the room, like the tick of an enormous clock, followed by a long, horror-movie door creak.

'If I look round and find that mirror has opened up

like a door,' Frankie told her little brother, feeling a chill on the back of her neck, 'I am going to freak out. Like, majorly.'

'It hasn't opened up like a door,' said Joel, looking over his shoulder.

'Thank crikey for that.'

'It's more kind of flapped downwards, like a hatch.'

'What?'

She spun round, suddenly realizing that the chilly feeling on her neck had nothing to do with fear. Cool air was blowing through the hole where the mirror had been. It had, indeed, pivoted on some hidden hinge along the bottom edge to reveal a large semicircular opening in the wall. And beyond, bathed in copper-coloured moonlight, was a tranquil woodland with tall trees stretching off into the distance.

CHAPTER 3

THE WOOD BEYOND THE WORLD

For a long, long moment, Frankie and Joel stared across the attic at the Mirror Door and the moonlit wood beyond. It's the sort of thing you need a bit of time to process.

'How come there's a load of trees in Grandad's attic?' said Joel finally, opting for the obvious question to start with. 'Why is it night-time there? Why did the door open when you told it to?'

Frankie's brain had been busily pushing all these questions away as fast as they occurred to her, particularly the last one. 'It's completely and utterly impossible,' she said softly, shaking her head in denial. 'It can't possibly be there. Grandad must have, I don't know . . . decided to play a trick on us or something. It's some kind of clever . . .' She floundered around for the right word.

There isn't a word for mysterious woodlands appearing behind mirrors in attics, Frankie thought, *for the very simple reason that it Just. Doesn't. Happen.*

'But it's *there*,' Joel argued correctly – and therefore infuriatingly. 'It can't be impossible. It's right there.'

'I *know* it's right there!' Frankie actually stamped her foot with frustration. 'But that does not stop it being impossible. You can't just have a . . . a . . . I don't even know what you'd *call* that. A portal?'

'I guess you'd call it the Mirror Door,' Joel replied calmly, pointing back at the map. 'And it's theoretically possible. I've read about it. I assume you're not familiar with the Many-Worlds Interpretation? Quantum decoherence?'

'You are so infuriating,' Frankie told him, walking gingerly across the wooden attic floor to peer at the wood. 'What is quantile decompression, or whatever? Does it make woodlands grow behind mirrors? I don't remember doing that in science last term.'

Beams of moonlight hit the soft forest floor, making a web of shadows, and as her eyes grew accustomed to the gloom, she could see tiny dark shapes flitting to and fro across the nets of orangey moonlight cast by the branches. Dotted here and there in the trees were much larger shapes – patches of pale golden light. And suddenly there came a high, clear hooting.

Joel, who had moved across the attic to join her, grabbed her hand and shrieked. **'WHAT'S THAT?'**

A second hoot sounded from further away.

'Oh, now you're worried?' she asked him acidly. 'Welcome to my world.'

'Actually –' Joel visibly steeled himself as he stood on tiptoe to peer through the opening – 'I'm not sure whose world that is. Unless it's . . . No.' He shook his head.

'What?' Frankie prompted him. 'Come on – if you've had some kind of nerdy mental breakthrough, share it with the rest of the class.'

'I think if I say what I just thought you'll get annoyed with me,' Joel reasoned. 'You hate talking about it and you'll get cross with me if I say it.'

'Hate talking about *what*?' she demanded. 'Look, I promise I won't be cross with you. What do I hate talking about?'

'Erm . . . *Spingle's Quest*.'

'Oh, shut UP!'

'Told you.'

'OK, OK.' With a considerable effort, Frankie mastered her irritation. It was true – the mere mention of her mum and dad's game was enough to make her stomach fizz with a cocktail of different feelings: annoyance, frustration, embarrassment and a hidden, secret dash of sadness. 'So what's this got to do with the stupid game, anyway?'

'Well, remember I said Grandad's house looks like

Spingle's cottage? And how, when he sets out on his quest, Spingle goes through the secret doorway into Owl Forest?'

'Yes.' Frankie had to wrestle a pang of nostalgia as she remembered how exciting that moment had been the first time she'd ever played the game. Back before the pre-teen hive mind at her school had decided it was pathetic and pointless.

'So –' Joel stood up even higher on his toes and pointed – 'that's a forest, right? And those are owls.'

Frankie scoffed. 'They're not owls,' she said. 'Owls don't glow in the dark. Oh, hang on.' She squinted into the night and gave what started out as a gasp of delight, but swiftly got turned into a huffy little snort. 'Oh man. They actually are.'

Now her eyes had fully adjusted to the dim light of the other world, Frankie was taking her first proper look at it. And forever afterwards, when she closed her eyes, she was always able to picture the way it had looked that first day – that first night.

The silent forest stretched away in front of her, the thick trunks and curled branches of the trees burnished by the moonlight. The light from one world – the one where it was still late morning –

spilled through the semicircular opening. It stretched out across the mossy ground to form a high arch with their two tiny silhouettes picked out at the bottom as they peered through. Once again, that clear, high cry sounded through the night, and this time Frankie could see exactly where it came from.

Perched on a branch of the nearest tree, regarding her calmly with its large eyes, was a slender golden owl. Not simply gold-coloured, but actually glowing, like a hoard of magical treasure in some dream. Soft light spilled out from its neat feathers to light up the branch – that's what the patches of light among the trees were: numerous softly glowing owls. Not a phrase you hear every day.

Frankie's mouth had dropped open in astonishment, and suddenly something flew slap bang into it. **'Bleargh! What's that?'** she said, spitting and fanning a hand in front of her face. Hordes of tiny dots had begun to swarm round the opening.

'They're moths,' Joel replied from beside her. 'The light's attracting them.'

Frankie looked down to see that one of the dark shapes had landed on the frame of the mirror and was crawling downwards, fluttering its delicately patterned wings. 'You're right,' she said grudgingly.

At that moment, the owl nearest to her leaned forward slightly and snapped its beak. She saw a brief glimpse of a dark shape in its mouth before it tipped its head back and swallowed.

'Angel owls emit a soft glowing light which attracts the moths on which they feed,' said Joel. 'These beautiful creatures give their name to Angel Woods, the thick forest that covers the southern slopes –'

But Frankie interrupted him, startled. 'Wait a minute – how do you know this all of a sudden?'

'It's in here.' Joel lifted his right hand to reveal the black notebook he'd been trying to show her at the breakfast table. 'It's written in Grandad's Bestiary.'

Sure enough, on a double-page spread was a picture of one of the elegant owls and a detailed drawing of one of the dark moths, once again surrounded by dense black handwriting.

ANGEL OWLS

Angel owls emit a soft light which attracts the moths upon which they feed.

These beautiful creatures give their name to Angel Woods, the thick forest that covers the southern hills of Parallelia.

I'm told by local forest knelves that family groups of angel owls have been known to hoot in harmony, although I have never managed to witness this.

Angel owls appear to have only one predator, the voice~throwing ventrilo~hawk, which distracts them by impersonating their distinctive cry before attacking them from behind.

'This makes no sense whatsoever,' muttered Frankie.

'Beautiful, though, isn't it?'

'Yeah, that's how it starts,' she grumbled, peering round the forest. 'It's always beautiful to start with. I've read your nerdy books. At first, it's all "ooh" and "aah", but later on there's . . . I dunno. Monsters or something.'

'Goblins?' breathed Joel. 'Or actual elves?'

'Goblins and elves are not things,' Frankie insisted, sounding as if she was trying to convince herself rather than her little brother.

She strained her eyes into the darkness, trying to work out whether any more of this strange land was visible beyond the wood. Stars glittered through the branches of the trees, and far away she could make out a dull reddish glow above the horizon. The forest floor sloped gently downhill away from the Mirror Door, but the only things she could pick out in the distance were the tiny smudges of glowing gold that had to be more owls in trees down the hillside. As she watched, some of the furthest ones began to float upward as if drawn by a magnet into the night sky.

'The owls are flying off down there.' Joel pointed. 'Look. Why are the owls flying off?'

'Something's scaring them,' said Frankie grimly.

Her scalp prickled. Something had indeed entered the forest and was coming up the hill towards them. 'I hate being right all the time,' she complained softly.

More points of light had now appeared – lower down, sharper and more defined than the diffuse, golden owl-glow. Spots of flickering yellow, bobbing rhythmically up and down, and growing larger frighteningly fast – torchlight. Flaming torches being carried by several people. (*People? Definitely people?* thought Frankie. *Not monsters?*) People who were, apparently, running up the hill towards them. Clear owl cries rang out as more and more of the glowing birds took wing, zigzagging upward through the branches to merge with the stars.

At that moment, booted footsteps thundered on the staircase behind them. Frankie tore her eyes away from the night-time wood and turned to see her grandfather plunge through the door, wide-eyed and clutching a muddy trowel in one hand.

'What on earth have you done?' he wailed, racing to the Mirror Door, dressing gown flapping, and watching as the torches grew closer. 'How did you get up here? How did you open the door?' he went on wildly, gripping the edges of the opening with whitened knuckles and peering out into the dark wood. 'Oh my stars. Your mother is going to absolutely murder me. And not in a good way. This is terrible.'

'I'm . . . sorry, Grandad.' Frankie shuffled her feet, not quite able to tell whether the old man was completely furious or utterly terrified, but either way it was clearly her fault. Guilt tightened clammily round her like a damp wetsuit. 'I just kind of . . . told it to open. By accident, though. We were just joking around.'

But her grandfather was only half listening. Grabbing a wooden chair, he perched on it to swish a long, thick curtain across the high windows, plunging the room into a darkness that matched the wood beyond the doorway. 'But, Frances –' he began.

'Frankie.'

'Frankie then.' His muddy black boots thumped loudly on the wooden floor as he hopped down off the chair, running back to the opening and peering through. 'You said the Mirror Door opened for you? It wasn't already open when you got in here?'

'No. Like I said, I just kind of asked it.'

Her grandfather turned to grasp her shoulders

and stare deep into her eyes. 'Well, petal' he said, his face crinkling up like paper and his eyes glistening as he smiled, 'that's a curve ball, isn't it?'

'What is?'

'No time now,' he told her, eyes snapping sideways at the sound of harsh voices from the wood. 'Seems like someone's interested in the portal. They must have seen the sunlight. You two, hide under there. I'll go and speak to them.'

He herded the two children towards the map table. 'Whatever happens,' he warned, 'don't make a sound. If anything goes wrong, talk to the Archers. They're my Sentinels – they'll know what to do.'

Rapidly, he shoved both of them underneath the table, kicking boxes across the floor to seal them in. And now a firm memory of playing with her grandfather in this very house came back to Frankie. He'd pulled all the cushions off the sofas to make a fort for her – she remembered them chortling with delight together as they hid from her parents. Now, though, she was hiding for real.

Peering through a crack between two boxes, she saw her grandfather straighten up, smoothing back his long white hair. 'Not a sound now,' he told them as, with a surprisingly agile movement, he vaulted through the Mirror Door to stand in the forest clearing. Frankie could only see his head and shoulders as the voices among the trees grew louder.

'It's him!' There was a clanking and the thumping of heavy footsteps as a high-pitched, reedy voice spoke. 'It's the custodian! I knew I saw a light up here.'

Someone grunted. 'Two down, two to go,' said a much deeper voice in a satisfied tone.

'Can I help you with something?' asked Grandad calmly, but with a hint of steel behind the bland words.

Frankie strained forward with all her might, but couldn't see who he was talking to without moving the boxes – and she was far too confused and terrified to do that.

'Help us, hmm?' asked a soft voice sarcastically, and there was a ripple of laughter. It was a peculiar voice – every few words, the speaker broke off to hum parts of a strange, high-pitched little tune.

'Yes, I rather think you can, ah, help us, hmm.' And, once again, there was a snatch of a peculiar, mournful melody before he continued. 'You can get in this cage, you see, so we can take you to Tramont Castle, hmm?'

'Oh yes?' Grandad's gaze flicked back over his shoulder for a split second to the room where his grandchildren were hidden. 'And what if I don't fancy getting in a cage?'

'Well, in that case, hmm,' continued the voice calmly, still with that high, thin humming breaking in from time to time, 'my large friend here will have to, how shall I put this? Hmm. *Persuade* you. Allamort, add this one to the collection.'

A loud thudding and a faint vibration in the floorboards told Frankie that someone very, very heavy was moving. And then she had to clamp a hand over her mouth to stop herself from crying out as the owner of the huge footsteps appeared in the opening beside her grandad. He was enormous, towering above the old man, with his yellow eyes blazing. His skin was bone white, and on top of his smooth, bald head two short, sharp horns curved upward. Without fuss, he grabbed Grandad with thickly muscled arms and flung him over his shoulder like a sack.

'Good. Now, get the helmet, quickly,' instructed the sneering voice, its owner still out of sight, and there was more commotion somewhere to the right.

'Don't you dare touch that!' said Grandad

furiously. **'What on earth do you think you're doing? You can't move the Talisman!'**

'You know, I rather think we can,' the voice replied, still infuriatingly calm, before once again he hummed a short snatch of that peculiar high-pitched tune.

'Got it!' said the reedy voice that had spoken first, and there was a raucous cheer.

'Well, that was easy,' the sneering voice replied. 'What's this?'

Frankie felt Joel stiffen in fright beside her as the thin, high voice came closer. 'Look at this – the custodian's got himself a little hidey-hole in here.'

Long fingers grasped the lower sill of the Mirror Door and a thin pale face with a pointed nose appeared in the opening. The man had greasy, straggly hair and quick, darting eyes. Frankie froze, terrified that his constantly moving gaze would fall on their hiding place at any second.

'What do you think he keeps tucked away in here, then?' the man said over his shoulder. 'Treasure? A few more nice shiny pretties like this? What do we reckon, eh?' As he spoke, he brandished an elegant, shining silver helmet in his other hand.

'Stop – hmm, stop waving that around and come back here,' snapped the second voice, its calm, sneering quality now edged with irritation. 'It's a long march to the coast, and there'll be plenty of treasure for all of you when my, hmm, work is done.'

Reluctantly, the rat-faced man withdrew from the doorway. 'All right, Haggister, no need to get angry. I was only looking.'

'Well, look another time,' the man who seemed to be in charge told him. 'Focus on the job. The sooner you follow me to the next custodian, hmm, the sooner you'll earn your reward.'

More cheering greeted this pronouncement, gradually fading as the kidnappers turned and headed back down the hill. Frankie could see their bobbing torchlight reflected on the attic wall, casting huge shadows as they moved away through the trees. But after a few minutes it – along with the sound of their voices and clomping feet – had faded back into darkness and silence. One single, pure cry sounded from one of the angel owls in the distance.

After a moment, Joel kicked aside the boxes and scuttled out from under the table.

'HEY!' Frankie grabbed at an ankle and missed. 'What do you think you're doing? Never heard of the "pretend we've all gone and wait till they come out of their hiding place" trick?' But, when nobody appeared through the Mirror Door to snatch her little brother, she reluctantly decided it might be safe and crawled out herself.

'Grandad's been kidnapped by orcs!' said Joel dramatically, raising his eyebrows.

'He has not!' Frankie's brain was simply refusing to process all of this. 'Those weren't orcs.'

'Goblins then.'

'What's the difference?'

'Well –' Joel clasped his hands behind his back, preparing to enter lecture mode – 'technically, *orc* is an elvish word . . .'

But Frankie interrupted him. 'You know what? Save it, OK? This is not the time.'

Panic was now floating round her like a cold mist. Desperately, she squinted through the Mirror Door and down the hill into the trees. The mossy ground was torn up by heavy footprints – divots of earth lay scattered here and there – but the wood now seemed utterly deserted and silent. When the doorbell rang, they both jumped so sharply that it was a miracle nobody hit their head on the actual ceiling.

'That's the doorbell,' Joel said.

'Oh bravo.' Frankie applauded him sarcastically. 'Congratulations, Great Wizard Obvioso. Incredible deductive powers.'

'I'm going to see who it is,' said the Great Wizard Obvioso with a sniff, pulling open the attic door and disappearing down the snaking staircase.

His sister continued to look out through the trees. She could still see that dull reddish gleam far away and glanced across at the map, remembering the tiny picture of a volcano. Was that what was causing the sky to glow a moody red? Or was dawn on the way in this strange place?

After a few seconds, she heard voices downstairs,

and footsteps moving rapidly through the house. Joel was bringing someone upstairs with him – and they were running. Leaving the Mirror Door, she looked down the attic stairs. The first thing that came into view was a bright yellow hat.

'What do you mean, "kidnapped"?' a woman's voice was saying from below Frankie. 'What was he doing with the Mirror Door open, anyway? I've told him I-don't-know-how-many times. That's how these bloomin' things keep coming through. Took us hours to catch this one, it did. Anyway, who was out there? Who took him?'

Frankie steeled herself. Clearly, all the questions that were currently echoing round the stairway were about to be asked directly to her face in approximately fifteen short seconds.

The yellow hat came higher up the stairs, bringing its owner along for the ride. It was the gangly boy who'd been up the tree on the village green, and he was carrying a wooden cage. Behind him – puffing and panting like a steam engine racing a bullet train – was the woman from the general store. It was she who was asking the constant questions, directing them over her shoulder at Joel, who was bringing up the rear, having apparently opened the front door and been railroaded by this incoming stampede. The flaps on her purple and orange hat were whanging to and fro like the ears of a speeding dog.

'How long ago was he taken? Is there any sign of him? Is the door still open? Did he leave the . . . Oh hello, dear.' The question cavalcade briefly halted as she reached the attic and saw Frankie. 'Did you enjoy your metal sugar-drinking goblet?'

Of all the questions she could have started with, this one was so unexpected and weirdly phrased that it nearly floored Frankie. 'Erm . . . yep. Yes. Thanks,' she mumbled.

'Lovely.' The shopkeeper's exhaustion – having been left a couple of stairs behind – seemed to suddenly catch up with her, and she bent over, placing her hands on her knees and panting. The boy in the yellow hat, meanwhile, put down the cage on the attic floor and, without hesitation, hopped through the opening and into the wood.

'Any sign?' the woman called in between deep, gasping breaths.

'No,' he replied, kicking at an uprooted piece of

mossy turf. 'The trail's fresh, though.'

'Well, that's something,' she said, still panting.

Frankie's eye was caught by a flash of movement inside the wooden cage, and she squatted down to stare through the bars. Staring back at her was a small, furry face with bright eyes that glittered with fury.

'What's this?' Frankie reached out a finger gingerly. 'Is it a cat or something?'

At this, the creature's eyes widened and it chittered at her angrily. Small hands reached out to grip the bars and shake them, and the tufted ears on the top of its head quivered.

'Not sure it likes that comparison,' said the yellow-hatted kid, sticking his head back through the opening and grinning at her. 'No, that's not a cat. That, there, is a parallelian pook. A tree pook, to be precise.'

'A parallel Ian WHAT the actual?' asked Frankie, getting back to her feet.

'Pook,' he told her. 'A pook, as in that's what it is. And Parallelian, as in it comes from Parallelia.'

'And where is Parallelia, in fact?'

'This is Parallelia,' he replied, stepping back from the Mirror Door and spreading his arms to take in the moonlit woodland and the night sky above. 'The Kingdom of Parallelia. My home.'

'OK, good one,' said Frankie, holding up her hands in a gesture of submission. 'You had me going for a moment there, I admit it. I was really starting to think there was some mystical portal in Grandad's attic. The guy with horns on his head was a nice touch, by the way. Now, where's the camera? Come on. You've played your joke. Out you pop.'

As she said this, she was turning on the spot, scanning the attic in preparation for a camera crew to emerge from some secret hiding place to reveal she was part of a very elaborate prank show. At the same time, though, a small voice inside her head was talking in a dry, matter-of-fact voice.

There's no camera crew, it was saying. *This is real. This is all real.*

Angrily, she ignored it. She hadn't spent the last few months cleansing her mind and personality of all things to do with magical kingdoms in order for an *actual* magical kingdom to materialize in the attic and ruin her holiday.

'What's that, dear?' said the woman from the shop. 'You want to find a camera? It won't work through there, you know.'

'Frankie.' Joel had moved up beside her and was clutching the sleeve of her shirt. 'I don't think we're in a hidden-camera prank show. I think we're in, you know –' his voice dropped to a whisper – 'an actual adventure.'

'We are NOT,' she told him decisively, 'in an actual adventure. There are no portals to magical kingdoms. There are no big tough guys with horns who go charging about the woods, kidnapping grandparents. There are no magical silver helmets.'

'But remember in *Spingle's Quest* –'

'Gargh!' she said furiously, her frustration boiling

over. 'This is not *Spingle's Quest*! Listen. There must be a proper explanation for all of this. Elves. Do. Not. Exist. Got it?'

In reply to this, the boy reached up and, grasping the tuft at the top of his yellow woollen hat, pulled it sideways off his head. Underneath, his hair bounced up in soft dark puffs, and protruding from the locks on either side of his head were two distinctly, unmistakably pointy ears.

'You have got to be actually KIDDING me!' wailed Frankie, sinking to the floor.

CHAPTER 4

Elsewhere in Parallelia, beyond the woods and across the wide, wet wastes of the marsh called the Insurmountable Slodge, it was raining. It had been raining for several days and it showed no signs of stopping. Fat, sky-fridged drops came pelting down from clouds the colour of bruises, smacking into the earth as if it had personally offended them. The drops joined together into chilly streams that ran along a rough track, mingling with the churned soil to create a rich, silky mud that stuck to anything and smelled like the ends of horses. And one day, sending a sharp nose between the raindrops and a pair of stout boots through the mud, there came walking a woman in grey. She was not so very old, but her faded blue eyes looked tired and sad. Her name was Justice, and she was completely and utterly sick to death of soup.

Justice had been walking for days through the flat, characterless countryside of Nor'Where – the lands to the north of the town of Where. In fact, though she didn't know it, she was more or less exactly in the middle of Nor'Where. She didn't know that because she didn't have a map. But she did have a sword – a long and very, very sharp sword – beneath her long and very, very wet grey cloak.

At exactly the same time as – in another world – Frankie Best entered a shop, Justice stopped at the top of a small hill and wiped the raindrops from her face. In the valley ahead, her keen eyes could make out the lights of a village shining palely through the haze as the miserable, wet late afternoon shaded into a horrible damp evening.

A tinging, tapping noise came from somewhere beneath the sodden cloak. It was hard to hear above the constant hissing of the rain, but Justice immediately dipped a hand to her sword belt, pulling a small metal device from its leather pouch. She held her hand out flat in front of her, balancing the silvery-grey disc on her palm. It had a glass top, and inside a small needle wavered gently back and forth. One end was painted red and was pointing directly at the village ahead. If you're thinking it was a compass, you're right. But only half right.

As Justice watched, the tiny tapping noise came again as the needle jerked excitedly, hitting its red end on the glass above it. It was almost as if it was tapping deliberately, trying to tell her something. Which, of course, it was.

'Down there? You're sure?' asked Justice, peering through the downpour at the cluster of roofs below.

Ting, ting, tap.

'I hope it's something decent this time.'

Tap, tap, ting.

'Because, I've got to be honest with you, I'm almost done with this.' She sighed briefly, pulled her left boot from an unusually enthusiastic patch of mud with a slushy splat, and plodded off downhill.

In the centre of the village was a large inne. Justice knew it was an inne because of the large letters reading

on the door. On the other side it said

In the grimy window to one side, a crudely painted sign read:

and, in smaller letters in the bottom right-hand corner,

John Crude, Sign Painting.

Justice clicked her tongue in irritation. She had been walking across Parallelia for weeks now, and the only thing these innes ever seemed to serve was soup. She was, as we found out a minute or so ago, completely and utterly sick to death of it. It wasn't as if the recipe ever varied.

If you're thinking, *Ooh, maybe it's cream of tomato today, yum*, you're barking up the wrong ladle. In every Parallelian inne, there's a huge cauldron that sits by the kitchen fire. Any stray vegetables get thrown into it, with a bit of meat from time to time if the innekeeper's feeling particularly flush. So we're not talking soup of the day here. It's soup of the week. Soup of the month. Perpetual soup, in fact. Never-ending, ever-tasting-more-or-less-the-same soup.

At the same time as – in another world – Frankie Best accidentally uttered the words 'open the Mirror Door', Justice pushed open the inne door.

'Soup,' she muttered furiously as she shouldered her way inside. 'Why does it always have to be soup?'

The interior of the inne smelled like damp mushrooms, and there was something decidedly fungal about the customers as well, as they huddled round tables with their brownish clothes and pale faces. Justice wrinkled her nose as she stomped in, holding the metal disc on her outstretched palm. It clicked and whirred some more, before finally pointing to a round table full of men with piles of greasy-looking coins stacked in front of them.

She marched over and plonked the device down in

the centre of the table. The needle swung decisively, pointing firmly at a short man in a green hood who was holding a pair of dice in one hand, while the other protected a pile of coins much larger than its neighbours. There was a further tapping and tinging from the metal disc.

'I am a Justice of Parallelia,' said Justice to the green-hooded man, whose face had drained of all colour like a cheap ice lolly after its first lick. 'You have been detected as the source of an injustice. As such, you are required to make amends or face punishment. The Kingdom is the King.'

'The Kingdom is the King,' repeated everyone within earshot, except for the green-hooded man, who started pushing the pile of coins round to his neighbours, mumbling apologies.

'He's been cheating you,' Justice told the other people sitting round the table. 'Make sure you get all your money back, won't you?' And, swiping the metal device up from the table, she made for the bar and plonked herself down on a stool.

What is this strange device? you are probably now shouting at this book. *I must know!*

To which the response is: *Don't shout at books – it*

makes you look mad. But you can stop shouting, anyway, because the answer is coming up right now.

Each Justice of Parallelia – and there are many of them, all taking the name Justice – carries a powerful magical object that directs them to any injustices that need correcting. This device, with its metal casing and free-swinging needle, is known – for obvious reasons – as a Moral Compass. The Moral Compass not only points the way, but is also able to communicate with its Justice and tell them a few details about the crime in question.

Obviously, Justices hope to make their name solving large and very bad crimes, not simply minor cases of cheating at dice. Which is why this particular Justice was having some fairly stern words with her own Moral Compass as she reluctantly accepted a bowl of soup from the landlady.

'Loaded dice at some grimy little inne in the middle of Nor'Where?' she said crossly. 'This is small-time stuff. I'm better than this! Can't you track down a proper, big injustice for once?'

The Moral Compass tapped apologetically, and Justice returned to her perpetual soup. As she spooned up the hot, tasteless liquid, she gradually became aware she was being stared at. The kitchen door was partly open, and a pair of wide yellow eyes was gazing through the crack.

'Basin!' snapped the landlady. 'Don't stare at the Justice! Sorry,' she said to the woman in grey. 'He's always bothering travellers, asking questions about where they've been and what they've eaten.'

Basin was fascinated by the wide world outside the inne, and particularly by the food that might be available there. He was always suggesting different herbs or ingredients to try and make the soup better, but nobody ever listened to him. This was a pity, because it would have been almost scientifically impossible to make it taste any worse.

'Don't apologize,' replied Justice, privately thinking to herself, *If you're going to apologize for anything, it should be for the quality of this soup*. 'Come on out,' she called to the kitchen door, 'and say hello.'

Gradually, the door opened, and a young boy shuffled out. He had a plump, pink face with, as we know already, bright yellow eyes. Two sharp horns stuck out of his tousled brown hair.

'Always a pleasure to meet a young gnoblin,' Justice told him as he approached.

'Basin's one of our dish pigs,' said the landlady, primping her curly hair. 'He's a hard worker, ain't you, Basin?'

Basin didn't reply, instead staring, fascinated, at the Moral Compass sitting on the bar in front of Justice.

'Ever seen one of these before?' she asked him.

'Never a real 'un,' whispered Basin, looking like a fan of Christmas who had just been ushered into the actual North Pole workshop. 'A traveller did show me a picture once in a book.'

He reached out a trembling finger and poked the side of the compass's case. At that exact point, the Moral Compass launched into a frenzy of clicks and taps; its needle jerking and swinging so violently that it actually propelled itself across the bar like a clockwork toy.

'I never done nothin'!' squeaked Basin in a panic, drawing his finger back sharply and retreating like a scolded puppy.

'Don't worry,' Justice reassured him, bending over

the compass and listening to it intently. As she did so, her eyes widened. 'Are you serious?' she murmured to the metal disc. 'You're absolutely sure?'

The tinging and tapping reached a crescendo – it sounded like stick insects fighting inside a tin can.

'An enormous injustice?'

She could scarcely allow herself to believe it. Before tonight, she'd been on the verge of giving up Justicing for good. A series of boring petty crimes had begun to convince her that she was wasting her time.

'It threatens . . . what?'

'What's it say?' whispered Basin, who had crept back up again and was now so close that his yellow eyes were reflected in the Moral Compass's surface, his breath fogging up the glass.

'An injustice has been committed that threatens the very future of Parallelia,' Justice replied.

A cold wind blew through the inne until someone yelled, 'Shut the door!' and it stopped. But the shiver that was running down Justice's back had nothing to do with the draught.

Finally, she thought to herself. *Finally, this is it. The one I've been waiting for. A proper, big injustice. No more sheep rustling. No more dice cheats. This is what I trained for.*

'Where?' she asked the compass urgently, receiving another series of taps in reply.

'I need to travel south,' Justice said as she listened, raising her voice so the whole inne could hear. 'Without delay. What's the quickest way to Angel Woods from here?'

'Ar, bant ee farn the slodge, marm,' said an old man at the table behind her. He had a face like an apple that had seen better days a decade ago.

'I'm sorry?' Justice replied.

'Bant ee farn the slodge!'

Oh great, thought Justice. *Just what I need at this crucial stage of the mission. Dialect.*

'He do say you mayn't cross the Insurmountable Slodge, Madam Justice,' explained Basin shyly. ''Tis a huge marshland, but 'tis the quickest way to Angel Woods. I –' He hesitated, reaching up and fiddling nervously with one of his horns. 'I could show you how,' he blurted finally.

'Garn!' Apple-faced dialect villager butted in again. 'Toe barnt nen farsh'n nay gannick cross no slodge!'

'I will too,' Basin protested hotly, being fluent in Villager.

'How can you get across the slodge?' Justice asked

Basin. Something in his eyes made her hopeful he was telling the truth.

Basin, for his own part, had sensed a way out of his miserable life in the kitchen. Maybe this woman in grey would even listen to some of his recipe ideas. He had lots and lots of those.

'I do go picking herbs there, madam,' the kitchen boy replied in his shy, squeaky voice. 'For to try and make the soup taste better. But they never do want to use 'em.' He looked crestfallen. 'Cook did threw them on the compost heap,' he added quietly. 'But there's one plant – marsh radish – what it only grows on drier patches.' He brightened up. 'I followed they flowers ever so long into the slodge, and I never even lost me boot. If we follows them marsh radish flowers, we can get all the way across, Madam Justice. I knows it. They shows the way through.'

'Well, Basin,' said Justice, making up her mind, 'your mistress says you like hearing travellers' tales, is that right?' The boy's horns bobbed as he nodded. 'Ever fancied going on an adventure of your own?' The horn-bobbing increased in speed dramatically.

And so, after a brief and heated financial transaction with the landlady, Justice and her new squire headed back out into the rain. There was an injustice to track and not a second to lose. She was finally needed for something important. Parallelia was in danger . . . and, best of all, there wasn't time to finish the soup.

• • •

At the same time as – in another world – Justice and Basin took their first tentative steps across the Insurmountable Slodge, Frankie Best sank to the floor of her grandfather's attic while wailing the words, **'You have got to be actually KIDDING me!'**

She was overwhelmed by a feeling that the entire universe had started moving much too fast and in completely the wrong direction, stranding her out in the open like the slowest gazelle in the pack. And, if you've ever watched a nature documentary, you know how it ends for *that* guy.

She pleaded with her little brother. 'Could we just back up a bit here for a minute?'

Joel had been staring without speaking for several seconds, but at this point he broke his silence. 'P-pointy,' he stuttered, stabbing a finger wildly in the general direction of the yellow-hatted youth's head. **'Pointy. Pointy, pointy, pointy.'**

'Yes, Joel,' Frankie soothed him. 'I know. Pointy ears.'

At this moment, the woman from the village shop pulled off her own purple-and-orange woollen hat.

'Pointy too!' burbled Joel as her ears came into view. 'More pointies. Four pointies.'

'So, you're an elf, then, are you?' Frankie asked, desperate to regain some kind of control over the situation.

'No, dear,' replied the woman. 'Elves are fictional.'

'Well, that's something at least.'

'I'm a knelf – silent k at the beginning. We're knelves.'

'Fine.' Frankie decided, for the time being, to just go along with this and see what happened. 'What are your names, then?' she asked, hoping it might help if she established the basics and worked from there. 'What sort of names do, er, *knelves* have? If you're called Spingle I will actually scream,' she warned, pointing to the boy with the yellow hat dangling from his hand.

'Of course I'm not called Spingle,' he retorted. 'That's a ridiculous name.'

'What then? Globulin? Mithramblart? Fantalemon?'

'Ooh, that's nice, that,' said the woman. 'Very lemony.'

'It's Garyn,' the youth replied.

Frankie hooted. 'Gary?' she said, forgetting her confusion for a moment. 'What sort of a name is that for an elf? Sorry –' she corrected herself – 'a *knelf*.'

'It's **Gary-nnnnnnnnnn**,' he told her, stressing the final syllable.

'And you can just call me Mrs Archer,' the woman added. 'I'm his mum, in case you hadn't worked it out.'

'The ears were kind of a giveaway,' said Frankie. 'Don't get too many of those round here. Speaking of which,' she went on, 'what are you doing running a shop in a perfectly normal village? Some kind of fairyland exchange programme, is it?'

'We're Sentinels,' Mrs Archer explained. 'If anything gets through the portal –' she pointed at the Mirror Door through which Garyn was leaning – 'then we help the custodian put it back in the right place. Like this little chap.' She moved her finger down to indicate the furry creature in the cage, which had been listening to the conversation with interest, tufty ears quivering.

'Grandad's the custodian!' said Joel excitedly. 'That's what those people called him. When the man with horns grabbed him.'

'Horns?' Garyn asked. 'Sounds like a gnoblin. Right,' he told his mum, 'there's no time to lose. We've got to follow them to Tramont – that's where you told me they were headed?' He looked questioningly at Joel, who nodded. 'And get the custodian back. I don't know who could have wanted to take him, but we can work that out on the way. If we make a quick start, we might be able to catch them before they reach the bay.'

'Oh, thank goodness.' Frankie felt relief flooding through her like hot chocolate. 'I thought for one terrifying minute that you were going to expect me and Joel to go off on some mad adventure behind that mirror.' She gave a short laugh. 'Well, just make sure Grandad's here before Mum and Dad get back, won't you?'

There was a long silence.

'That's next weekend, by the way,' she added, slightly more nervously, feeling a little of the relief leak away.

There was another silence, fifteen per cent longer and eighty-three per cent more awkward than the first.

'You are talking about the two of you going to rescue him?' Frankie asked finally. 'Right?'

'Oh no, dear,' said Mrs Archer kindly. 'I'm far too old to be gallivanting off on adventures. And, besides, who'd mind the shop? Mr Bentall will be in for his sausages!'

'Wait!' Frankie leaped to her feet, the faint panic that had been swirling about her now assuming solid form and coiling itself round her insides like a snake. 'You don't mean you want me to go? Me and Joel?'

'I think you're going to have to, dear,' Mrs Archer replied.

'I'll come with you, obviously,' Garyn added, grinning from ear to ear. 'I know the quickest way to Tramont. Plus – I can't wait to get back into Parallelia! I'm sick to death of this stupid place.'

'Oy!' Despite not being the biggest fan of her grandad's village, or indeed the world in general at this point in her life, Frankie felt rather stung to hear it being criticized by an elf. *Sorry* – she mentally corrected herself – *a knelf*.

'It's not that bad!' she muttered rather lamely.

'The snack food is amazing – I'll give you that!' Garyn's mother piped up enthusiastically. 'I still can't get over those noodle pots. You just add the hot water . . .'

'Yes, yes.' Frankie was keen to avoid another glowing tribute to instant, kettle-based cuisine. 'The question is . . . what are we supposed to do? I've never been to Magical Pixie Bunnyland, or whatever it's called . . .'

'Parallelia,' Garyn corrected proudly. 'The Kingdom of Parallelia.'

'And I don't know what to do!' finished Frankie weakly, fully aware that she was sounding kind of helpless and annoying.

'Yes you do!' came a voice at her elbow. Joel was looking up at her, bright-eyed. 'You leave the cottage, you journey through Owl Forest, and eventually you reach Darzil's Dragon Fortress, remember?'

'JOEL!' She placed a calming hand on her forehead. It didn't work. **'FOR THE LAST TIME, THIS IS NOT SPINGLE'S QUEST.'**

'Well, the game's all about an elf going on a quest,' said her brother reasonably. 'That's a knelf,' he added, pointing at Garyn, 'and this is –'

'Don't you dare,' Frankie warned him, 'call this a quest.'

'Well, it is,' he replied. 'What else would you call it?'

She searched for the right word. 'It's a trip. A jaunt. A going from one place to another place and then coming back again. Not,' she reiterated, 'a quest.'

'It kind of is a quest,' Garyn pointed out.

'It really is.' Joel nodded his head vigorously.

'It is a quest, dear, really,' Mrs Archer agreed apologetically.

Joel was now actually hopping from foot to foot in excitement. 'We're going on a quest,' he was chanting to himself under his breath. 'We're going on a quest. Questy, questy quest.'

'First rule of this journey,' his sister told him sternly, 'is that the word "quest" is now banned. I hate quests. I already hate *this* quest and it hasn't even started yet.'

'Sorry, *Princess*,' he replied, raising an eyebrow. 'OK, OK,' he added quickly, seeing her expression darken. 'I think I can guess the second rule. Make sure you take the map, though.'

Frankie was about to make an angry retort about

the map being stupid and made-up, but then realized with a fizz in her brain that it wasn't. This wasn't some imaginary map from a story. Those were *real places*.

'And I've got the Bestiary,' said Joel, 'in case we encounter fascinating animals of some kind. We can tick them off as we go.'

'It's not a safari, Joel,' his sister scolded.

'I know,' he told her cheekily. 'It's a quest.'

'Gah!'

'Well, sounds like you're all set,' said Mrs Archer in a satisfied tone. 'Garyn, you'd better change into Parallelian clothes and get your stuff together, and I'll pack some food. Noodle Pots all right for everyone?'

CHAPTER 5

It's hard to describe what it feels like stepping through a portal to another world, even to yourself. But there was no doubt in Frankie's mind as she climbed reluctantly through the Mirror Door later that day that she was entering somewhere that was indescribably *other*. The air on her face became cooler and somehow softer, and she felt a strange tingling in her scalp, like the static electricity when you rub a balloon on your hair. Her trainers landed on soft, mossy turf and she turned round to see the smiling face of Garyn's mum. She had grasped the mirror with both hands and was starting to lift it back into position.

'HEY, WAIT!' Frankie cried, suddenly feeling

panicked at being shut out.

'Nothing to worry about, dear,' said Mrs Archer soothingly. 'My lad'll take good care of you.'

Frankie looked round at Garyn, who was now wearing a large rucksack, his yellow hat with ear flaps now back in place. 'Shouldn't I have . . . I dunno . . .' She was stalling, trying to put off the moment when the real world would be sealed off to her. 'A sword or something?'

'Can you use a sword, dear?'

'Well, no,' Frankie admitted.

'Best not take one, then,' said Mrs Archer. 'You'd probably do yourself a mischief. Bye now!' she trilled. 'Have a good quest!'

'This is not a qu–' Frankie began to say, but she was cut off by the sound of the Mirror Door being slammed shut. With a loud click, it completely disappeared, becoming part of the ancient stone wall in which the semicircular opening had been set. Frankie placed a hand on the lichen-covered stones, but all that was left was a faint indentation the same shape as the mirror.

'Hey! We're trapped! How do we get back through?' she yelled to Garyn, who had already followed Joel somewhere out of sight round the other side of the wall.

'When the time comes, you'll know,' he replied irritatingly.

'That is exactly the sort of dumb, enigmatic thing people always say in this kind of fantasy scenario,' she raged, stomping off to find him. 'Irritating thing about fantasy number one: nobody gives a straight answer to a straight question. Why can't you just –' But the words caught in her throat as she realized where he'd gone.

The Mirror Door, she could now see, was set into the back of a squat, square stone tower – one of five identical structures that surrounded a glade in the forest.

Frankie Best was not a huge fan of the word 'glade' – especially as one of the first levels in *Spingle's Quest* was called Grassy Glade – but even she had to admit that the hilltop clearing in which she was now standing was, without a doubt, best described by using the g-word. Tall trees encircled a mossy, sheltered circular space surrounded by the five weathered stone towers. You couldn't call it a clearing, or an opening – there really was only one word to use, and that was the word 'glade'. It was the gladiest glade Frankie had ever set eyes upon.

In the centre of the glade was a stone plinth with a statue on top of it. Joel and Garyn were already examining it and Frankie ran over to join them, casting a quick look back over her shoulder. Something about this place felt deeply unsettling. The other-worldliness of it all was creeping her out.

Joel, on the other hand, appeared to be in his element. 'Look at this, Frankie,' he said in an awed whisper as she approached. 'It's brilliant.'

The statue, like the towers, was ancient – worn down by wind and weather. But Frankie could clearly see that it was a woman in full battle armour. She was seated, cross-legged, with her hands resting peacefully on her legs and her eyes closed.

'Ilvatar,' read Joel in a hushed, reverent voice, squinting in the dim pre-dawn light at the carved letters on the plinth. 'Is that her name, Garyn? Is this Ilvatar?'

'This is where Ilvatar's Helm is kept. Or at least it ought to be,' the knelf replied. 'This statue should be wearing it.'

'What's a helm?'

ILVATAR

'You know – a helmet,' he explained. 'A silver helmet.'

'JUST SAY HELMET, THEN!' snapped Frankie. 'There's no need to give it an olde-worlde name to make it sound all fantasy. Silver helmet. Yeah, we know. We saw that creepy-looking guy waving it about. The same people who took Grandad stole the helm. *Helmet, gah!* You've got me doing it now!'

'This is really serious.' Garyn pushed his yellow hat back from his forehead, which was furrowed in concern. 'That helm is one of the Talismans of Parallelia.'

'Talismans? Magical protective items?' Joel asked. Garyn nodded silently in reply. 'Cool. Who would want to steal it, though?'

'It doesn't matter,' said Frankie crossly. 'We didn't come here to hang about gawping at statues. If we waste time sightseeing and asking dumb questions, we'll never get anywhere. Focus,' she told Joel, knocking a fist gently on the top of his head. 'Remember the mission! Enter Magical Fairytale Kingdom. Rescue Grandad. Go home – that's it. Statue appreciation and helmet rescue are not on the flight plan. Now, Gary . . .'

'Garyn.'

'Whatever. Which way did they take him? Let's get moving, yeah?'

She pulled her phone out of her pocket, with the vague idea that the maps app would spring into life and help them plot a route. But the phone was completely dead. Frankie mashed the power button – the battery had been full a few moments ago; she'd glanced at it in the attic while Garyn had been strapping a sleeping bag to his rucksack.

'It won't turn on,' the knelf informed her. 'Magic from your world won't work once you're more than a short way past the portal. Just as magic from Parallelia won't work if we travel the other way.'

Frankie scoffed. 'Phones aren't *magic*,' she said.

'Oh really?' He raised his arched eyebrows until they vanished beneath his yellow hat. 'How do phones work, then?'

'Well, you know . . .' She huffed, realizing she'd backed herself into a bit of a corner here. 'It's, ah, radio waves, isn't it?'

'And what are those?'

'Everyone knows this stuff!' she told him hotly. 'You know, invisible waves – and they go through the air, and transfer, um, power . . .'

'Sounds a lot like magic to me,' said Garyn smugly, high-fiving Joel, which made Frankie's stomach boil with irritation. 'Anyway, take my word for it: that phone will not turn on until you get close to the portal again. Right, let's get going. One thing you said does make sense – we need to hurry. I can tell you about Ilvatar some other time. You need to hear the *Tale of the Warrior* to understand what our quest is.' He strode out of the glade and began to pick his way through the trees.

'Count me out,' Frankie requested as she and Joel followed him. 'That sounds like a three-page poem if ever I heard one.'

'As you wish,' replied Garyn with an infuriating air of calm and a slight bow.

There was no track to lead the way through the forest, but the high, gnarled trees were widely spaced enough for them to easily set off down the hill. Between the trunks, the ground was soft and mossy, and here and there clods of earth that had been kicked up showed the kidnappers' route. It had been late afternoon back at Grandad's house – but here in Parallelia it was early morning, and shafts of lemon-coloured sunlight angled themselves through the foliage.

As they walked, Frankie had been hoping the creeping feeling of unease and anxiety would diminish. But instead it grew. *What's the problem*? she wondered to herself. *Just think of this as a nice hike in the woods, OK? Worry about everything else later.*

The trouble was, this was not just a hike in the woods. Frankie didn't know much about trees, but she knew enough to tell that the ones now surrounding her were a variety she'd never seen before, with thick, fist-like clusters of purple berries among their golden leaves. And, she realized, it was too quiet here. Whenever her parents dragged her and Joel out for a walk in the country, there was always the distant hum of a road or the low whistling of a plane. Here, behind the unfamiliar birdsong and the soft thumping of their footsteps, there was a huge silence, so enormous and so complete that it felt almost oppressive.

Shaking her head to clear it, Frankie jogged slightly to catch up with Garyn. 'What's our first stop, then?' she asked him.

'We're heading for Artleknock,' he told her. 'It's a

knelvish village – it's where I grew up, actually. Can't wait to head back there. We've nearly finished our five-year stint as Sentinels; it's almost time to go home. Ah, which reminds me.'

He reached round and slipped off his backpack. The wooden cage with the tree pook inside was fastened to the top of it with bungee cords. 'This should be far enough away from the door,' he decided, unclipping the cage and setting it on the ground. 'Off you go, then.' He unfastened the door. 'And stay in your own world this time, OK?'

Tentatively, a furry face peeked out from the cage and sniffed the air. Then, with a delighted squeak, the Tree Pook scurried across the forest floor and leaped straight upward, catching a branch with its thin arms and vaulting higher into the tree.

'Whoa!' marvelled Joel. **'Excellent climbing skills!'**

'Thanks,' replied a tiny voice from somewhere above him.

Frankie moaned. 'Oh, for pity's sake,' she said.

'What's the problem now?' asked Garyn, reshouldering his pack and setting back off down the hill.

'Talking squirrel creatures? I mean, seriously? Could this place get any lamer?'

Joel chipped in at this point. 'There are several different varieties of pooka,' he said. He had pulled the Bestiary from his pocket and was reading aloud. 'That one is a tree pook, which means it lives in a small house high in the tree branches.'

'You really hate all this, don't you?' said the knelf, half turning to give Frankie a quizzical little smile. 'I thought you'd be just as excited as your brother.' He nodded at Joel, who was scanning the branches as he walked in case any more pooka decided to stop by for a chat.

'What is there to be excited about?' retorted Frankie glumly. 'I absolutely hate all this fantasy, swords and sorcery nonsense. It's childish and it's stupid.'

'What's so stupid about it?'

'Well, for a start,' said Frankie, warming to her theme as she realized that talking was making her feel a little less anxious, 'how come it's always, like, the Middle Ages?'

'What do you mean?'

'I mean, why is it always castles and princesses and

no properly functioning infrastructure? For example –' she jerked a thumb over her shoulder in the direction of the Mirror Door – 'you've got a portal to our world right there. Why doesn't some enterprising dwarf ever sneak through and make a fortune selling smartphones to the centaurs or whatever?'

'Well, for a start,' Garyn replied, 'as I've already explained, the smartphones wouldn't work. Magic from your world –'

'Yeah, OK, but you know, there must be tons of cool stuff from our world that *would* make this one better.' She circled her hands as she tried to think of a good example. 'Got it!' She clicked her fingers. 'Water. Clean water.'

'We drink water straight from the spring,' he shot back airily. 'It doesn't get any cleaner than that. In your world, you get someone else to go to the spring for you, put the water in a plastic bottle and then charge you for it.'

Frankie thought about this for a second and found, to her frustration, that he was right. 'All right then,' she said, 'what about aeroplanes? You could avoid all this slogging through the woods to get anywhere.'

'What – spend a few years zipping round the

world, pointing at bits and going, "**Oooh!**", not caring if you melt large parts of it?' said Garyn with a sniff. 'No thanks. We only borrow ideas from your world if they actually make things better.'

'Music then,' she said. 'We have truly excellent music. If my phone worked in this stupid pixie dell, I'd play you some stuff that would blow your little knelvish mind.'

'We actually play our own musical instruments in Parallelia,' he threw back over his shoulder as he strode away from her. 'Rather than paying huge amounts of money to pop stars who just end up complaining about how miserable fame has made them.'

'What about social media?' Frankie was getting slightly desperate by this point.

'You're not serious? Social media? Give me a break.' Garyn vanished among the trees, and Joel and Frankie had to break into a trot to avoid being left behind.

'Why do you hate this place so much, Frankie?' her brother panted as they ran. 'You used to love this kind of thing. You completed all the *Spingle's Quest* games – and I remember you reading me that story you wrote about the magic sword –'

'That was years ago, Joel!' She sounded angrier than she felt as she tried to mask an undeniable feeling of regret. 'Just because I liked all this nonsense when I was little doesn't mean I like it now. **It's so lame!**' She gestured towards the tranquil, sunlit woodland and he crinkled up his face in puzzlement.

'You know what I mean!' she blurted. 'Not this part specifically. This part's actually quite pretty. Just the pointy ears and the statues and the, er, helm, and a quest. It's ridiculous!' By now, she had caught sight of Garyn's back through the trunks. 'Come on,' she urged. 'If we get left behind, I'll abandon you to be eaten by dragons.'

'No dragons in these woods,' replied Joel confidently. 'They live further out to the west, beyond the borders of Parallelia. You should read this sometime.' He waved the Bestiary at his sister. 'You might learn something.'

The Journal of Frankie Best (continued)

Here's a few things I've realized on my first day in this ridiculous place:

Going on a quest through a Magical Fairytale Kingdom is very much like going camping. There's a lot of walking about through the countryside, you sleep on the floor and there's nowhere decent to go to the toilet.

I hate camping. I absolutely hate it.

Therefore, I also hate quests.

About the toilet thing. It's something they never talk about in this kind of story. Where you go to the toilet? Am I right? I don't remember any of those details in the fantasy books I used to love so much when I was little. And, to be honest, I didn't think about it much when we set out into Parallelia. But by the middle of this afternoon, it was kind of pressing on my mind, if you know what I mean.

By this stage, the trees of Angel Woods had begun to thin out a little. We had been walking steadily downhill all day, following a track that seemed to come and go whenever it felt like it. Garyn never got lost, though – every time the path disappeared, he would stop and look carefully around, sometimes squinting up at the sky, before confidently setting off again. My anxiety had started to fade very slightly – at least our guide knew what he was doing. I was also feeling relieved that, after several hours of walking, Joel had finally got bored of making endless jokes about stopping for Second Breakfast.

But, as I say, the question about toilet arrangements had started to occupy my mind a little. And, just because I want you to get the full experience of what this was like for me, I don't intend to gloss over the whole issue as most fantasy authors seem to. I need to give this to you with both barrels, if you'll forgive the expression.

'Garyn, wait!' I broke into a trot to catch up with him as he strode between the slender trunks. 'I need to . . . you know. Go.'

He stopped and turned round. 'You need to go where?' he asked, planting his hands on his hips.

'Oh, come on,' I pleaded. 'Don't make this more awkward than it already is. You know – *go*. Even elves – knelves, sorry – must need to go sometimes, right? Or do all the waste products from your digestive system get magically extracted overnight while harps play or something?'

'Oh, I see!' he said, his eyes widening. 'You need to *go*.' He swung his rucksack off his shoulders and started rummaging in one of the side pockets.

'Cool,' I said, 'so what are you looking for? A map to see when we might pass somewhere with a bathroom, or . . . ?'

My sentence dried up as he pulled out a small garden trowel and held it aloft as if it was a magic sword or something.

'What do you want me to do with that?' I asked woodenly. I was already working out what the answer was for myself, but I guess my brain just refused to accept it.

'Well,' he said, knitting his brow, 'I assume you don't need a complete set of instructions. But this is to dig a hole and, you know, fill it in afterwards.'

'But, but, but . . .' I still couldn't believe I was hearing this. 'What about hygiene? Washing my hands and . . . everything . . .' I trailed off rather lamely.

'Yeah, I think there's a couple of washbasins just behind that tree over there,' he told me, handing over the trowel with a rather pitying expression. 'Let me know if the hand soap's running low and I'll call housekeeping.'

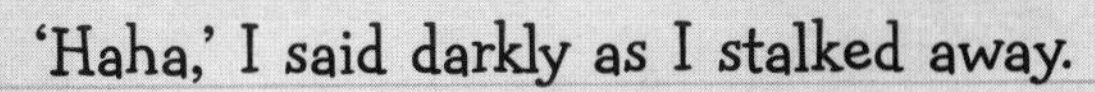

'Haha,' I said darkly as I stalked away.

'You're hilarious, you know that?'

'Insider tip from the Magical Fairytale Kingdom,' he called after me. 'Those leaves are particularly good.'

I turned to see that he was pointing at a large shrub with luxuriant dark-green foliage.

'Good? Good for what?'

Yes, I know I was slow picking up on all of this, but give me a break. It had already been a very long day.

'You know,' replied Garyn, who had now been joined by Joel. I was annoyed beyond measure to see that they were both grinning widely at me. 'They're soft and strong. Not particularly long, though, so make sure you pick a few.'

'Walk away!' I shouted furiously as I began to dig with the tiny trowel, hearing them ineffectually trying to stifle their laughter on the other side of the thicket. 'Walk away right now!'

CHAPTER 6

Frankie was writing in her notebook, lying on her tummy beside a flickering campfire. One hand was cupped across the page to shield it from prying eyes reading over her shoulder, although, to her slight disappointment, neither Joel nor Garyn was showing the slightest interest in what she was scribbling.

After what seemed to Frankie like about a thousand hours of plodding gently downhill through Angel Woods, the knelf had finally announced they were stopping for the night. By the time the sky in the west had begun to redden – though it still wasn't quite as flaming as Frankie's face after her recent bathroom experience – the ground had levelled off and the green clearings between the trees were growing wider and wider. The path, too, had been widening – like a stream growing into a river. At times, you could almost call it a track.

As the shadows lengthened, Garyn had led them away from the path to a low hill dotted with scrubby trees and a few low, weathered stones. 'We'll stop here tonight,' he announced, pointing towards the distant lights of a small town. 'Artleknock's not far away, and I can get you some proper clothes there in the morning. Can't have you running into anyone dressed like that.'

Frankie sighed irritably, looking at the knelf's homespun clothes and suddenly realizing there was going to be more hessian in her immediate future than she was completely comfortable with.

Joel and Garyn had built a fire as she huddled huffily up against a stone, hands round her knees and heart in her sneakers as the twilight deepened. She looked at her little brother's face, almost visibly glowing with happiness as he watched Garyn blow gently on a pile of twigs and send a twirl of smoke skyward, followed by a lick of flame. He was living out his wildest, most exciting dreams, she realized.

And what was happening to her? The complete opposite. She was being dragged against her will through a place that confused, frightened, and most of all really, really irritated her.

Half an hour later, Frankie realized that she was absolutely starving. And another forty-five minutes after that she realized something else: cooking anything on an open fire takes a really long time. Joel spent ages happily trotting off among the trees, looking for fallen branches and dragging them back, while Garyn carefully coaxed the flames into a cheerful blaze. But it wasn't until the first logs had crumbled into white-hot embers that he balanced a pot of water on three large stones he'd placed near the edge of the campfire.

Frankie wondered what was for dinner as Garyn rummaged in his rucksack. He seemed to have a huge amount of stuff squirrelled away in there – in fact, she was slightly tempted to ask him whether there was some kind of enchanted holds-a-lot-of-stuff kind of a deal going on, but was fairly sure that, if she did, she wouldn't like the answer one bit. She was steeling herself for some kind of fantasy-story dinner – herbs and stewed rabbit, possibly. But instead he pulled out three pots of instant noodles and, using his sleeve as a makeshift oven glove, poured water into them.

'Here you go,' he told Frankie and Joel, handing the steaming pots over. He leaned sideways to dip a hand into his bag once again, and passed them both sporks.

'Aha!' said Frankie triumphantly as she blew on her pot. 'So, for someone who thinks our world is a load of rubbish, you're perfectly happy to eat noodle pots with a spork! Maybe it's not so bad after all.'

'I'll admit the snack food is fairly impressive,' he said grudgingly. 'But the spork's a Parallelian invention, you know. We've been using them for hundreds of years. These have been passed down through my family for generations.'

Frankie looked doubtfully at her spork, and was annoyed to see that it did indeed seem to be rather old, and was made of polished wood. To cover her embarrassment, she took a large mouthful of hot noodles and burned her tongue really quite badly.

'How often do you have to catch pooka, then?' Joel wanted to know. He'd pulled the Bestiary out once again, and was flicking through its colourful pictures of strange animals.

'Oh, they're always getting through,' said Garyn airily. 'We try to round them up whenever we can, but they're a nightmare. Always stealing small stuff and bringing it back to their pook houses. They seem to be fascinated with all the weird things you people carry around in your pockets. That one today was a tree pook, of course, but there's different types. You find peeky pooka mostly around farms or down wells. Cave pooka live along the coast . . .'

PARALLELIAN POOKA

TREE POOKA

live in small but immaculately kept houses high in the branches.

Curious and inquisitive, they have long fingers and a short, prehensile tail.

They plant nettles near their dwellings to avoid discovery.

PEEKY POOKA
live in the wall
cavities of human
homes and have an
unnerving habit of
peeking out at you
from cracks.

CAVE POOKA
have webbed fingers and are strong swimmers.

Generally found along coastlines but a freshwater variety is known to exist along the banks of Tygermere.

Fond of collecting shiny objects, escaped pooka in the Otherland are responsible for stealing car keys and other small items.

At this point, Frankie zoned out. Finishing the last dregs of noodles, she wandered off to the edge of the hilltop, perching herself on a rock and staring out into the night. Once again, the strangeness of this place filled her brain. It wasn't the big differences – the fantastical creatures and all the rest of it. It was more the small stuff. The different bird calls she could hear far off in the darkness. The fact that the lights of the nearby village flickered faintly, rather than shining constantly like the electric lights of her own world. Even the air smelled subtly different. Nothing here was familiar, and it was all she could do to stop it tipping her over into total panic.

It was at this point that Frankie had grabbed her notebook and started journalling again, desperate to somehow distract her brain. Garyn was still talking in a low voice about some of the creatures of Parallelia, pointing to a picture in Joel's book. A whisper inside Frankie's head tried to tell her that she should really be paying more attention. But a far louder voice countered that she was just here to rescue Grandad and get out again, so there was no point filling her brain with a lot of stupid fairytale nonsense. She certainly didn't plan on coming back.

She'd been putting off going to bed for as long as possible, fully expecting to have the most uncomfortable night's sleep. She remembered camping with her mum and dad, trying to get cosy on an inflatable mattress that squeaked as if it was full of mice every time she made a slight change of position. But a huge yawn crept up on her and Frankie realized that, after a hard day's walking in the fresh air, she was practically nodding off over her journal. She clicked her pen shut and put the notebook away.

'Night, nerds,' she called to the other two, unstrapping her sleeping bag and making herself as comfortable as possible on the springy turf, while staying close enough to the fire to feel safe. 'Speak to you in about half an hour when I fly into a tantrum because I'm too uncomfortable to sleep.' But, even as she said the words, Frankie realized she was drifting into a pleasant half-doze.

At home, her phone was usually charging by the bed. More often than not, she'd forget to put it on silent, and it would suddenly buzz midway through the night like a needy wasp trying to get her attention. Add to that the orangey glow of the street light right outside the window leaking through the blinds, and the knowledge that the radio was going to start burbling at 7.15 a.m. sharp, and you'd have to admit that her usual bedroom wasn't the most relaxing environment.

In contrast, here's what it was like going to sleep that first night in Parallelia. One side of Frankie's face was warmed by the fire; the other was nicely cooled by the fresh night air. In her nose was the smell of woodsmoke and, behind that, the fresh scents of the crushed grass and trodden herbs that grew around the clearing. She didn't know at that point, but Garyn had chosen this as a sleeping place because it was surrounded by a low-growing shrub called luller balm. With its gentle scent – a mixture of mint, lavender and clean linen – it was used by Parallelians to aid restful sleep.

Frankie lay on her back, the orange flicker of flames in the corner of her vision and the rest of it filled with a vast array of stars. From the other side of the fire came the soft voices of Joel and Garyn as they continued what had become a general question-and-answer session about the history and wildlife of Parallelia. Frankie caught the occasional word –

maeriona, Celidon, Lomea, Hickathrift – as she began to drift.

Then she let out a deep breath, almost feeling like she was breathing out the day's irritation and bad temper and replacing them with the subtle scents of the Parallelian night. She closed her eyes for a second. And, when she opened them again, the fire had burned down to cold ash, Joel and Garyn were lying fast asleep not far away and the first fingers of a bright red dawn were beginning to claw at the clouds. Frankie felt as if all the sleeps she'd had before this one had just been rehearsals, and not particularly successful ones, either. This was the first night she'd really, properly nailed it.

For a long while on that first morning in Parallelia, Frankie Best didn't even sit up. She just lay on her back, gazing up at the sky as the last stars faded and the blackness started to edge ever so gradually into a rich blue. There was a whirr of wings and a small brown bird with a bright red head landed on a nearby branch, puffing out its chest and launching into a silvery cascade of song.

Frankie just stayed there, feeling like time had briefly stopped as the music washed over her. At any moment, she knew Joel and Garyn would wake up and another annoying day of this journey would begin – something she wasn't looking forward to one tiny bit. But until that happened she was determined to hang on to this one peaceful moment in the dawn, when the air felt so clean it smelled like it had been scrubbed.

'Frankie?' came Joel's voice a while later. She turned on her side and waved a hand vaguely at him. 'Oh, thank goodness,' he said. 'You were just lying on your back with your eyes open – I was starting to worry.'

'Just listening to the bird,' she replied, pointing to it and inadvertently scaring it away. It took flight, vanishing towards the distant houses of the village.

'That's a little off-brand for you.' Joel looked puzzled as he sat up and looked around him. 'Morning, Garyn.'

'How did everyone sleep?' asked the knelf, jumping straight to his feet and brushing himself down.

'Surprisingly well, thanks, Gary,' Frankie told him, also standing up. The knelf let that one slide.

By now, the sun was just showing a thin crescent above a distant hill. The morning air was chilly, but it felt refreshing rather than anything else.

What on earth is happening? Frankie thought to herself. *I never wake up in a good mood.*

'You both stay here,' Garyn told them. 'I'm heading into Artleknock to pick up some clothes, and I'll grab us some proper breakfast as well. This should keep you going in the meantime.' He dug a couple of cereal bars out of his pack and threw them over.

'Does this mean we're actually going to have Second Breakfast?' asked Joel excitedly as he munched.

'I guess so,' Garyn said, smiling. 'Until then, just keep quiet, and stay out of sight, OK?'

'What should we do if someone attacks us?' asked Frankie, suddenly feeling a little apprehensive about being left alone in this strange place. 'Should we – I don't know – hoot like an owl or something?'

'Sure, if that would make you feel better,' said Garyn. 'Hoot away.'

'And you'll come and help?' Frankie pressed.

Garyn shrugged. 'No, I'll be at the village, out of owl-shot. But don't worry. I'm sure nothing will attack you and I won't be long.' And he loped off down the hill with his long-legged knelvish strides, soon disappearing among the low trees and shrubs.

'Let's get the fire going again,' said Frankie, feeling the need to do something practical to stave off the anxiety that was fluttering at the edges of her brain once again. 'Why don't you go and drag some more branches over? Then, when Garyn gets back, we can help him make breakfast. Come on!' She strode confidently over to the nearest patch of trees and began grabbing sticks.

Half an hour later, they had managed to build a very smokey and very small fire. 'How did he make it look so easy last night?' Frankie complained, kneeling down and blowing to try and coax some flames into life. All they seemed to have created so far was a pile of slightly hot wood that emitted a thick plume of dark grey smoke. It was a long way from the comforting blaze that had lulled her to sleep the previous evening.

'He said to stay out of sight,' said Joel, looking around. 'This is giving away our position to every monster in the vicinity. It's a classic rookie adventurer's mistake.'

'Don't worry,' his sister soothed him. He was darting round the hilltop, peering off in different directions and muttering something about

'Weathertop'. 'There aren't any monsters, I'm sure. Garyn wouldn't have left us here if there were.'

'You should have listened to him last night,' Joel retorted. 'This place is full of monsters. It's like a monster safari park, only we're not in a car. And there's no gift shop.'

Suddenly a loud cracking and rustling sounded from a thicket just down the hill. Frankie felt as if a very cold hand had clutched at the back of her neck. 'What kind of monsters?' she hissed.

Joel moaned. 'Something's coming,' he said, grabbing a stick from the fire and waving it in front of him. It wasn't fully alight, so it didn't look especially threatening. A thin stream of smoke was drifting from the very end, but that was all.

'What are you planning to do with that?' she asked him acidly. 'Send a smoke signal spelling out "please don't eat us"?'

'It may fear fire,' whispered Joel as the rustling came closer.

'If it fears fire,' Frankie retorted, 'we're in real trouble. If it fears very, very mild heat and a lot of smoke, then we're golden.'

By now it was clear that someone, or something,

was forcing its way through the vegetation at the very edge of the clearing.

'Maybe it's just Garyn coming back,' Frankie added doubtfully, knowing full well the knelf would never make that much noise – and, besides, he had gone off in a completely different direction.

A patch of bushes nearby was shaking and rattling furiously. They parted, and Frankie let out a sigh of relief. A very innocent-looking and rosy-cheeked old man was walking towards them. He was small and bent, carrying a wicker basket covered with a red checked cloth.

'Oh, good morning, friends,' said the old man, apparently catching sight of them for the first time. 'It's a fine morning to be out gathering mushrooms, is it not?'

'Morning,' Frankie replied.

Her brain had started to fill with images of terrifying monsters, so it was a massive relief that something human had emerged from the undergrowth, let alone such a harmless and charming-looking one. His kindly eyes smiled at her as he looked round the clearing with the benevolent expression of a lovely old tortoise.

'Out on an adventure?' he asked, crinkling up his face to an even-higher level of apple-cheeked non-threateningness. 'Perhaps you'd like some of these mushrooms for your breakfast, yes?'

Without thinking, Frankie started to edge forward. If Garyn came back and they had mushrooms already sizzling on the fire, perhaps he'd be a little less dismissive of her adventuring skills.

'Careful, Frankie,' said Joel in a low voice.

'Don't be silly. It's just a friendly old mushroom guy.'

'Here's a wise young man,' observed the mushroom-picker with a chuckle. 'Wise to trust nobody when you're out adventuring. But you've nothing to fear from me, I promise you.' He slipped the edge of the cloth away from the basket.

'Frankie,' Joel said in a more serious voice. 'Come away from him right now. It's Rule One.'

'What do you mean, "Rule One"?' she replied, turning back to face him.

'Rule One of any adventure,' he told her. 'If someone tells you to trust nobody, then they're definitely a baddie. At some point, they will turn on you and invariably utter the phrase, "I did warn you to trust nobody." Remember in *Spingle's Quest Two* when . . .'

'Joel!' She rolled her eyes. 'How many times? This is not *Spingle's Quest*. And there isn't some set of stupid rules for . . .'

But at that point she stopped talking. Because the apple-cheeked, tortoise-faced old gentleman had done something rather unexpected. Moving with surprising speed, he had pulled a short, fat dagger from his basket and grabbed Frankie's arms firmly in an incredibly strong grip.

'Sorry, little lady,' he said. Out of the corner of her eye, she could see that his face was no longer innocent and kindly, but his eyes were now glittering with cold triumph. 'You really should have listened to your brother.'

CHAPTER 7

THE GOOD GUYS OF LAWLESSTON

One day a week or so earlier, a man in a black cloak had arrived at the gates of Lawlesston. Nothing very unusual there – black was definitely this season's colour in the small, dirty town with its winding, unswept streets. Yes, black was definitely the new black in Lawlesston. It was also the old black. A black cloak helps you pass by unseen, you see. It allows you to do very bad things on a very dark night without getting caught doing them. And bad things were what people in Lawlesston liked doing best. The people there would rob you as soon as look at you. In fact, most of them wouldn't even bother to look at you first.

So, when this tall man in his black cloak knocked

at the gates, the gatekeeper didn't bat an eyelid at his choice of outfit. He simply peered out through his hatch and grunted. 'Are you carryin' any concealed weapons?'

'Hmm . . . no,' replied the on-trend visitor smoothly, beginning his answer with a strange little hum, as if he was picking out a snatch of some odd high-pitched song.

'You got a sword?'

'I have not.'

'What about a dagger, then? You got a dagger?'

'No.'

'What, not even a little one tucked in yer sock?'

'No, no dagger at all, hmm.'

The gatekeeper screwed up his face in puzzlement. 'What about an axe, then? You got an axe? Or one of them big 'ammers 'angin' orf of yer belt?'

In reply, the man spread out his black cloak to reveal his axe-less, hammer-less belt beneath.

'A mace then?' The gatekeeper hazarded another hopeful guess. 'Throwin' stars? Bow and arrer?'

The stranger shook his head.

'Trident? Siege catapult? Trained attack wolf?' He was clutching at straws by this point. 'Do you mean ter say,' he said huffily as he pulled the gate open to inspect the man more closely, 'that you're comin' into Lawlesston with no concealed weapons at all?'

The stranger drew in a breath as if he was about to give a long and detailed answer to this, but in the end he simply shrugged and said, 'Yes.'

'Well,' replied the baffled gatekeeper, standing aside to let him through, 'you'd better borrow this.' He pulled a long, narrow dagger in a leather sheath from his own belt and handed it over. 'Don't know what you think you're doin', swannin' into Lawlesston with no concealed weapons. Flamin' death wish.'

With a nod of thanks, the man vanished up the dark street. The gatekeeper, looking after him, shook his head sorrowfully. 'That'll be another one for the guards ter fish out o' the moat come mornin',' he predicted gloomily.

Lawlesston lies just outside the boundaries of Parallelia, with the high, treacherous northern mountains on one side and the untracked vastness of the Forests of the Neon Tyger on the other. Every undesirable who finds that the peaceful Kingdom of Parallelia is no place for them tends to end up there – congregating in the dirty little town like hairs clogging up a plughole. And it's every bit as unpleasant as that simile makes it sound.

The man in the black cloak strode confidently through the winding streets, pausing every now and then to check the buildings and make sure he was heading in the right direction. He had been given very detailed instructions about where to go, and the people he needed to find when he got there. Eventually, he stopped and looked up at a large, grubby building with tall windows. The windows gave an excellent view of what was going on inside, which was a shame because at that precise moment two large men were fighting each other with chairs and it was more than a little disturbing.

The building was the meanest, most dangerous, most frightening inne in the whole of Lawlesston. As you can imagine, it was up against some fairly stiff competition. And, if you're wondering whether it had an amusingly ironic name like the Fluffy Baby Badger, you're wondering in vain. It was called the Dead Man's Arms.

In traditional pub names, the word 'arms' refers to a coat of arms. In this case, it actually referred to a pair of arms, and there was a crudely painted picture of them on a wooden sign hanging above the door. Those are the only arm-based details it's really possible to give without this book needing to come with a warning sticker on the cover.

The man with no hidden weapons – apart from the dagger he'd been forced to borrow – pushed his way into the Dead Man's Arms and walked calmly up to the bar. This in itself was an impressive feat because his route wasn't exactly straightforward. He had to make a detour round the men fighting with chairs before stepping over two figures on the floor who had been previous participants in the same chair fight until they'd felt inclined to have a lie-down for a while.

The landlord – who had a wide, flat face with a clumpy brown beard at the bottom that made it look like an uncleaned shovel – sidled forward, wearing a stained apron and a doubtful expression. He gave a grunt that meant *what do you want?*

'I'm looking for the Good Guys,' said the man casually.

Immediately, every single person in the inne stopped moving as if somebody had pressed pause. Even the men with the chairs halted in mid-swipe. A wave of fear swept through the tavern, so strong you could almost smell it. You couldn't because of the way the Dead Man's Arms already smelled, which for the record was very bad indeed. There was a silence so complete you could hear a pin drop. Normally, that's just an expression, but in this case it was absolutely true.

There was a tiny tinkling noise from one of the tables over by the window and everybody turned to see a huge man in a loincloth, who was blushing furiously. 'Sorry, I dropped a pin,' he whispered in an embarrassed fashion, holding up his embroidery.

Everybody turned their heads back to the man at the bar who had just uttered the words that were, surely, about to get him turned into something that resembled – but tasted worse than – a rich beef casserole.

You see, nobody ever came into the Dead Man's Arms and said they were looking for the Good Guys. The Good Guys were NOT, in capital letters, the sort of people you wanted to go looking for. If you found out that the Good Guys were looking for *you*, you emigrated. If they caught up with you, you gave them all your worldly possessions and hoped they'd leave you at least a couple of limbs to try and escape with. Because the Good Guys were the nastiest, meanest, most evil group of thugs, thieves and general all-round bad pieces of work in the whole of the lawless town of Lawlesston. There were five of them – four of whom were identical, and all five of whom were thoroughly horrible.

Let's take a look at them, shall we? You're allowed to take a look because you're reading about them in a book. If you'd actually been in the Dead Man's Arms and dared to even glance at the Good Guys, you wouldn't be walking away afterwards. Not with the same number of limbs you started with, anyway.

The main thing that every gang of villains needs is muscle, and a lot of it. The Good Guys had a great deal of muscle, mostly distributed among the eight huge arms belonging to the four Mort brothers. They were enormous gnoblins from the mountains to the north – identical quadruplets fully twice as big as a normal-sized gnoblin. They were dressed identically in nothing but thick boots and rough woollen trousers, and they were so huge that at first glance it looked like a gigantic pile of whitish boulders had been dumped in a corner of the inne for some kind of indoor rockery. Their names were Gammort, Hackmort, Allamort and Titch. Titch's name was ironic, but if you smiled at it he would sit on you.

The fifth member – and leader – of the Good Guys was more interesting, but only in the way that really horrible things are interesting. His name was Slytely Good, which explains the misleading nickname given to his gang of ne'er-do-wells. Slytely Good was clever, the way a nuclear bomb is clever, and small, the way a very, very sharp knife is small.

At that exact moment, he was sitting quietly on a nearby bar stool, wondering whether he should have the stranger murdered immediately, or whether he should listen to him for a couple of minutes first. Fortunately, he was in an uncharacteristically benevolent mood that night, and he got silently to his feet.

The man in the black cloak turned away from the barman – who was still staring at him wordlessly with his beard quivering like brown jelly – to see a pair of eyes boring into his own from a couple of metres away. They looked like the kind of eyes that would steal all your money – possibly even without the rest of the face getting involved.

'Are you one of the Good Guys, hmm?' the man asked calmly, humming a short burst of a sad little tune at the end of his question. 'I was told I would find them here.'

'You're either unusually brave or unusually foolish,' replied Slytely Good, the dim light of the bar reflected in his mean green eyes. His voice was as thin and sparse as his long, straggly hair.

'In my experience, they're, hmm, the same thing,' the man in the black cloak shot back. Good inclined his head in agreement. 'I was hoping to hire you and your, hmm, men for an interesting little job.'

Everybody in the inne was still completely motionless, listening anxiously to this conversation. Even the embroidering barbarian hadn't yet stooped to pick up his pin. The men holding up the chairs were beginning to struggle by this point, despite their impressive upper-body strength. When the man in the black cloak told the leader of the Good Guys he wanted to hire him, everybody felt a slight sense of relief. The Good Guys weren't for hire. Within a few seconds, this would be made quite clear to the man in black – probably with the aid of a large metal instrument that was either very, very heavy or very, very sharp, or more than likely both.

'I don't think it's going to be interesting enough, sadly,' husked Good, signalling with a finger. Two of the enormous gnoblins stood up from a nearby table and moved forward with the air of people who were about to do something extremely painful.

'It involves, hmm, the complete destruction of Parallelia,' the man continued in the same casual tone, 'and you getting more money than you've ever seen before in your entire life.'

Good's finger inched slightly to the left and the two hulking gnoblins stopped in their tracks. Of all the things the man in black could have said, the phrase 'the complete destruction of Parallelia' was the only one that could possibly have prevented him from getting squished. Slytely Good, like all the other villains in Lawlesston, hated Parallelia. Every time they tried to commit a crime inside its borders, one of the many Justices would immediately be led towards them. And being stopped from committing crimes was Slytely Good's least favourite thing in the entire universe.

'I'll give you two minutes,' he said after a moment, beckoning the other man towards a quiet table in the corner. And two minutes was all it took for the man to outline his plan.

Precisely two minutes later, the man in the black

cloak stood up. His name, it now seems reasonable to tell you, was Haggister. 'So, hmm, we'll start first thing in the morning?' said Haggister, reaching down to shake Slytely Good's hand. Good nodded, eyeing the fat pouch full of bright gold coins that had been left on the table in front of him as a down payment.

This was the easiest job he'd ever been offered – four kidnappings and four thefts. It was like asking the rest of us to pop to the shop for carrots. And most important of all, when the job was over, the entire Kingdom of Parallelia – a prosperous, peaceful land filled with contented people – would be open and unprotected. It made Slytely Good's mouth water just thinking about it.

• • •

A week later, the tranquil surroundings of Angel Woods were being completely spoiled by the thudding of twelve feet as the Good Guys stampeded down the hill. Haggister led the way, his face set in an expression of grim determination. Behind him, the four enormous Mort brothers ran tirelessly, like white boulders rolling down the slope. Each of them carried a huge backpack with a wooden cage lashed to the top of it.

Two of the cages were occupied. In one of them sat a stocky man in rough brown clothes. He had a wise, calm face beneath a thatch of untidy black hair and his arms bulged with muscle. You don't actually need this information at this point in the story, but his name was Jon Topham and he was known across Parallelia as the Custodian of Tygermere. He was watching his captors closely but didn't speak, only giving a slight frown and a shake of his head every now and then. The occupant of the second cage was a little more vocal. This man, dressed in striped pyjamas and a purple dressing gown, was clutching the bars, his long white ponytail jerking to and fro as he cried out to Haggister.

'OY!' Frankie's grandfather – the Custodian of Angel Woods – was shouting. 'I'm supposed to be looking after my grandkids this week! You can't just go snatching people out of their houses and running off with them! My daughter will flipping well kill me when she gets back. Plus, who's supposed to look after my vegetables?'

'Your, hmm, vegetables are the least of your worries, you old fool,' Haggister countered.

By now, they had reached the bottom of the slope and the trees were beginning to thin out. Their pace slowed slightly as the rooftops of a small village appeared in the distance. 'You and your fellow, hmm, custodians are going to help me out, you see. When we get to Tramont Castle, I will perform a ritual that will transfer your powers to me. Your precious, hmm, Parallelia is finished. So enjoy the last days while you can.'

'Oh, you're kidnapping all the custodians, are you?' Grandad looked thoughtful for a moment. 'That's an interesting plan.' A slight smile flickered across his face.

'What are you smirking at?' asked Haggister sharply. 'Do I need to get, hmm, Allamort there to open up your cage and hit you on the head until you learn some manners? Hmm?'

Frankie's grandad considered this prospect for a moment. He could see just how enormous the gnoblin carrying his cage was. The horns on its huge head were each as thick as his forearm.

'Nothing – don't mind me,' he told Haggister blandly. 'Just hope my seedlings will be all right, that's all.'

'What's going on?' asked the final member of the Good Guys, who was jogging to catch up with Haggister.

And now it's worth having a slightly longer look at the man called Slytely Good. If you remember, back in the Dead Man's Arms he had been a small man with long, straggly hair and a rat-like face. Well, he was still small and his hair was still straggly. But he was now completely unrecognizable. You see, Slytely

Good was a very rare and rather creepy individual: he was able to change his appearance. If you were to glance at him, then look away, then back again, you'd have the unsettling impression that someone else had swiftly taken his place. He seemed to look different every time you saw him.

Some said that Slytely had learned a very ancient and very mysterious thieves' trick – a way of moving the bones of his face into different shapes the way the rest of us would twiddle our fingers. Just have a think about that for a second – yuck, right? Anyway, whatever the reason, he was the most cunning thief in the whole known world. As well as being a master of disguise in literally the creepiest way imaginable, he was also an expert swordfighter, a tireless and rapid long-distance runner, and completely and utterly devoid of any sense of human kindness or compassion. If there was some kind of International Villain Championships, he would have won so many medals he'd have had to ask the Mort brothers to carry them for him.

'This old fool looks like he's, hmm, laughing at me,' complained Haggister petulantly. 'I don't trust him.'

'Think you know something we don't, old man?' Slytely Good sneered at Grandad, pulling out a long, curved dagger and running it along the wooden cage bars. 'I wouldn't bank on it.'

'Maybe he thinks someone's coming to rescue him,' ventured Titch, the largest of the Mort brothers, in his deep, heavy voice.

'Is that it, old timer?' asked Slytely Good, screwing up his elastic face into a parody of concern. 'Think your friends are going to follow you and break you out?'

'What if, hmm, what if he does have helpers?' said Haggister, peering back up the hill. 'Warriors, perhaps? Lots of knelves live in these woods, don't they? I don't trust them.'

Slytely cocked his head to one side – his long, greasy brown hair waving wetly as he did so – and listened. 'Someone's moving high up in the forest,' he told Haggister. 'But don't worry.' He waved his dagger in front of Grandad's face mockingly. 'I'll hide out here and give them a lovely welcome.'

'Make it quick,' Haggister instructed him. 'And make sure you catch up with us before we cross the bay. Meet us at Bethcar Lighthouse.'

'Oh, don't worry,' said Good with a mean smile. 'I'm sure it won't take long.'

'HEY!' Grandad grabbed the bars of his cage again as the Mort brothers broke into a lumbering jog. **'That might be my grandkids up there! What are you going to do?'**

'Oh, don't worry,' Slytely repeated, slinking backwards into the bushes. 'I'll make it quick.'

Grandad's furious shouts receded as the rest of the Good Guys jogged away. This was quite lucky as they were far, far too rude to write down here.

CHAPTER 8

THE FELLOWSHIP OF THE BACON ROLL

'I did warn you to trust nobody,' snarled the man with the dagger, who, as you may have gathered from the previous chapter, was not an apple-cheeked old mushroom fancier but the dangerous criminal Slytely Good. He dragged Frankie across the clearing and flung her to the ground beside the fire.

'I told you he was going to say that!' yelled Joel. **'I warned you about Rule One!'**

But before he could say anything else, Slytely grasped the front of Joel's purple centaur T-shirt in a burst of speed and dumped him beside his sister.

'I thought I'd wait until your friend had left you alone,' Good gloated. 'So much easier to deal with you two first. Then I can dispense with him when he gets back from his little errand.' By now, he had completely thrown off his old-man persona. He was no longer bent and frail; his face no longer wrinkled or kindly.

'I don't suppose there's a Rule Two?' Frankie asked, grabbing Joel's hand. 'Something that might stop us actually getting sliced into bits at this point?'

'Rule Two,' Joel replied, his lips pale with fear, 'is that every villain has a weak point. Remember all the boss fights in *Spingle's Quest*? There's always a way round their defences. Like that giant troll – the one you have to grab by the tail so it drops its club? Remember?'

'Every villain has a weak point?' snarled Slytely Good. 'How pathetically naive. I have you here, alone and helpless in the wilderness. I have a knife and you have nothing. Whatever do you think my weak point could possibly be?' He gave a thin laugh.

'How about failing to look behind you?' came a new voice. And along with the voice came a long, polished sword that appeared at Slytely Good's shoulder, looking very much like it meant business.

Frankie saw Good's eyes shift sideways like a trapped animal and, with a sudden twisting movement, he ducked sideways, turned a swift somersault and came up facing the other way to defend himself against this new enemy. As he did so, Frankie and Joel got their first look at their rescuer.

She was a tall woman of about their mother's age, dressed all in grey. Crouched slightly in a combat stance, she was waving her slim sword threateningly as Good began to slowly circle her.

'Justice,' he said, snarling. 'I knew one or two of your kind would catch up with us sooner or later once we entered Parallelia. No matter.' The snarl warped into a cruel smile. 'Your time is almost up. And, besides, you're no match for me.'

'You don't look behind you, and you're overconfident,' replied Justice, raising her eyebrows. 'That's two weaknesses and counting. Impressive.'

Goaded, Good leaped at her with his dagger. Immediately, the clearing was filled with that cool swordfighting sound as the pair spun and parried, Justice's grey cloak billowing behind her like a cloud of smoke as she twirled, expertly countering the rat-faced man's attack.

Although, as we know, Justice's Moral Compass had been directing her towards a seemingly endless series of petty, irritating crimes, that didn't mean she had been neglecting her training. Every day, without fail, she put in a tough hour of sword practice because somewhere inside her she knew that, one day, she'd be given a proper assignment – one that would make her name. That day was today.

'This is ridiculously, incredibly awesome,' breathed Joel as he and Frankie watched the two combatants whirl and clash, their boots kicking up clumps of mossy turf as they fought. 'Where did the cool sword lady come from? Why is she helping us? Who is she?

How did that man make himself look so old?'

The restful scent of luller balm filled the clearing as the whirling swordfighters crushed the herb underfoot.

At the start of the fight, it had seemed that the pair were fairly evenly matched. But, after a few minutes, Frankie could tell that the man with the dagger was outclassed – and he knew it. His eyes widened, and the hand holding the knife was slick with sweat. She was reminded of tennis players who start dropping points – it was the same gradual realization that, come what may, there could only be one eventual winner.

Slytely Good seemed to reach this conclusion at more or less the same time as Frankie. His face writhed strangely, as if made from heated wax, and he snarled in fear and frustration. At last, with another of those sudden duck-and-tumble manoeuvres, he somersaulted away from his opponent and pelted off down the hill, sprinting at incredible speed. Within seconds, he had vanished among the trees.

Frankie and Joel watched silently as the woman in grey sheathed her sword and dusted her hands together in a satisfied fashion. Then she ducked a hand to her belt and pulled something from a leather pouch, looking at it in her cupped palm. She nodded to herself and walked over to them, calling over her shoulder at the same time, 'Basin! Come and get this fire going, will you?'

There was a further rustling in the bushes and a small boy about Joel's age bumbled out, tripping over a log and regarding them with wide yellow eyes as he flailed himself upright. It was at this point Frankie noticed the short horns on his head.

She gasped. **'It's one of thore orcs! The people who took Grandad!'**

'What's an orc?' asked the grey-cloaked woman curiously. 'Basin's a gnoblin. He's helping me out.'

Frankie frowned. 'But aren't they, you know . . .?'

she said doubtfully before trailing off.

'Aren't they what?'

'Aren't they the *baddies*?' said Frankie in a stage whisper. 'In all the stories, your orc-slash-goblin type of person tends to be.' She turned to Joel in frustration. 'Help me out here, will you?'

'Our grandad was kidnapped,' said Joel, 'and it was a big giant goblin – sorry, gnoblin, did you say?' The woman nodded. 'It was a huge gnoblin that carried him off.'

'*Ri-ight.*' Justice looked at Frankie quizzically. 'And because you met one evil gnoblin you've decided that all gnoblins are – how did you put it? – *baddies*?'

'It is kind of unfair when you think about it, Frankie,' reasoned Joel.

'OK, OK, sorry.' Frankie held up her hands. Basin, looking confused, scurried over to the fire and started blowing on the twigs. 'This is all pretty new to me. We're not from around here.'

'You can say that again.' Justice examined them more closely. 'You're Otherlanders,' she said in surprise. 'What on earth?'

'Ooh,' said Basin, turning away from the fire, where a small lick of flame was already spreading.

'I never see'd an Otherlander before. Look at their strange garb, Mistress!'

Justice perched herself on a stone, still regarding Frankie and Joel with fascination.

'My name's Frankie,' Frankie told her, attempting to sound confident and adventurer-esque. 'This is my brother, Joel.'

'We're on a quest!' piped up Joel excitedly, which rather spoiled this air of cool casualness. If there's one thing that people on quests don't tend to do, it's exclaim the words, 'We're on a quest!' in the same tone of voice they'd also use to say the phrase, 'We've just won a lifetime's supply of chocolate!'

'I thought you must be,' replied the woman calmly. 'An injustice has been done to you. A huge injustice.'

'How the heck do you know that?' said Frankie incredulously, realizing there was no point trying to stay enigmatic any more.

'This told me,' the woman replied, holding up her hand to show them what she'd been examining so carefully. In it was a small, round metal compass.

Well, Frankie thought as she moved closer to take a better look, *I guess she needs a compass to get around. It's not like Parallelia has GPS.*

But, when she examined the squat, glass-topped disc, she realized there were no markings round the side to denote north, south and all the rest of it. The woman laid her hand flat to show the needle was pointing directly at Frankie herself.

'Oh, is that north, then?' she asked, moving to one side to look over her shoulder. The low morning sun was directly behind her. 'Does the sun rise in a different place here, or what? Because . . . hang on!' Frankie had looked back at the compass to see that the needle was tracking her movements. She kept on circling and, sure enough, the needle followed. 'What on earth is that thing? A Frankie Detector?' she asked suspiciously. 'Can't see there being much call for those, unless Mum loses me down the supermarket again.'

'This,' replied the woman, 'is my Moral Compass. It tells me when an injustice has occurred. And it tells me that you have suffered a very great one.'

As Frankie watched, the red-tipped needle inside the compass jerked upward to tap sharply on the glass, and then down to tick against the metal case. *Ting, ting, tap-tap-tap*.

'Very well,' said the woman solemnly. 'You said

your name is Frankie?' She nodded. 'Frankie, I am a Justice of Parallelia. And I and my sword are at your service until justice has been served.'

'Awesomely cool,' said Joel excitedly, once again completely spoiling the moment.

'Let's sit down,' Justice suggested, 'and you can tell me everything. Then we'll make a plan.'

• • •

'Second Breakfast, anyone?' cried Garyn cheerily ten minutes later, as he marched back into the clearing, laden with armfuls of clothes and a cloth bag swinging from one wrist.

Frankie Best saw a lot of incredible things during her journey through Parallelia, but the double take the knelf did when he saw the four of them sitting calmly by the fire was definitely up there with the most impressive. He actually jumped, jerking his arms upward and sending the clothes and the bag flying into the air.

'What's going on?' he squawked.

'Second Breakfast sounds lovely, thanks, as long as it isn't soup,' said Justice calmly. 'Basin, help this good knelf pick up his belongings.'

Basin began to skip round the hilltop, herding the scattered clothes together as the wind blew them back and forth.

'Garyn, this is Justice,' said Frankie, feeling a warm, proud feeling that she'd made such a cool Parallelian friend while he'd been away. The creeping sense of panic that had been surrounding her since Grandad had been kidnapped had loosened its grip very slightly, and as Garyn looked at her with wide eyes she felt a tiny seed of what might have been confidence. It was too small to tell at the moment, but she hoped it would keep on growing.

'I know it is!' he replied. 'How on earth did you manage to track down a Justice? I've only been gone an hour!'

Frankie's confidence seed swelled ever so slightly, even though she had to admit, 'I didn't actually track her down. But she's here to help!'

'I was somewhere over in Nor'Where,' said Justice as Garyn nervously joined them and they settled themselves on the soft turf beside the fire, 'when my compass told me about a great injustice. It says something very strange is happening to the whole fabric of Parallelia. And now this young lady tells me that one of the custodians has been kidnapped, and his talisman taken as well.'

'The Custodian of Angel Woods,' confirmed Garyn.

'He's our grandad,' Joel explained. 'He said it was the wind, but it wasn't. And he doesn't even have a cat. But Frankie opened the door by accident.'

Justice frowned in puzzlement. 'Well, I don't understand all of this,' she said, 'but the Moral Compass is very clear. We have got to rescue your grandfather. If we don't return him and his talisman, who knows what could happen? The Protections of Parallelia have stood firm for hundreds of years.'

Frankie could see out of the corner of her eye that Garyn was looking at her intently, almost as if he was daring her to ask for more details about these mysterious protections. She straightened her back, determined not to give him the satisfaction.

'Sounds too much like one of Joel's adventures in *Wyverns and Warlocks* for my liking,' she said with a sniff. 'I'm just here to rescue my grandad before Mum and Dad get back.'

'Frankie says she hates quests,' Joel explained.

'Though I think she's starting to enjoy this one a little bit.'

'I am most certainly not,' his sister retorted, catching Garyn's eye once again and giving a slight, involuntary smile and a shrug. 'Now, what was that about breakfast?'

'Second Breakfast!' Joel corrected his sister, beaming.

'Wonderful idea,' said Garyn. 'Well done for getting the fire going.'

As Frankie's seed of confidence put out a tentative green shoot, he delved into the cloth bag. 'Fresh bread,' he announced, turning to his rucksack and somehow producing a frying pan, 'and bacon.'

'It's definitely some kind of magic bag,' Frankie whispered to Joel suspiciously.

As the smell of frying bacon filled the hilltop, she got to her feet before wandering to the edge and gazing into the distance. Thin streams of smoke rose from the rooftops of the village of Artleknock, and far in the distance her eyes could make out a silvery gleam on the horizon that just might have been the sea. The land ahead seemed mainly flat, dotted with patches of forest and, further away, rows and rows of dark green blobs that looked like large bushes of some sort.

'Is that the way we're headed?' she asked Garyn over her shoulder.

'That's right,' he confirmed as he prodded the sizzling bacon. 'Straight to the coast. You heard the kidnappers say they were heading to Tramont Castle – and that's the fastest way. They'll be heading across the bay – and if we don't catch them before we get to Fishsmelling we can pick up a ship there.'

'Good plan,' said Justice approvingly, looking longingly at the contents of the frying pan.

'Maybe even cut them off before they reach the city,' Garyn continued. 'Hand me a roll, will you?'

Basin was already standing at his shoulder with a bread roll ready in each hand. Garyn speared the rashers two at a time and handed round the best bacon sandwich Frankie could ever remember tasting – bread fresh from the bakery and bacon fresh from the wood fire. Though she did make a mental note that next time she was sucked into an adventure in a Magical Fairytale Kingdom, she'd bring ketchup.

'I'm just glad it's not soup,' said Justice through her first mouthful. 'I've been travelling from inne to inne for weeks – it's all they ever seem to have. I'm sick to death of it.'

'So, are you going to come with us, then?' Frankie asked her, a little nervously.

'Of course!' Justice replied. 'I told you my sword was yours, didn't I? That means I come with you, help you, fight for you. Whatever you need. Until justice is served.' There was a thin tapping as her Moral Compass signalled its agreement.

'Shall we get going, then? Finish these on the way?' said Frankie, getting to her feet.

'You're very keen to start,' noted Garyn, grinning. 'Maybe Joel's right – maybe you're starting to enjoy this quest after all. Just a little bit?'

Frankie marched over and lifted up one of the flaps of his yellow woolly hat, speaking directly into a pointy ear. 'Stop calling it a quest,' she said, though without realizing it she was returning his grin. 'Rescue Grandad. Go home. That's the plan. So let's get on with it.'

'As you wish,' he replied with a mocking bow, 'though you'd better get changed before we go.' He pointed to the clothes he'd brought from the village, which Basin had arranged in two immaculate piles.

Sighing theatrically, Frankie grabbed one of the piles and took herself off behind a patch of undergrowth to get changed. Garyn had brought comfortable leather boots, a pair of trousers that felt unexpectedly soft – like really old jeans – and a faded blue top that fastened with a thick leather belt. If she appeared back in her own world dressed like this, she'd immediately explode from embarrassment, but at least they would enable her to pass through Parallelia without attracting too much attention.

'Perfect!' Garyn congratulated her as she appeared sheepishly round the bushes, and once again her mouth smiled, even though she hadn't told it to. He carefully wiped down the frying pan with leaves and wrapped it in cloth before stowing it in his backpack and kicking dirt over the fire.

Joel was already tying his sleeping bag on to his rucksack, dressed in a dark red top, black trousers and a faded green cloak, and clearly enjoying this bit of real-world role play immensely.

'Five of us now,' he pointed out as the others also got ready to leave. 'That's got to be enough to call this a fellowship.'

'We are not,' his sister told him sternly, 'referring to this as a fellowship. Not under any circumstances.'

'The Fellowship of the Bacon Roll,' urged Joel, waving his half-eaten Second Breakfast in her face.

'I like it,' decided Garyn. 'Forward, Fellowship of the Bacon Roll. It's a long, tough day's march to the coast – let's get moving.'

'That name will never catch on,' Frankie muttered as she trailed down the hill after Justice's flowing grey cloak.

•••

Frankie's mind filled with a million questions as the fellowship started their journey towards the coast, but for most of the day she was too out of breath to ask any of them. Garyn hadn't been joking when he'd talked about a tough day's march and, as the miles crept by, it became clear the landscape wasn't quite as flat as it had looked from the hilltop that morning. The ground undulated in a series of low hills and Frankie's legs – usually used as a convenient phone stand – soon learned to dread the shallow uphill stretches.

Justice and Garyn were setting a fast pace, with Joel and Basin plodding just behind them, deep in conversation most of the way. Frankie was reduced to bringing up the rear, feeling rather like a spare part as the sun reached its highest point and her feet grew more and more sore.

'Where are we?' she finally asked Justice, breaking into a jog to catch up with the front of the group. They were now walking across a wide, grassy valley, making for a series of slightly higher hills in the near distance. She noticed the dust their boots kicked up was a lighter, more yellow colour. The soil was growing sandy – the sea couldn't be very far away.

'We're crossing the edge of Bethcar,' Justice replied.

'Yeah, I have no idea what that is,' Frankie said, unable to stop herself getting a little snappy after long hours on the march with no food. The bacon roll was now merely a distant, albeit very tasty, memory.

'There's a large map in your rucksack, remember?' Garyn pointed out.

'Bethcar is right in the south-east of Parallelia,' Justice explained kindly. 'At the bottom end of Calmwater Bay.'

'Great ships do take the Bethcar pears right around the world every harvest time,' added Basin. 'We got some at the inne once. Don't think I never tasted nothing so wonderful, neither.'

'Bethcar pears are a local delicacy,' said Joel. 'They're used to make pear wine. Basin says if we pass some of the orchards we might get to taste one.'

'I'd rather have another Mumbai Madman . . .' Frankie was still feeling grumpy after the long march, trailing at the back of the fellowship.

Her mood didn't improve over the next hour, either. The soil grew sandier still as they reached the hills and began to climb. With every step, her new leather boots sank up to the heel, and she was soon sweating and sulking in just about equal quantities. But when she reached the top of the ridge, she forgot to sulk. She let out a small gasp at the view now spread out before them.

The land sloped away towards the sea in what looked for all the world like a giant set of shallow steps covered in a fine, light green carpet. The slopes were scattered with untidy rows of huge, spiky bushes with glossy dark leaves – the dark shapes they'd seen from the hilltop that morning. And at the bottom of the stairs, so to speak, was the sea, batting the sunlight back into the air like a sheet of polished metal. Numerous rocky outcrops and small islands broke the surface, ringed with white waves as if someone had circled them with paint. The sun was dipping low, giving the entire scene a serene golden glow.

'Welcome to the pear orchards of Bethcar,' said Justice, hitching up her sword belt. 'Only an hour or two to the coast now – we should be at Fishsmelling by nightfall. Come on.' And she strode off down the slope.

'They don't look much like pear trees to me,' muttered Frankie as they passed the first of the towering bushes. In between the thick leaves, sturdy, twisted thorns stuck out at all angles, ridged and extremely sharp-looking. 'I can't even see any fruit on them.'

'The pears grow on the inside,' said Garyn, coming up to join her.

'Mayn't we get one, Mister Garyn?' pleaded Basin, looking longingly at the threatening spikes. 'Just a small 'un, mebbe?'

'Be careful then,' said Garyn, nodding. And, without further ado, Basin dropped to the ground and rolled underneath the bush, scrabbling at the sandy soil to avoid the lowermost thorns.

'It's a great defence mechanism,' said the knelf, reaching out a finger to test a thorn and immediately drawing it back and sucking it. 'Ow! Yes, they're sharp all right. The Bethcarians have to dig underneath – like Basin's done – to carry out the harvest. It's dangerous work.'

There was more scrabbling and Basin reappeared with two large golden fruits clutched carefully to his chest with one arm.

'There you go, missus,' he told Frankie, labouring to his feet and holding out one of them. 'Wager you never did taste the like, like.'

She took it from him uncertainly and examined it. It didn't look like anything they'd describe as a pear in her local supermarket. It was bigger, for a start – the size of a mango – and covered with fine hair like a kiwi fruit. She sniffed it uncertainly.

'T'aint hurt you!' Basin laughed, taking a bite out of the other pear and capering off down the hill, yelling, 'Joel! Get yerself outside o' this.'

Bethcar pears won't grow anywhere outside Parallelia, which is a pity because if anyone was able to cultivate them in our world they'd make a fortune. It was, quite simply, the most delicious piece of fruit Frankie had ever tried. The skin was soft, but the sea air had given it the very slightest hint of salt. Inside, the flesh was cool and tasted something like elderflowers, something like lime and something like the scent of blossom. It was pretty darned great, basically.

'WHOA,' she said in amazement. 'No wonder the people here risk getting impaled on thorns to pick these things.'

Garyn smirked. 'Told you,' he said. 'Come on, race you to the cliffs.' And he dashed away from her down the slope, where the figures of Justice, Basin and Joel were already diminishing in the middle distance.

Frankie broke into a half-hearted trot for a few seconds, but soon slowed down again so she could give the pear her full attention. And she was still lagging behind an hour or so later when she pushed noisily through a thicket to see the rest of the fellowship turning round and shushing her. All four of them were crouched down near the edge of a low cliff – one of those sandy ones you get beside dunes that are such fun to jump off. It led to a wide beach, but it wasn't the beach they were all looking at.

Right on the lip of the cliff sat a row of small, plump birds. They were covered in orangey-brown downy fur somewhere between fuzz and feathers, and had short, stumpy wings. One of them, apparently a parent as it was much larger than the others, was waddling up and down the line, uttering a series of sharp, squeaky cries. The smaller ones – seven of them, she quickly counted – were shuffling about nervously.

'Ping wings,' Garyn told Frankie in a whisper as she crouched down beside him. 'Stay very quiet – don't scare them away. The mother bird's trying to teach them to fly.'

'With those?' she hissed back, peering at the stubby, blunt appendages – more like slightly flattened arms than wings.

'Yeah, they're flightless. But it doesn't stop them trying. Look!'

Encouraged by a series of squawks from their mother, the babies all started to whirr their wings frantically, some windmilling them, some beating them up and down. Once they were all flapping frenziedly, the larger bird hopped along the line behind them, lifting a webbed foot and booting each tiny ping wing squarely in the small of its back. With a startled *peep*, each of them disappeared over the edge of the cliff. There was a series of dull thuds as they hit the beach, then a shuffling and squeaking.

After a few minutes, during which the mother fussed up and down, peering over the edge, the babies reappeared a little way to her right, toiling up a shallower part of the slope and lining up once again in preparation for another flying lesson.

Joel, who was lying on his stomach at the other end of the row, beckoned her over. 'Look, Frankie,' he whispered. 'Grandad wrote about them in the Bestiary.'

He had pulled the black notebook out of his pocket and smoothed it out in front of him. Sure enough, as Frankie lay down beside her brother, she could see a delicate watercolour sketch of the birds now lining themselves back up in front of them.

PING WINGS

are the most optimistic creatures I have ever encountered. They seem to have a constant belief that they will, at some point, evolve so they are able to fly. Each parent bird is convinced that their children will be the first generation to do so, and become the ancestors of a whole new species of flying ping wings.

Parallelian children sing a nursery rhyme about them, which goes as follows:

> *Ping wing, ping wing, will you fly?*
> *Ping wing, ping wing, won't you try?*
> *Ping wing, ping wing, though you drop,*
> *Ping wing, ping wing, never, ever stop.*

It's all very inspiring.

'I think it's incredible,' said Joel, looking as if his brain might explode with the effort of fitting all these marvels inside it.

'I think it's completely and utterly mad,' said Frankie crossly. 'Their mum is literally kicking them off a cliff!'

'She believes that – one day – one of them could become the first ping wing to fly,' Garyn countered, crawling over to lie beside her. 'Isn't there any part of you that might find that just a teensy bit wonderful?'

Frankie crinkled her nose at him. 'Teensy bit,' she admitted.

Briefly, she wondered what would happen if she brought her school friends here and showed them the ping wing flying lesson. What would they do? Make fun of them, like she'd been tempted to do? Maybe it was better to react like Joel and Garyn. Perhaps there was nothing so very terrible about finding things wonderful every now and then. Even just a teensy bit.

CHAPTER 9

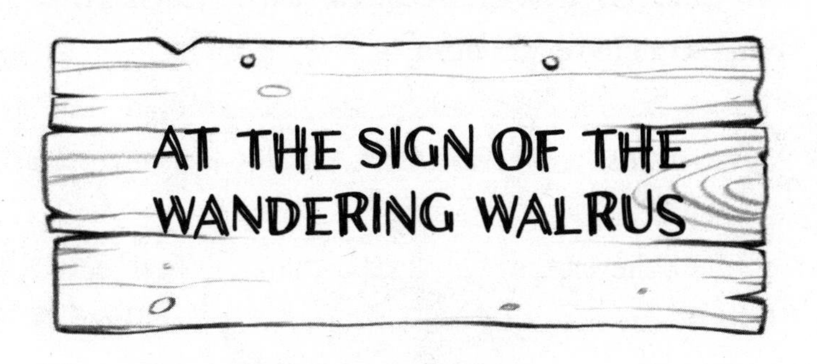

The Fellowship of the Bacon Roll passed several more family groups of ping wings as they followed a wide, grassy track along the edge of the beach. The squeaking and thumping as the young were kicked over the cliffs filled the early-evening air, and the sea began to reflect a burning sunset. Frankie's stomach was beginning to tell her it was time for dinner, and she was relieved to see plumes of chimney smoke rising from somewhere not far ahead along the coast.

'So that's – what do you call it – Fishy Town?' she asked Justice, who was striding along beside her.

'Fishsmelling-on-Sea,' she said. 'Biggest port in Bethcar. We should have no trouble picking up a ship that will take us north.'

'No need to ask how it got its name . . .' Frankie grimaced as a waft of breeze carried a strident porty pong straight up her nose.

• • •

The Journal of Frankie Best

So, for tonight's entry, I've got to start with the smell. That's something else they never tell you in this kind of story – along with the toilet arrangements. They never tell you that a lot of the time Magical Fairytale Kingdoms *smell*. I mean, they smell really, *really* bad. Partly because of the toilet situation, of course. But also due to a lot of other factors – the general use of horses as transportation; the fact that people don't have kitchen bins with properly closing lids; and the fact that if you used the words deodorant, toothpaste or shower gel they'd probably think you were talking about some faraway land or legendary hero: 'Come listen to my ballad, and hear of the marvellous adventures of Deodorant the Mighty! And his valiant steed, Shower Gel!'

Anyway, what I'm getting at is that the port of Fishsmelling-on-Sea smelled fairly

ripe, as if someone had taken a sardine, put it inside a sock they'd been wearing for a year or two, and then left the fish-stuffed sock atop a cowpat in the sun for about a fortnight. Apart from that, it wasn't a bad sort of place once you got used to its trademark scent.

We got our first proper look at it as we crested a sandy hill, passing one final group of adrenaline-junkie ping wings who had selected a worryingly high cliff for their evolution practice. Ahead of us, jumbled round the head of a large cove as if dropped there by a toddler, was a ramshackle collection of houses. A wide stone jetty curved around the seafront, and bobbing about in the bay was a motley collection of boats. Many were proper big sailing ships – you know, real *Pirates of the Caribbean* kind of things. But clustered round and between them were loads more – little rowing boats, rafts, canoes – all

sploshing back and forth, laden with chests, barrels and piles of Bethcar pears.

I knew Joel was going to cry out the word 'awesome', but here's the funny thing. For the first time, I was almost tempted to join him. Despite its unpleasant name and even more unpleasant signature fragrance, Fishsmelling-on-Sea was . . . kind of cool. I liked it the first time I saw it – and not just because I was, by now, completely and utterly starving.

'Let's find an inne,' suggested Garyn. 'See if we can get something to eat.'

Justice wasn't optimistic. 'It'll be soup,' she told him. 'It's always soup.'

'Then I'll look for a ship,' continued the knelf as we approached the first houses. 'Looks like some of these are getting ready to sail. If we're lucky, we could be halfway across the bay by this time tomorrow.'

If you ever find yourself in the bustling port of Fishsmelling-on-Sea – which is rather unlikely, but if you do – then I can highly recommend you stay at the Wandering Walrus. You'll find it in a prime location right on the quay, just behind a large pile of semi-decomposed fish heads. Look for the badly painted sign of a walrus with a spotted handkerchief on a stick over its shoulder, and you're there.

From the very moment you walk through the door, Mrs Mumpish will ensure you're treated like absolute royalty. No, not royalty. What's the word I'm looking for? Ah yes, manure – that's it. Mrs Mumpish will ensure you're treated like absolute manure. And don't forget to try the house speciality – starfish soup. You'll feel like you're actually eating a slightly warmed-up rock pool. Frankie's review: five starfish out of five. A must-stay (sarcasm).

'Ho, just what I need,' growled Mrs Mumpish as the Fellowship of the Bacon Roll pushed through the door and into the large, wooden-floored inne. 'More flamin' customers.'

Looking around, Frankie couldn't help thinking that more customers was exactly what the innekeeper of the Wandering Walrus did, in fact, need. A swift headcount revealed no more than seven people scattered round the room – a couple of old sea-dog types propping up the bar and a few more clustered round the rickety tables.

The owner herself was a tiny woman, who was dwarfed even by Joel and Basin. She had a red, weather-beaten face with a crop of wispy white hair on top – not unlike a tomato that had been forgotten at the back of the fridge for a couple of decades and gone wrinkled and mouldy. When they first entered the Wandering Walrus, Frankie could only see her head poking above the bar – at first glance thinking she was one of those novelty charity money boxes you see sometimes. It was only when the money box started speaking that she realized there was a body attached to it – and the body in question was soon stomping across the room towards them.

'I'm Mumpish,' she declared as she approached, her wide skirts swishing threateningly. 'I expect you're wanting food and lodging, is it? Just what I need, that is.'

'That is what innes usually offer,' said Justice, looking a little confused at this hostile welcome.

'Ho, is it now?' Mrs Mumpish placed her hands on her hips and craned her neck painfully backwards to glare furiously into the taller woman's face. 'What innes usually offer, is it? Just what I need, that is. To be told what I should be offering. Ho yes.'

'Maybe we should go somewhere else,' proffered Garyn politely.

'Go somewhere else?' shrieked Mrs Mumpish. 'Just what I need, that is. Five customers coming in, giving a poor old widow a meagre shred of hope that her struggling inne might get a bit of business, then to have even that crumb of possibility hoicked back out of her mouth just when she was starting to get a taste of it. Ho, just what I need. Soup of the day is starfish.'

She pointed with an air of finality at a large, empty table beneath the grimy windows along the front of the pub.

Justice moaned. 'Told you it'd be soup,' she said bitterly, selecting the least uncomfortable-looking chair and stretching her long legs out towards a pale, disappointing fire that flickered in the grate. 'It's always soup.'

'Five soups then.' Mrs Mumpish had decided without asking. 'And five ales. I don't know. Pouring ales all afternoon like a bloomin' skivvy. Just what I need.'

She swept back across the room and vanished behind the bar, where clanking, complaining and sploshing noises mingled as she began to pour drinks.

Frankie Best was not a big ale drinker. You'd

presumably be quite worried if she was, considering she was twelve. *How on earth do people drink this for fun?* she thought, taking a tentative sip from the pewter tankard that Mrs Mumpish had plonked aggressively in front of her. It tasted like a tablespoon of Marmite stirred into a mug of stagnant pond water.

'I wonder if I might just have a glass of tap water?' she called after the innekeeper's retreating back, but Mrs Mumpish either didn't hear or – and let's be honest, this is a lot more likely – simply ignored her.

'I'll drink yours if you don't want it,' said Garyn, who was taking long pulls at his tankard with every appearance of enjoyment.

'Though you might want to hang on to it,' said Justice darkly. 'You'll probably need it to take away the taste of the soup.' As it turns out, she was absolutely right.

After the fellowship had disposed of their bowls of starfish soup, Garyn went out to try and find a ship that would take them as passengers. (By the way, saying they disposed of their soup isn't just a fancy way of saying they ate it. They took a couple of mouthfuls between the five of them, then paddled their sporks around in it for a while. Next they sat there staring at it, hoping it might eventually evaporate. But it wasn't nearly warm enough to do that, so in the end they literally disposed of it by tipping it out of the window when Mrs Mumpish had harrumphed out of the bar to go and prepare their room upstairs. The following morning it was still there in globulous puddles on the quay outside, proving that whatever creatures roam Parallelia at night looking for scraps, they must at least have some standards.)

Justice sat back in her chair, propping her high grey boots on a low stool, pulling up her hood and producing a long pale pipe from somewhere. She sat, calmly blowing smoke rings, as the faint firelight illuminated her sharp-featured face, looking so much like a character from *Wyverns and Warlocks* that Joel stared at her, open-mouthed, for fully half an hour, only blinking when absolutely necessary.

In the meantime, Frankie chatted quietly to Basin about his life back at the inne in Nor'Where and his journey with Justice across the Insurmountable Slodge. She'd started the conversation as a way to fill time, but in the end she found the young gnoblin to be a bright and friendly companion. Eventually, she ended up trying to explain some details about her own life to him, but to her surprise they already seemed a little remote and other-worldly. The concept of messaging someone on a phone, which she thought the little gnoblin would find fascinating, didn't interest him at all.

'Just go and speak to 'em proper, like,' he said, frowning. Only when Frankie started talking about supermarkets did his eyes light up. 'What, they do sell all foods?' he asked eagerly. 'All from one room?'

'Yes, all foods,' she told him.

'Not fish, though.'

'Yes, Basin. *All* foods.'

'Not herbs.'

'All foods. All of them. Herbs, fish. All of it.'

'Well, 'tis a thing I would dearly love for to see,' he said breathlessly.

Frankie smiled warmly, imagining leading him into their local superstore, as around them the patrons of the Wandering Walrus ambled in and out – mainly the latter.

When it was completely dark outside, Garyn came bursting through the door, rubbing his hands against the cold, followed by a very tall man in a bright blue jacket.

Mrs Mumpish, who by now was back in position, mostly hidden behind the bar, muttered, 'And now another one. Wantin' serving and expecting me to wait on him hand and foot, I'll be bound. Ho, just what I need.'

'Captain Fry here has a ship that might suit us,' said the knelf. 'And he's due to sail on the morning tide.'

'Horatio Fry,' announced the man, casting an eye round the table. 'Master and commander of the good ship *Spindrift*.'

He had a long, thin, oblong head that did, in fact, look not unlike a giant French fry – burnt a rich golden brown by the sun and salted by the sea breeze. If it was indeed a fry, it had been dunked in a generous pool of mayonnaise – very continental – because the bottom half of his face was enrobed in a luxurious white moustache and beard.

'Won't you take an ale with us, Captain Fry?' said Justice, sitting forward and setting down her pipe.

'Aye.' The captain pulled up a chair and accepted a foaming tankard from Mrs Mumpish, who sulked off, muttering something about endless drudgery.

'So you good people are after passage across the bay?'

Frankie was a little disappointed that he didn't have a proper pirate voice. She'd been expecting Garyn to come back with someone who peppered their speech with the word 'arr' at random intervals. In fact, his voice was deep and rather cultured. He didn't sound as if he'd ever shivered a timber in his entire life. But, as she was beginning to learn, Parallelia was full of surprises.

'I'm not even going to ask why a Justice, a knelf and three children want to cross Calmwater Bay so badly,' said the captain in the tone of voice that implied that he was, in a very real sense, asking that exact question. He raised both his tankard and a pair of quizzical eyebrows, but Justice cut him short.

'Best not to,' she told him curtly. 'A wise man would accept their generous payment and keep any questions to themselves.'

At this point, Garyn, who had once again been rummaging in his possibly-magic rucksack, plonked a leather pouch on the table in that dramatic way payment always seems to be offered in this kind of story. In fact, it's happened twice in this one already and we're only halfway through.

'Just as you say, Madam Justice,' said Captain Fry solemnly, grabbing the pouch and weighing it in his hand. 'Well, my cargo is almost loaded. If you can be on board at two bells of the morning watch, I'll take you and gladly.' He slammed the empty tankard back on to the wooden table and got to his feet. There were two of them, and Frankie was slightly sad to realize that he lost even more pirate points because neither of them was wooden.

'We'd better get some sleep, then,' said Justice as the sea captain left the pub. 'Early start tomorrow.'

'What's two morning bells, then, or whatever he said?' Frankie wanted to know.

Justice translated. 'Five o'clock in the morning,' she said, deadpan.

'Sorry?' said Frankie. **'Who o'clock in the – WHAT THE ACTUAL HECK?'**

• • •

Sleeping on the bed at the Wandering Walrus felt like lying on an old sack stuffed with sand – and Frankie highly suspected there was an excellent reason for that. But she was so tired after the day's march through Bethcar that she didn't much care. She wrote in her journal for a while, by the light of a flickering candle but, by the time she'd finished her fake online review of the inne, exhaustion was lapping at her brain like the slow waves of the dark sea outside the window. She stuffed the book back into her rucksack and was asleep within seconds – even Basin's snoring from across the room didn't wake her.

What did wake her was being gently shaken by the shoulder just a few short hours later. Feeling like her eyeballs had been stuffed with room-temperature sawdust, Frankie blinked and grimaced into the face of Garyn, who was bending over her, already fully dressed and with his (possibly-magic) backpack on.

'Time to go,' he whispered apologetically.

Automatically, Frankie's hand reached out to grab her phone from the bedside table, until she remembered where she was. The phone was tucked into her trouser pocket, blank and lifeless. It wouldn't turn back on until she was close to a portal out of Parallelia.

She sat up groggily to see Justice perched on a stool, gazing out of the wide windows that were made of thick, diamond-shaped panes of glass. Levering herself out of bed like an insomniac zombie, Frankie tiptoed over to join her, cracking a yawn so enormous that it felt as if it might flip her entire head open.

Outside, the sun was just coming up – a hazy lemon above the bay – and in the pale dawn light she could see that a ship had been moored right in front of the Wandering Walrus. It was so close that she could clearly see the name *Spindrift* picked out in gold paint on the black prow. In front of the name was a large, carved wooden figurehead, but it wasn't the usual generously chested lady that old-time sailors in our world seemed to favour. It was a long horse's head, surrounded by intricately carved waves that had been painted a bright blue.

Frankie could see people moving about on deck and, as she watched the first proper rays of sun picking out the top of the tall mast, something rather unexpected happened. A surging excitement began to fill her up at the prospect of a sea voyage on a sunny day. It felt like Christmas. In fact, even better. It felt like she'd woken up to be told it was a brand-new, secret holiday even better than Christmas, one that celebrated sunlight and sea spray and sand. An orange dawn washed over the wide bay, catching the millions of wavelets and flinging light up at the window like handfuls of thrown gold.

What on earth is wrong with me? she thought as another grin ambushed her half-awake face. *This is the time of the morning when I'd usually get up and go for a quick wee before sinking back under the duvet.* She was slightly concerned by the strong possibility that Parallelia was turning her into a morning person.

''Spec' you'll want breakfast?' said a voice from the doorway. 'Just what I need.'

'Morning, Mrs Mumpish,' said Justice calmly. 'We'll be down in ten minutes.'

There was a general rustling of bedclothes as the rest of the fellowship stirred sleepily under their blankets, and a long groan from Joel, who was normally even worse at getting up in the morning than his sister.

Downstairs, despite the ridiculously early hour, the wooden floor of the bar had already been scrubbed clean. Mrs Mumpish certainly liked to complain, but she kept a tidy inne. If she went off on a short residential soup-making course, she might show real potential.

Breakfast, luckily, wasn't more starfish soup. (Though, if any of them had wanted some, they could simply have popped outside and scraped up one of the splats on the cobbles.) There was a tray of little flat oaty cakes, and a big pottery jug of a golden liquid that was – Frankie realized as soon as she sniffed it suspiciously – Bethcar pear juice. It was the second-best breakfast she'd ever eaten – the previous day's unexpected bacon roll still just about hanging on to the top spot.

''Spec' you'll want to pay? Just what I need,'

muttered Mrs Mumpish as Garyn approached with yet another pouch of coins, pulled once again from the depths of his rucksack.

'He's got a lot of pouches of gold, hasn't he?' mumbled Joel to Frankie through a mouthful of oatcake.

'Hmm,' she agreed, absent-mindedly gazing out at the *Spindrift* bobbing gently on the quayside. 'I don't know what kind of a salary he pulls down as Sentinel for one of the portals of Parallelia, but it clearly isn't too shabby. You should look into it when you're old enough. Weird creatures, Magical Fairytale Kingdoms . . . It'd suit you down to the ground.'

'Time to set sail,' said Justice, throwing open the door and admitting a smack of salty air and a glutinous trickle of starfish soup.

'Bye, Mrs Mumpish,' called Frankie as she got to her feet and shouldered her bag. 'See you again soon! Thanks for the soup! I'll leave you a great review online.'

The innekeeper simply glared and carried on counting the coins Garyn had handed her.

'A review on what line?' queried Justice, holding the door open.

Captain Fry was leaning over the *Spindrift*'s rail,

deep in negotiations with a man on the dock who'd dragged a cart laden with pears right up to the side of the ship.

'Look lively there! Handsomely, now!' he shouted over his shoulder, and a group of burly sailors quickly vaulted over the rail and started loading the cargo. At that moment, a bell began to ring and the captain noticed the Fellowship of the Bacon Roll weaving their way across the quay towards him.

He congratulated them. 'Ah, right on time, right on time,' he said, waving his hand at the gangplank. 'Come aboard, smartly now. We sail as soon as these pears are loaded.'

The wide deck of the *Spindrift* was busy as the ship's crew dashed around, doing what looked like very complicated things mainly involving rope. Captain Fry, having tossed a few coins down to the pear farmer, accompanied the passengers towards one of the doors set into the front of the quarterdeck.

'Through my cabin and down the stairs,' he told them. 'That's where you'll sleep. Drop your gear off, and then I'm sure you'll want to be on deck as we pass through Shipwreck Shoals.'

'Sorry?' said Frankie. 'We're passing through the wh–' But even that fairly urgent question died in her throat as her eyes adjusted and she got a proper look at the inside of the ship.

Captain Fry had ushered them into a wide room, with windows right across the *Spindrift's* stern. A table filled the centre of the space, and various cutlasses, telescopes and other bits of seafaring tat were attached to the walls. But it wasn't the table or the maritime accessories that had caught Frankie's attention. It was the sheer number of rats scuttling around on the floor. Large rats, too – unusually sleek and clean-looking, running here and there as if they actually owned the place.

'GAH!' she screamed, taking a couple of steps backwards and reversing hard into Justice. **'YOUR SHIP IS FULL OF FLIPPIN' RATS!'**

Captain Fry, who had walked straight to the table where a chart was spread, weighed down with lumps of coral, threw out his arm as if to say *ta-dah!*

'Aye, indeed,' he said proudly. 'More rats than any other ship afloat, I'll be bound. Yes, young lady. The rattiest sloop in the harbour, or my name's not Captain Horatio Fry.'

Frankie stared at him uncomprehendingly, the rats in her peripheral vision making it look as if the captain's cabin was equipped with a gently moving brown carpet.

'You're acting like it's a good thing,' she pointed out lamely. His enthusiasm for his ship's rodent quota had – if you'll pardon the old-time ship metaphor – rather taken the wind out of her sails.

The captain seemed surprised. 'It is a good thing,' he said, looking down at the rats as if seeing them

properly for the first time. 'Rats hate to get wet, you know. The more rats there are, the drier the ship.'

'It's very impressive, Captain Fry,' said Justice soothingly, moving past Frankie and joining him at the table. 'I don't think I've ever been on a ship with more rats on it.'

He puffed up with pride as if she'd just told him he'd been nominated for the Sea Captain of the Year Award, before pointing down some stairs.

'You'll find hammocks slung for you on the lower deck,' he told them. 'Don't leave any of your belongings on the floor now, will you?'

'Why?' Joel wanted to know. 'Is it because you keep a tidy ship and hate mess?'

'Not really,' replied Captain Fry, screwing up his long face. 'It's just that if you leave anything on the floor, the rats will eat it.'

'That's brilliant,' decided Joel.

'That's completely revolting,' contradicted Frankie, her earlier enthusiasm for a sea voyage evaporating – unlike her bowl of starfish soup, which was still stubbornly puddled on the cobblestones outside the Wandering Walrus.

CHAPTER 10

THE VOYAGE OF THE *SPINDRIFT*

The cabin assigned to the fellowship was small, dark and cramped. Not only that, it smelled like half a dozen goats had been shut inside it for the past week with nothing to eat except a very garlicky fondue. Add to that the rats scuttling hither and yon on the wooden floor, and Frankie was extremely glad to dump her bag on one of the five swinging hammocks and dive back up the stairs towards the sunlight and fresh air of the top deck.

It wasn't that she was scared of rats particularly – she just wasn't relishing the thought of sharing sleeping quarters with, like, a thousand of them. She resolved not to go below deck until it was dark enough to simply pretend they weren't there. If she stepped on one, she could just put it down to squeaky shoes or something.

The sailors on deck had stopped running about and were now manning their posts, keenly awaiting the captain's orders. Several of them had lowered long oars into the water; others were standing beside the thick ropes that fastened the *Spindrift* to the dock; and a group of five had taken up positions at the very front of the ship, hands clasped in front of them as if they were about to give a performance of some kind.

'Stand by to cast off!' bellowed Captain Fry, emerging from his cabin and allowing everyone on deck another brief glimpse of the rat-themed safari park in full swing behind him. 'Oarsmen ready! Songsters ready!'

'Songsters?' Frankie turned quizzically to Garyn, who was leaning on the rail beside her, gazing out to sea next to Joel, who looked slightly apprehensive.

'Ah yes, you're about to see something pretty impressive,' the knelf told her, a fresh sea breeze tugging at the ear flaps of his yellow hat. 'Before the crew can hoist sail in the main part of the bay, they need to steer through Shipwreck Shoals.'

'Shipwreck Shoals, right,' said Frankie doubtfully.

'I take it that the name's ironic in some way?'

'Not really. You see, just outside the harbour the sea's full of hidden rocks, reefs, currents . . . All kinds of dangerous stuff. But ships have been sailing these waters for generations, and gradually the mariners worked out the safest route through. They passed the secret down from captain to captain, and now most ships can get through safely, as long as they remember all the words, that is.'

'All the words to what?'

'To the song,' he told her. 'The safe route to get out of Fishsmelling and through Shipwreck Shoals has been passed down in a song. Those men and women at the front of the boat are getting ready to guide us.'

'What about coming from the other direction?' Joel piped up. 'What if you're trying to get back into Fishsmelling?'

'Well, if they're rowing in the other direction,' said the knelf, 'they have to sing the song backwards, of course.'

'Ah one,' bellowed Captain Fry at the top of his voice, 'ah two, ah one two three four . . .'

Frankie sighed. 'You have got, once again, to be actually kidding me.'

As the huge oars dipped into the water – and as the sailors at each end of the ship cast off their ropes and coiled them neatly on deck – the five people at the front of the *Spindrift* began to sing in harmony:

'Oh row, oh row, oh row (two three four).

Row, oh, me hearties, row.

Row and row, then row (two three four).

Row, row, row some more.'

'Takes a while to get to the interesting parts,' said Captain Fry, striding over to join them. 'We need to get out of the harbour first, but we must start the song as soon as we cast off, or the timing goes all wonky.'

The sailors at the front took up the song again:

'Continue rowing, me hearties,

Row, row, row, row, row.

Do not stop rowing under any circumstances.

Failure to row at this point would have extremely serious consequences.'

'Give me strength,' muttered Frankie, turning her back on the captain and propping her elbows on the rail. Already the ship was moving at a surprising pace past the other boats in the harbour and, as she watched, the high stone walls that guarded the entrance to the port of Fishsmelling-on-Sea slipped past. She leaned out further, reaching up a hand to shield her eyes from the low morning sun as she gazed ahead across Shipwreck Shoals. Everywhere she looked, spray fountained into the air from numerous rocks, and rows of creamy white waves showed the location of underwater reefs. It just didn't seem possible that a ship this size could find its way through the maze.

'The reef ahead means certain death,' went the song at this point. The smallest of the sailors diverted into a brief freestyle, warbling 'certain, certain, certain, certaaaaaiiiiin deeeeeeee-he-he-he-he-heath' on his own while the waves pounded behind him like the distant roar of a stadium crowd.

'We're going to hit it!' yelled Frankie, peering through the spray and getting a faceful of sea into the bargain.

The *Spindrift* was heading full tilt towards the breakers, which were now so close that she could actually see the jagged rocks half buried among the waves, like chunks of cookie dough and chocolate peeking out of a posh tub of ice cream – only considerably more fatal.

She was extremely relieved to pick out the lyrics to the next line of the song carried across the deck above the roaring of the waves:

'Unless we steer immediately left.' ('Immediately left, imm-ee-eee-eeee-eeee-diately left,' quavered the smallest sailor.) At once, the short, wide woman holding the wheel threw it dramatically to her left, and the entire ship heeled sickeningly over on to one side.

'Clap on to a sheet there,' called Captain Fry as Frankie was sent sprawling on to the deck. 'It gets a little choppy from here on in.' He was holding firmly on to one of the numerous ropes that rose from the deck to the tall mast, and as she scrambled to her feet she decided that would be an excellent example to follow.

'And now a second reef is ahead,
Another hard left or we'll all be dead.'

This time Frankie kept on her feet, clinging desperately to the rope as the ship once again rolled to one side, so far that the rail on the opposite side actually dipped underneath the greenish foam.

'And now row forward for a count of seven'
(Littlest sailor: 'One two three four fiiiiive six seven')

'Before turning right to avoid ship heaven.'

You don't need to be burdened with the entire Shipwreck Shoals song – it goes on for eighty-nine stanzas in total. Frankie could testify to this because she counted them to try and keep calm as the *Spindrift* careered crazily through reefs, rocks, whirlpools and, at one point near the end of the song, through a narrow channel between two barren islands. The channel was called the Tyger's Mouth, and it was lined on either side with terrifying sharp rocks that stuck out at all angles like teeth.

The ship had to constantly steer left and right to avoid being punctured. Several times, the rocks loomed so close that Frankie could have reached out and touched them if she'd been willing to risk losing a finger or three. They were formed from what looked like a volcanic rock of some kind, dark and shiny and extremely pointy. But finally they were through. The Tyger's Mouth receded behind them, and for the first time she could look ahead across the open sea without identifying at least eight things within a biscuit's throw of the *Spindrift*'s prow that could sink it.

'And now the shoals have been navigated.

(Na-ha-ha-ha-ha-ha-ha-ha-haaaaa-vigated.)
The Gods of the Sea hath been placated.
(BINNN placated, BINNN placated.)
The rolling deeps are now our friend,
And our song
(And our song, and our so-ho-ho-ho-hong)
Is at . . .
(Is HAT, is HAAAAAAT)
An . . . end.'

Joel clapped enthusiastically and Frankie found herself joining in, more out of relief than anything else. For the first time in an hour or two, the ship was on an even keel, floating calmly with nothing ahead but flat ocean. The sky overhead was a washed-out blue, with a few clouds in the distance that looked like they'd just been put there to complete the effect, though one did have a curtain of greyish rain hanging off it like dirty lace.

'Any minute now, we'll pick up the Dragon's Breath,' said Captain Fry, stomping across the deck and pointing up at the mast. 'Then you'll really see something.'

'Shipwreck Shoals was quite enough of a thing for one day, thanks,' Frankie told him, shivering slightly.

'I am no longer taking auditions for new things.'

'That was too scary,' complained Joel. 'I thought we were going to crash and sink!'

The captain was indignant. 'We haven't crashed and sunk yet!'

'Well, obviously not,' said Frankie reasonably. 'Every captain probably says that, until they actually do crash and sink. Then they don't say anything apart from, "Help, help, I'm drowning, *blub-blub-blub*."'

Fry inclined his head in agreement at this unanswerable piece of logic, and at that point a clean, sharp gust of wind blew across the deck.

'All hands prepare to hoist sail!' he bellowed suddenly. And, at once, sailors began swarming up the ropes like monkeys, calling out things to each other that sounded extremely complicated, full of words like *jib*, *reef* and *main brace*.

'SHEETS HO!' screeched the captain as the sailors spread out along the wooden crosspiece set near the top of the mast.

At this, they all leaped off it at the same time, holding on to the ends of ropes and dropping like some complicated acrobatics act at a very contemporary circus. As they plummeted towards the deck like nautically attired bungee jumpers, a huge white-and-purple striped sail that had been folded up beneath them leaped into life and soared upward, fastened to the other end of each rope. The sail rose into position, catching the wind, puffing out dramatically and slowing the sailors' descent just before they slammed into the wooden planks below. Instead, they each made a delicate landing and ran backwards to tie up their rope ends round metal rings set into the deck.

As soon as this happened, the *Spindrift* leaned forward like a racehorse that really, really means business. There was a hooshing roar from the front of the ship as it dipped downwards into the waves and began to surge forward at an increasingly exciting pace.

Joel and Frankie whooped – yes, that's right, Frankie whooped. It's true that she's not come across as much of a whooper thus far in the story, but at this point she whooped like a good 'un. The feeling of speed, the sunlight diffused through the huge expanse of the sail and the sting of the salt spray on her face – you would have whooped, too.

'The Dragon's Breath will carry us all the way across Calmwater Bay,' said Captain Fry, holding on to a rope and leaning right out into the spray. 'By this time tomorrow, you'll be looking at the fair port of Splendidness.'

A quick note here that the name is pronounced with the stress on the middle syllable – so it's Splen-DID-ness not SPLEN-didness. Not that it really matters, as they never actually got there.

• • •

Meanwhile, from a balcony at the top of a stone lighthouse on a rocky headland to the south-east, the Custodian of Bethcar gazed out over the calm waters of Calmwater Bay. She fixed her keen, far-seeing eyes on the distant sight of a black ship clearing the very last hazards of Shipwreck Shoals and hoisting its sail to begin the journey north towards Splendidness. As she watched, it began to move more quickly through the water, a white feather boa of foam appearing underneath its prow as it cut through the waves.

The custodian ducked through a low wooden door into the room at the top of the lighthouse. It was octagonal, with a round convex window in every wall. The oddly fashioned glass filled the dusty air with rainbows as she directed her gaze to the north, where she could make out a very, very far-off glimmer of white houses in the sunshine where the prosperous port of Splendidness spread itself out luxuriously beside a wide sandy bay. Then she turned to stare to her right, out at the open sea. There the picture was very different.

Brought into sharp focus by the curved glass, she watched towering, distant waves rise up to crash against each other as lowering clouds boiled and churned in the angry sky. Out there, the ocean was plagued with huge storms – tempests that could pluck a ship from the surface and send it to the bottom within minutes. It was a wild and dangerous place. But no storms could ever enter Calmwater Bay. It was protected by one of the Talismans of Parallelia – the Talisman that it was her duty to safeguard.

The Talisman in question was a bright blue shield. It was attached to a stone statue of a warrior that stood in the very centre of the lighthouse where the custodian lived. And, as long as the Shield of Ran stayed in place, Calmwater Bay would remain safe and protected.

Ah yes, about that.

At that exact moment, the lighthouse door burst open and a huge gnoblin charged in, followed by a man in a long black cloak.

'Good morning, hmm, Custodian,' said Haggister.

• • •

Frankie and Joel spent most of the afternoon on deck as the *Spindrift* bucked and smashed through the waves. The speed was exhilarating as the taut sail boomed and cracked above them, and they ran backwards and forward, leaning out over each side of the ship with the wind in their hair, drinking in the view.

Shortly after lunch, Basin reappeared. 'I can't wait to see Splendidness,' he told Frankie, 'because I did hear tell that the taverns there do serve the finest feasts in all o' Parallelia –' not realizing, of course, that he was just rubbing it in as they were destined never to get to Splendidness at all.

'What's THAT?' Joel squealed suddenly, pointing a little way out from the *Spindrift*'s side. Basin and Frankie leaned over the rail, each holding up a hand to shield their eyes from the spray. Two enormous, long, dark shapes were visible in the water, keeping pace with the ship.

'Ah, now that's an extremely lucky omen,' said Captain Fry in a satisfied and not at all ironic tone of voice. 'They say that if you sight maeriona at the start of the voyage it'll be a safe and prosperous one.'

Joel had already pulled Grandad's Bestiary out of his pocket. 'I've seen these,' he muttered to himself,

MAERIONA *are sea serpents with a horse~like head. Note the large fins on either side of the neck, which aid steering. When leaping out of the water, these fins lie flat, giving them the appearance of a horse's mane.*

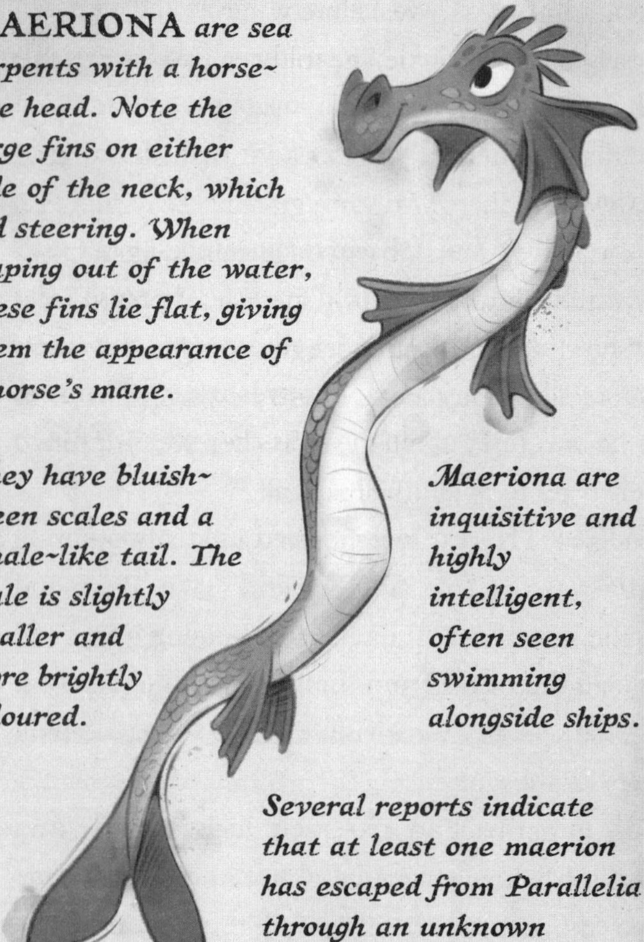

They have bluish~green scales and a whale~like tail. The male is slightly smaller and more brightly coloured.

Maeriona are inquisitive and highly intelligent, often seen swimming alongside ships.

Several reports indicate that at least one maerion has escaped from Parallelia through an unknown underwater portal somewhere to the north.

Otherland legends speak of a strange creature in a lake.

flicking through. 'Ah yes! Here we are!'

'Sea serpents, Frankie,' he told her, pointing to the page. 'Look!'

At that moment, a huge head broke the surface, looking for all the world like a giant horse with calm, intelligent eyes. Frankie gasped in pure delight. And yes, you're entirely correct – she just whooped, and now she's gasping in pure delight. Frankie Best was, at this point in her not-a-quest, beginning to veer hopelessly off-brand. Her role as cynical quest-hater was really hanging in the balance.

Far away to the left, the coastline of Parallelia swept by; they passed a wide river estuary, and after that the shoreline became more and more jagged, with patches of distant woodland visible above the grey cliffs. Finally, Frankie decided that it was, at last, time to take an interest in the map that she'd carried this far in her backpack without once consulting it. Breathing shallowly through her mouth and tiptoeing round the constantly scurrying rats, she ducked downstairs to the cabin to fetch it.

Justice was lying in one of the hammocks, looking decidedly green. 'I hate sea voyages,' she moaned, 'almost as much as I hate soup.'

Frankie gave her a comforting pat on the arm as she passed, feeling a sudden warm affection for this serious swordswoman who had sworn to help her.

When Frankie reappeared on deck, Joel and Basin had moved over to the left-hand rail of the *Spindrift* and were pointing excitedly at the coast. She rushed over to join them, unrolling the map at the same time. They were staring at an enormous structure on the distant shore. She caught a flash of sunlight bounding off bright white walls – a series of buildings rising into a kind of flattened pyramid at the top of some steep, impassable-looking cliffs. It was too distant to make out many details, but the gleam of gold seemed to come from a smaller structure right at the top.

'Ah,' said a voice from over her shoulder, 'the Temple of the Warrior's Tomb. The very central point of Parallelia.' Garyn had moved quietly up behind her. He pointed at the map. Sure enough, right in the centre of the star-shaped pattern that covered Parallelia there was a small drawing of a pyramid.

'Temple of the Warrior's Tomb,' read Frankie. 'Who was this warrior, then?'

'I'm glad you asked,' the knelf replied. 'Because the Warrior and her five Talismans are the reason for our entire quest. Want to hear the story?'

Frankie sighed. She knew when she was beaten. 'Fine,' she said. 'As long as you promise to skip the boring bits.'

'Knelf's honour,' he said seriously. 'I'll tell you the whole tale before we get to Splendidness.'

Which, in case you missed this detail earlier, they never did.

CHAPTER 11

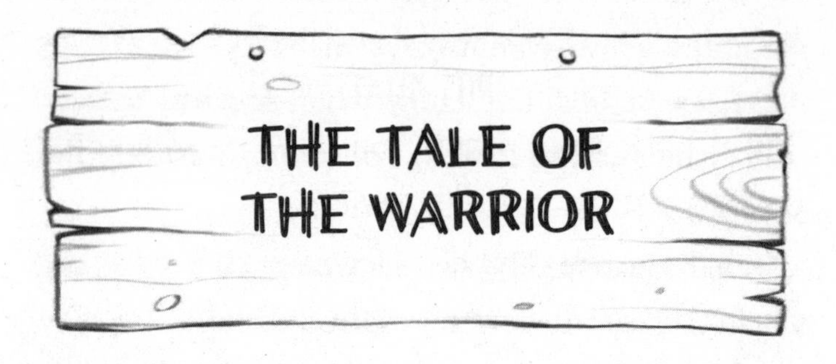

THE TALE OF THE WARRIOR

On the narrow shingle beach below the lighthouse where, until five minutes ago, the Custodian of Bethcar had been guarding the Shield of Ran, a boat was tied up. It was a large fishing boat that, until an hour ago, had belonged to some fishermen. It now belonged to the Good Guys because they had stolen it. The four enormous Mort brothers were standing in the shallow water, preparing to cast off. Arranged carefully in the front of the boat (even these villains didn't want their prizes to get damaged) were four wooden cages. One was empty and one contained the woman who lived in the lighthouse. One contained the Custodian of Tygermere and the final one, of course, contained Frankie's grandfather.

The Custodian of Bethcar watched in fury as the man who seemed to be in charge of this crew of thieves scrunched his way down the beach, carrying a bright blue shield. **'PUT THAT BACK!'** she stormed. **'Put it back this instant! You have no idea what powers you're meddling with!'**

'Oh, hmm, oh yes, I do.' Haggister sneered at her, placing the shield carefully in the bottom of the boat alongside a shining silver helmet and a pair of highly polished black leather boots. 'I'm stealing the Talismans, you see.'

'But,' the woman sputtered, 'you'll destroy the Protections of Parallelia!'

'That's the general idea, yes, hmm' replied Haggister, humming his odd little tune absently as he took his seat at the back of the boat. He craned his head round, scanning the shore impatiently. 'Where is he?' he muttered to himself.

At that moment, Hackmort raised a finger and pointed mutely to the low hills behind the beach.

'Ah!' Haggister sighed in satisfaction. 'Just in time.'

A distant figure could be seen running towards them along the clifftops, moving with surprising speed. Such speed, in fact, that within a couple of minutes there was a scattering of shingle as Slytely Good sprinted down the beach towards them. As he drew closer, Haggister could see that his face was grave and sheened with anxious sweat.

'What's happened?' he said sharply. 'Were we pursued? Did you deal with them?' And the subtle emphasis he put on the word 'deal' would have made your flesh creep if you'd been there to hear it.

'We need to hurry,' said Good tersely as he splashed through the shallow wavelets and leaped nimbly into the fishing boat. 'There's two children and a knelf chasing after that one.' He pointed jerkily to the second cage along, in which a white-haired man in a purple dressing gown was sitting calmly, watching him with clear, bright eyes.

'Two . . . hmm – *children*?' queried Haggister. 'I can't imagine they posed much of a challenge. Two children against the, hmm, the deadliest villain in Lawlesston?'

Slytely Good's face writhed unpleasantly. Within a few seconds, his appearance changed rapidly, as different characters and expressions kept replacing each other so fast that it was difficult to keep track. But each one of the different faces was alive with anger and hatred. 'They had help,' he spat. 'A Justice. She . . . she bested me.'

There was a low chuckling from the front of the boat. Both men turned to see that Frankie's grandad's eyes had filled with tears of laughter. 'Oh, that's the funniest one yet,' he said, reaching up a knuckle to wipe his eye. 'You call yourself, what was it? The most dangerous villain in Lawlesston? And you can't even get past my grandkids. I think you should give it up now, lads. You're not cut out for this kind of thing.'

The Good Guys regarded the custodian furiously. They were, they felt, very much cut out for this exact kind of thing.

'Never mind that old fool,' said Haggister scornfully. 'When I take control of the, hmm, Talismans, he'll soon stop laughing.'

'Stop it,' begged Grandad, laughing even harder. 'I need a wee already. You're hilarious, you know that? You really don't get it, do you?'

'Get, hmm, get what?' Haggister couldn't help asking.

'Parallelia's protected by more than just the Talismans, you idiot.'

And now, for the first time since his capture, the Custodian of Tygermere spoke. 'He'll never understand, Jim,' he said in his deep, calm voice. 'Don't waste your time. He's only interested in what benefits him. You see it with pigs sometimes.' (Jon Topham was a farmer, by the way, before he was chosen by Celidon, the Spirit of Earth, to be the custodian. Just so you know why he's suddenly going on about pigs.)

'SILENCE!' said Haggister sharply. He rounded on Frankie's grandad. 'You think a pair of pathetic children will be able to help?'

'I was listening to them talk,' added Slytely Good scornfully. 'The girl hates Parallelia. She finds the whole place ridiculous.'

'And yet you said she has a Justice helping her. One that beat you in a fight?' mused the Custodian of Angel Woods. 'Well, it's shaping up to be a very interesting week, that's for sure. Though I hope Mrs Archer remembers to water my marrows.'

'Enough!' Haggister controlled his temper with difficulty.

Within days, I will be all-powerful, he thought to himself. *All-powerful beings don't worry about old men in cages laughing at them.*

'It doesn't matter,' he continued slyly. 'Even if they do have a Justice with them – even one impressive enough to, hmm, beat Good here – it won't help them. In a few short hours, hmm, nobody will be able to follow us, you see.' He reached out and stroked the polished surface of the bright blue shield.

'You must put it back!' said the Custodian of Bethcar desperately, pointing towards her lighthouse. 'Without the Talisman in place, there's nothing to keep the great ocean storms out of Calmwater Bay! You'll sink every ship out there!'

'Exactly!' said Haggister smugly. 'As I said, hmm, nobody will be able to follow us. Now there's nothing to keep the storms out, Calmwater Bay is about to become a little less calm, shall we say? Hmm.'

He hummed as he looked over to the east, and everyone else in the boat followed his gaze. Far out to sea was a huge bank of cloud like a shadowy mountain range. Flashes of lightning sparked here and there inside the glowering mass.

'If that storm overtakes us,' said the Custodian of Tygermere matter-of-factly, 'we'll sink.'

A sudden darkness fell over the afternoon sun.

There was a thin scream as a biting wind swept across the headland.

'Oh, we'll be ahead of the storm, never fear,' said Haggister. 'Morts, to your oars!'

Without speaking, the four giant gnoblins took their places along both sides of the boat. Each grabbed an oar and, as Slytely Good untied the painter, they began to row.

We already know that the Mort brothers were incredibly strong. But they were also incredibly fast. Their oars churned the water like four outboard motors, and the fishing boat shot out across Calmwater Bay at breathtaking speed. Within a minute, it was far from land, heading directly north towards the distant, looming shapes of a chain of high islands. It was going so fast that it did, indeed, outrun the gigantic ocean storm that was about to lumber across the bay like something out of a weather-based disaster movie.

Other slower boats would not be so lucky. Boats like the *Spindrift*, for instance.

• • •

On board the *Spindrift*, which was skimming across the bay, unaware of the horrifying mass of black clouds approaching it from the east, dinner was being served in Captain Fry's cabin. The sea chart had been replaced with a set of shining metal plates and goblets, and the wide windows showed off a gleaming panorama of the sea, which was just beginning to turn golden in the lowering sun. It wasn't a bad setting in which to have your tea, basically.

Frankie was ravenous after a day of fresh sea air, but her hopes weren't high. She'd once read in a story when she was younger about something called ship's biscuit, and she had a vague idea that was what sailors always ate. She wasn't even really clear as to what ship's biscuit was – possibly something like those rusks you give to babies, only much staler and probably with weevils in it. So she was pleasantly surprised when a sailor tottered in, carrying a huge tray laden with fried fresh fish. Behind him was another man with a basket of bread and some creamy yellow butter, and bringing up the rear was a third steward with a platter of ham, cheese and grapes.

With breakfast at the Wandering Walrus feeling like it had happened a week ago, Frankie dived in and – there's no delicate way of putting this – gorged herself absolutely stupid. Justice, who'd edged rather reluctantly into the cabin and only managed to nibble a grape or two, watched her queasily.

After the meal, Garyn sat back with his goblet of wine. 'I promised Frankie here that I'd tell her the *Tale of the Warrior*,' he announced.

'Wonderful!' said Captain Fry. 'Yes, you can never hear the old tales too many times.'

'I think you'll find some of the answers you're looking for,' Garyn told Frankie. And although she'd just eaten a really impressive amount of cheese, and all she really felt like doing was curling up for a nice after-dinner nap with the sunset sea spread outside the window, she resolved to listen. After all, Garyn had told her this would explain their quest. *Their not-a-quest*, she quickly and silently corrected herself.

'But,' she warned the knelf, 'you did promise to skip the boring bits.' He sighed and nodded reluctantly.

'*Once was a people*,' Garyn began in a dramatic voice, '*war-weary, famine-fearful* –'

'Whoa, whoa, wait a second,' said Frankie, holding up the hand that wasn't reaching for another piece of cheese. 'That sounds like a poem.'

'It's the ancient saga of Parallelia,' said Garyn indignantly, 'handed down by bards from generation to generation.'

'I thought so!' she said triumphantly. 'You almost tricked me into listening to some super-boring epic poem there. No way, Mr Pointy-Ears. Nobody wants the verse version. Even Joel skips over those parts in fantasy books.'

'I do not!' said Joel hotly. 'Well,' he admitted, 'sometimes I do. But I go back and read them later. Almost always.'

'You heard the arch-nerd,' Frankie told the knelf. 'Just give us the headlines, OK?'

Garyn broke into a slight smile in spite of himself. 'Fine, fine,' he told her, 'have it your way, Princess.' She held up a warning finger, but couldn't help returning his grin. 'So, a long time ago,' he summarized, 'in a country far, far away . . .'

Joel congratulated him. 'Excellent intro!'

'. . . there had been a war that raged for generations. Great and greedy families battled and schemed to become great and greedy kings and queens. The people were downtrodden and miserable – and so it continued for hundreds of years. War followed war as dynasty overthrew dynasty. Until, one day, a warrior appeared.'

'See?' said Frankie. 'The prose version's better already. Bet in the poem that doesn't even happen until verse nineteen.'

'Though the part where the warrior first appears is wonderful in the saga,' said Captain Fry, who had enjoyed a few goblets of wine with his dinner and was looking slightly misty-eyed and emotional. '*Swift was her sword, sturdy her shield,*' he quoted from memory. '*Bright her breastplate with its red ruby raging. Lore-learned, spirit-strengthened, into the city she strode. A new path she promised to the few who would follow.*'

'Nice,' admitted Frankie grudgingly. 'But let's stick with the abridged version, OK?'

'Nobody knows who this warrior really was.' Garyn picked up the story. 'Some say that she had once been part of one of those great and greedy families. There's even a theory that she was the rightful queen, but had been tricked out of the crown by her younger brother. Anyway, whoever she was, she had left years before on a journey of discovery, and when she returned to the country's capital city she was not alone.'

In spite of herself, Frankie found herself drawn in by this tale of long ago. Not enough to ask for the poetry back, but definitely enough to stop eating cheese temporarily.

'Surrounding the warrior when she marched into the city,' the knelf continued, 'shimmering in the air, were five Guardian Spirits: Andrasta, the air-spirit. Celidon, the spirit of earth. Ilvatar, the spirit of light. Ran, the spirit of water. And, burning with a bright red flame, Fornax – the fire-spirit of power.'

'This is BRILLIANT,' Joel whispered.

Garyn went on with the tale. 'The warrior stood in the middle of the city, with the five spirits clustered in the air around her. She told the people that she had decided to renounce wars and scheming forever. She planned to leave, and form a new kingdom. A kingdom with no single ruler, and no ceaseless vying for control. Who would join her?'

'We would totally have gone,' Joel decided. 'Frankie, we'd have gone with the warrior on her quest, right? Right?'

Frankie pondered this question. A couple of days ago, she'd have unhesitatingly said, 'No, of course not. The quest sounds dangerous. I'll be right here if anyone needs me.' Now, though, she wasn't so sure. A small but growing part of her brain was excited about the thought of adventure, about new places and new beginnings.

'Many set out with the warrior,' Garyn continued, 'but it was a dangerous journey.'

'Across long leagues they laboured, mountains they mastered,' intoned Captain Fry dramatically, waving his wine around for effect and sloshing some of it on to the cheeseboard. *'Monsters they met in the fearsome forests; fearlessly, they forded rivers roaring.'*

'But the warrior led them through,' said Garyn, 'because each of the five spirits poured their powers into the different parts of her armour. They linked themselves to her helm, sword, shield, boots and breastplate. And those items became the five Talismans that protected the people on their long journey. And even now, they still protect the place where the warrior and her followers eventually settled.'

'In a lost land, at last they lingered –' a couple of no doubt very salty tears were trickling down Captain Fry's sunburnt cheeks – *'a kingdom there to kindle.'*

'A kingdom without a king or queen,' said Garyn. 'The warrior's people decided that never again would they let one family rule over them. So the spirits agreed to choose a custodian each.'

'The custodians would keep the five Talismans safe,' said Justice, who had been largely silent throughout the whole tale apart from the odd small burp. 'And these five custodians would also share the leadership of Parallelia.'

'Every five years, the rule switches between the custodians,' said Garyn. 'At the moment, Princess Prince is ruler in the great city of Tramont. Before that, we had Princess Alika of the Islands.'

'Hold up.' Frankie was putting the pieces together. 'Does that mean my grandad used to be, like, a king?'

'Parallelia has no king,' said Justice, shaking her head. 'The Kingdom is the King.'

'The Kingdom is the King,' repeated all the Parallelians round the table.

'But he was certainly Prince of Parallelia, yes,' said Garyn. 'Before I was born. He ruled from the Forest Court in Angel Woods and by all accounts it was amazing.'

'Whoa,' said Frankie and Joel in unison. It seemed the most appropriate response.

'And that's how the Kingdom of Parallelia works,'

concluded Garyn. 'A kingdom that has been happy and peaceful for hundreds and hundreds of years because it's been protected by the five Talismans – the fragments of the warrior's armour that were made magical by their link to the five Guardian Spirits.'

Excitedly, Frankie reached down for the map that she'd been carrying around with her all day and was now beneath her chair. Shoving a platter of grapes to one side, she unrolled it on the table, weighing the corners down with plates and glasses. 'And that's what this pattern is,' she said, tracing the coloured lines with her finger. 'This star shape joins up the five Talismans! Here's Angel Woods, where Grandad looked after that silver helmet.'

'Ilvatar's Helm,' confirmed Garyn. 'Then the Boots of Celidon are kept over there, to the west, on an island in the lake of Tygermere. When they're in position, the Talismans cast a protective web across all of Parallelia. Though now, of course, one of them is out of place. And that's why we need to chase these kidnappers and put the helmet back where it belongs.'

Justice, still looking the approximate colour of lettuce, spoke up at this point. 'That's what the Moral

Compass meant when it told me the future of Parallelia is at stake.'

Frankie was just about to respond to this, but was distracted by the entire contents of the table suddenly sliding into her lap as the *Spindrift* heeled sharply over to one side. There was a crashing and tinkling as plates and goblets went flying, and a brief frenzy among the rats as, in their world, it began to rain cheese. The timbers of the ship cracked and croaked alarmingly.

'What's going on?' cried Joel, who had been catapulted out of his chair and was sliding rapidly across the floor.

'Feels like a storm's blowing up,' replied Captain Fry, struggling to his feet with difficulty and looking extremely confused.

'I thought you didn't get storms in Calmwater Bay?' bellowed Garyn above the creaking and banging.

At this point, the ship tilted crazily in the other direction, which meant Joel's sliding was reversed and he headed back past Frankie. She grabbed his cloak and pulled him up on to her chair.

'We *don't* get storms in Calmwater Bay!' yelled

Captain Fry in a disbelieving tone, tottering to the door and throwing it open. Immediately, a huge wave burst into the cabin, startling all the rats except one that ended up surfing along on a coaster. 'The Talisman of Bethcar keeps the bay protected!' the captain added, before putting his head out of the door and bellowing to his crew, **'All hands to reduce sail! Man the lifelines!'** There was a thudding on deck as the sailors began to stampede for the mast.

'I should not have eaten that grape,' moaned Justice, swallowing nervously as the ship gave another enormous lurch. 'This is going to be bad.'

Captain Fry nodded. 'I think we might be in for a tolerable blow,' he said. 'Best if you passengers get yourselves down to your cabin. Lash yourselves into your hammocks and ride it out.'

Frankie was alarmed to see that the colour had drained from his face above his now-soaked moustache. *He looks completely terrified*, she thought as the *Spindrift* bucked like a horse trying to unseat its rider.

At that point, she got a brief glimpse past the captain at the conditions outside on deck. The sailors were labouring to pull down the sail, but struggling to keep upright on the soaking deck. Beyond, Frankie could see what looked like an entire city made of water coming towards them – skyscrapers and all – beneath huge, boiling black clouds.

'Come on,' she told Joel, dragging him towards the stairs. 'Let's do as he says. Get in our hammocks and wait for the storm to pass.'

'Frankie? I'm scared,' he whimpered as they struggled down towards the cabin.

She patted his shoulder, trying to sound more confident than she felt. 'It'll be fine,' she told him, privately wondering who she was trying to reassure.

Garyn followed them, carrying Basin, and Justice, whose skin colour had now deepened to the rich verdant shade of a carefully nurtured lawn, was bringing up the rear, puffing out her cheeks and clutching a hand to her mouth.

By the time the fellowship made it down to the lower deck, the ship was plunging and rearing through such enormous waves that their feet actually left the floor at times. Cataracts of foaming, freezing water followed them down the stairs as the raging sea broke right over the deck. Frantically, they climbed into their hammocks, wrapping the material round themselves to avoid flying out when the ship plummeted downwards.

For the next four hours, they were unable to move. It was physically impossible to get out of the hammocks as they spun and jerked like crazed puppets. Rats pinged round the cabin like pinballs, at times floating past in zero gravity as the ship plunged down the surface of another gigantic wave. Also floating round the cabin in zero gravity were a few globules of Justice's grape – it looked like that trick astronauts sometimes do in space with water. Apologies if you happened to be eating while reading this paragraph, but it's important you realize just how terrifying the storm in Calmwater Bay really was.

Joel, in the hammock next to Frankie, yelled across to her during a brief lull.

'SOMEBODY'S TAKEN THE SHIELD!'

'What?'

'Captain Fry said the Talisman of Bethcar – the shield – keeps the bay safe from storms, right?'

'Right!' She thought back to the star-shaped pattern on her map, grateful to have something to focus on.

'So – whoever took Grandad didn't just want one talisman. It's like *Spingle's Quest Three*, remember?'

It was on the tip of Frankie's tongue to scream over the noise of the storm, **'THIS IS NOT. SPINGLE'S. QUEST!'** But something stopped her. This very clearly wasn't a game – the flying rats were proof enough of that. But it was pretty obvious that her mum and dad had been basing a great deal of *Spingle's Quest* on this incredible, somehow real-life place called Parallelia.

She thought back to *Spingle's Quest III*, which she'd played the previous year. 'When Spingle had to gather the five lost jewels?' she asked her brother.

'Right!' he said. 'Those big gnoblins, and whoever's in charge of them, they didn't just come for Grandad and that one talisman.'

'They're stealing ALL the Talismans!' Frankie realized. **'All five of them!'**

'All of the warrior's armour. They're putting it back together.'

'But who would want to do that?' his sister asked as a rat flew past her face, doing an elegant breaststroke in the air.

'We didn't see him,' her brother recalled, 'but

remember that man who seemed to be calling the shots the day Grandad got kidnapped? It must have been him who sent that greasy-haired creep back to try and finish us off! That's our bad guy.'

'Right!' Frankie felt a sudden anger at this villain who was plunging Parallelia into such danger. 'What was his name again? Hag-something, right? Hag . . . Hag . . .'

But at that point she was interrupted by a gigantic, splintering crunch. Their hammocks were all flung wildly forward as the ship stopped in its tracks. There was a deep, deep groaning from the strained timbers, and almost immediately water began to bubble up through the floorboards of their cabin. The rats made a beeline – or to be more accurate a ratline – for the stairs. And among the carpet of fleeing rodents, Captain Fry appeared.

'QUICK!' he urged the fellowship. **'Quick, get on deck! We hit rocks! We're sinking!'**

'I'm not sure Captain Fry's Relaxing Sea Cruises is really going to catch on as a tourist attraction, are you?' Frankie asked Joel as they spilled out of their hammocks and, grabbing what possessions they could, stampeded for the stairs.

He smiled at her thinly, grateful for her attempt to lighten the atmosphere.

And in the mad rush on deck, and the turmoil of heading for a lifeboat, Frankie never did finish off the name of the man who was apparently trying to reassemble the armour of the warrior. *Hag . . . Hag . . .* But it's now come to the point in the story where you need to find out a little more about him. So let's finish the name off, shall we?

His name, as you already know, was Haggister.

CHAPTER 12

The city of Tramont lies in the deep, shallow basin between three mountains, close to the icy-cold waters of Lake Gah. A long, curved wall surrounds the city to the south, with the jagged slopes of the Sprudelhorn and the softer green foothills of Silknaw Pike protecting the west and east. But to the north, the city climbs steeply up the lower slopes of the glowering black volcano called Mount Perspective. The stone that makes up the houses becomes darker and darker the further through the city you go, and the streets get harder and harder to climb, eventually turning into what are basically staircases with pavements.

The man called Haggister lived in the lowest part

of the city, to the right as you went through the gates. In fact, it was by far the nicest part of town. Further away from the volcano, the houses were lighter-coloured and more spacious. And to the east, towards the green slopes of Silknaw Pike, the streets were wider and there were more trees and parks. But many people in Tramont still chose to live close to the castle – close to power. And these people tended to sneer at the people who lived down the hill and on the right – 'Downright nobodies', they called them. They considered themselves a cut above, these fine 'Upright' folks who lived on the high slopes to the east of the castle, even though their houses were smaller and darker and the air they breathed was far more polluted and sulphurous.

Wait a minute, you might be saying to yourself at this point. *I thought that Parallelia was a lovely, fair place where everyone got along? It doesn't sound like the warrior's original plan, all this snobbery?*

To explain what's going on, you need to remember that Parallelia is protected by five Guardian Spirits. And each spirit gives the area in which it resides a rather different atmosphere. Angel Woods, for instance, is calm and contemplative because it is the home of Ilvatar, the light-spirit of wisdom and inner peace. Tramont Castle, on the other hand, is the home of Fornax, the fire-spirit of power. And being close to power can do very strange things to people.

You see, as the centuries had gone by, Fornax began to tire of his role as a protector. He had grown restless in his deep home beneath the volcano – restless and angry. And that restless rage, seeping out from the mountain like an invisible heat haze, had started to affect some of the more weak-willed inhabitants of Tramont. That's why they clustered round the castle in their smaller soot-stained houses, somehow sensing that it made them closer to the seat of power, or that proximity to the castle gave their lives more meaning.

Each day, the man called Haggister left his house in the Downright district and climbed towards the castle that loomed above Tramont like bad weather. As he walked, the streets got narrower and steeper, and the air grew more and more choking when he moved into the more expensive districts. The houses grew smaller and more caked in soot, and the people looked less and less happy, even though they grew richer and richer the higher they lived.

Each day, Haggister nodded to the guards on the castle gate and slouched through the ornate audience chambers, with their high glass doors and their gold-framed paintings of princes and princesses of Parallelia past. Each day, he shot a secret sneer at the rows of faces – kind and noble faces, haughty and proud faces – before passing through the staterooms and into the darker, more secret chambers at the back of the castle.

Haggister was a tall, thin man with a tall, thin face. His long hair and his smart suit were both dark and carefully brushed. His mind, too, was dark, but that fact was carefully concealed.

You'll have noticed already that Haggister had a peculiar habit of humming short snatches of a strange little tune every now and then.

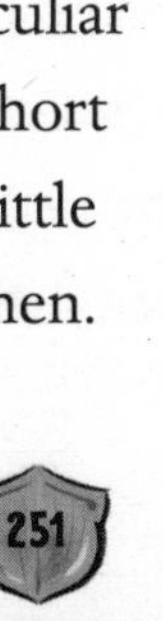

It was a habit he'd picked up during his long hours working alone in Tramont Castle or walking its long, dim passageways. The other staff knew he was coming when they heard the mournful air echoing from the stone walls. When he met the other castle workers, Haggister's face wore a habitual expression of obliging friendliness, a tilt of the head and a slight smile that said to the world, 'How may I help you?' But, if you looked very, very closely, you would see a different expression hiding just underneath, like a second face beneath a thin mask. And this face wore a very different expression – an expression of distrust and dislike, and a jarring jealousy that gnawed at Haggister like tooth-rot, digging down to his very soul.

And so, even though he said 'good morning' politely each day to Dr Contumelius, the portly and richly robed man who organized the castle staff, and to his colleagues, the man called Haggister was often left to get on with his work alone.

That work consisted of polishing the castle silver. Castles come with a lot of silver, so there's a lot of polishing to do. In fact, as soon as he finished polishing all the silver, he had to go back to the beginning and start all over again. As a young man, he had started off with an entry-level job polishing the castle bronze, and once the very old man who was in charge of polishing the castle gold finally retired he had excellent promotion prospects.

But Haggister wasn't happy. No, Haggister was about as far from happy as you could be without actually falling off the edge of the emotional world. Polishing a load of very expensive silverware, not one piece of which you could afford to buy, can do that to a person. Especially if you're doing it in close proximity to Fornax, the fire-spirit of power, who is looking for a discontented soul to corrupt.

It took nineteen days of hard polishing to get through every piece of silver in Tramont Castle. Nineteen days of humming his high-pitched little tune as he dipped his cloth in the polish and rubbed the silver until it shone. Haggister knew this because every nineteen days he got to do the only part of the job he liked. A secret part.

Right at the back of Tramont Castle, in a passageway that leads to the dungeons on one side and the saunas on the other (building your castle underneath a volcano does have some advantages after all), there is a huge door of ancient blackened wood studded with worn, tarnished nails. This door is strengthened with bands of thick iron and it has no lock or handle. It leads to a tunnel cut deep into the rock of the mountain, and at the end of this tunnel is a cavernous . . . cavern, for want of a better word. A natural cave, right inside the slopes of Mount Perspective. The hiding place of the most powerful piece of the warrior's armour – the Breastplate of Fornax. The *silver* Breastplate of Fornax.

Each of the Talismans of Parallelia is protected by a secret door, which can only be opened by one of the five custodians. And so, every nineteen days, Haggister had to trail through the passageways and staterooms of the castle like an unwanted wisp of smoke, searching for Dr Contumelius.

'It's time, Doctor,' he would say to him humbly, tugging his fringe of dark hair and snarling with jealous rage beneath his raised hand. 'Time to enter the chamber, if you please, sir. Hmm.'

'Yes, yes,' Dr Contumelius would reply, huffing beneath his richly embroidered doublet. 'Wait at the door, and the custodian and I shall be with you presently, ah, Haggister?'

Dr Contumelius had known Haggister for fully twenty-eight years, but he was one of those people who liked to give the impression that his brain was far, far too full of far, far too many important things to retain the actual names of the people who worked for him. If he could have got away with just calling Haggister 'silver-polishing servant', he'd have done it, but there was something about the tall man's obsequious manner that unnerved him. And, to be fair, rightly so.

And so, every nineteen days, Haggister would take up position beside the huge door with no lock or handle while Dr Contumelius went searching for one of the only five people who could open it. One of the five custodians.

The Custodian of Tramont Castle – and, at that time, the ruler of Parallelia – was Princess Prince. A quick note on her name is probably in order here. *Princess Prince*? It's not the most likely of monikers, so what's going on? A mix-up by a short-sighted midwife? A king with an unusually lively sense of humour? Neither of the above. Parallelia has no king, remember – the Kingdom is the King. And you're not a prince or princess unless you're chosen by one of the five Guardian Spirits – and who knows how they pick the person best suited to the job? So, until she had been selected by Fornax to be a custodian, the young princess had just been plain old Tammy Prince, a name that had sounded a great deal less confusing, but had come with much more basic accommodation.

Anyway, back to Haggister, waiting pretend-patiently in the passageway, cloth and silver polish in hand. Dr Contumelius, having sought out Princess Prince, would lead her in a stately fashion to the corridor between the dungeons and the saunas.

'Sorry to have kept you waiting,' he would say casually to Haggister, in the tone of voice that means *not in the least sorry to have kept you waiting.*

And Haggister would simply nod politely, humming his high-pitched tune all the while, and watch what happened next with hungry eyes.

Princess Prince would reach up and place her hand right in the centre of the door, where there was a star-shaped gap in the thick iron bands that reinforced it. For the briefest of moments, the iron would glow with a deep, deep red, and then the door would smoothly swing open.

'Make sure you close it when you've finished, won't you, ah, Haggister?' Dr Contumelius would say, before leading the princess away. 'Now, Your Highness, about the banquet for the Bethcar pear merchants next week –' his voice would recede down the passageway – 'I was thinking you could give a short speech about how it's so important that . . .'

Whatever piece of castle-based admin they were discussing, Haggister would pay it no attention. Grasping his polish and his greying cloth tightly, he would edge down the tunnel that led deep beneath the volcano, a tunnel that started out lined with black bricks. After a while, these gradually gave way to jagged, shiny rock. The air grew hotter and thicker, and the silence pressed on his ears. Haggister would emerge into an enormous circular cave and – this never changed, no matter how many times he went there – shiver from the top of his head to the soles of his feet to be in the Chamber of the Talisman.

The entire chamber was filled with a strange, almost visible field of power, like the electricity in the air before a thunderstorm. Haggister had never seen a light bulb, but if he had he might have imagined that if he brought it into this chamber it would light up of its own accord, powered by the particles that charged the air.

The cave was gigantic, as we already know, and circular. But this was no empty hole beneath Mount Perspective. Opposite the opening through which Haggister entered, the entire far wall had been carved into columns, pillars and arches, all formed of the same shiny black rock. Three doorways were cut into the bottom of the wall, and far above them was a huge space like a church window, only this was a window with no glass. Instead, it held a wall of rock, glowing red hot in several places.

In the very centre of the room was a circular plinth. Surrounding it were five roughly hewn stone chairs reinforced with more bands of thick black iron. And on the top of the plinth was a statue of the warrior, carved out of polished black rock. The statue stood, legs apart and hands held out in a gesture that said *kneel before me*. And fastened to her torso was a breastplate of shining silver with a single giant red ruby set into its very centre.

Haggister would climb up to the statue and begin polishing the Breastplate of Fornax – a lengthy process that involved rubbing polish on to it with a cloth in numerous little circles, leaving it to dry and then polishing it away with another softer cloth. And, for many years, Haggister carried out this ritual with nothing on his mind but jealousy for the owner of the bright silver and an uneasy feeling that he was not alone in the deserted chamber beneath the mountain.

And then one day, a year or so before this story began, Haggister heard a voice speaking to him.

It is not fair that they have everything and you have nothing.

Haggister whirled round to see who had spoken, although he had the impression that the words had not been said out loud. He gazed up at the huge, arched expanse of glowing rock set into the wall opposite him and rubbed his eyes. By some trick of the light, the glowing areas in the black stone almost looked as if a gigantic face was looking down at him. He glanced back down at his polishing, and rubbed his eyes again. It must just be a reflection, but it was as if the great ruby in the centre of the warrior's breastplate was glowing with a deep, pulsing light.

I have been watching you come here for many years, Haggister, the voice went on. *I have sensed your righteous anger and I, too, rage at the unfairness with which you have been treated. And I have decided to help you.*

'Help . . . me?' asked Haggister softly, still staring at the ruby. 'Help me with what?'

With power, said the voice that seemed to be both inside his head and everywhere else at the same time. *Power is all you lack, Haggister. With power, you can seize all you long for. And I can show you how to get that power. Think on how powerless you are until you return to me.*

And the light inside the ruby dulled, and the glowing rocks now looked simply like your regular glowing rocks that you get in the average cavern beneath a volcano.

Shaken, Haggister finished his polishing and left, allowing the door with no lock or handle to thud shut behind him. But over the next nineteen days he thought about what the voice had told him. He thought how unfair it was that other people held all the power and he was reduced to polishing the riches they didn't even enjoy. The jealousy inside him began to grow, and transformed into a bitterness and a hatred towards the people who held him back.

And so, next time Haggister eagerly entered the

Chamber of the Talisman, he was even more ready to listen to the voice from the glowing rocks. And, as the weeks went by, they made their plans.

The voice was that of Fornax, the fire-spirit that governs power, ambition and influence – all things that can be useful in small doses, but hugely toxic for people who desire or gain too much. Fornax had grown tired of protecting Parallelia, and was planning its escape. All it needed was a willing disciple, and Haggister was perfect.

The *Tale of the Warrior* tells how the five spirits linked themselves to the five pieces of armour that became the protective Talismans of Parallelia. Fornax had now decided to break that link, and it knew the ritual that would make that happen. It would need all five Talismans, along with their custodians, to be gathered together beneath the volcano on one certain night. No small feat. But Fornax had finally found someone with the ambition to carry out this plan. He tempted Haggister with the thought of wearing the armour of the warrior, and explained how powerful he would become – able to take whatever he wanted. All Haggister had to do was bring the custodians and their talismans to this sacred circular chamber.

Bit by bit, pieces of silverware began to disappear from Tramont Castle. Nobody noticed because there was a huge amount of it – nineteen full days' worth of polishing, to be exact. The silverware slipped into Haggister's pockets – first smaller things and then, as his crimes went unnoticed, he grew bolder. One day he walked out past the guards with a silver candlestick down each leg of his smart dark trousers. And, very soon, Haggister became one of the richest people in Tramont. Rich enough to hire some very bad people and make them go out across Parallelia and do some very bad stuff.

And that's when Haggister surprised Dr Contumelius with the news that, after twenty-eight years' solid work, he had decided to take a little holiday. And he took a trip just outside the boundaries of Parallelia, to a town not protected by the five Talismans. A town where he could hire the worst, most ruthless villains to bring him the custodians and the Talismans they guarded.

The town was called Lawlesston. And the bad guys, as you will have worked out for yourself no doubt, were called the Good Guys.

CHAPTER 13

ISLANDS OF THE SKY WOLVES

The storm had blown itself out at last. And in a small lifeboat five exhausted figures were drifting on the still-choppy sea. Four of them were slumped in the bottom of the boat, and the fifth – a woman in a grey cloak – was leaning over the side being very enthusiastically sick.

'Bleuuuurrrrrgh,' said Justice. **'Phwoooooargh. Pluph. Ptchah.'**

'Would you be likin' a glass o' water, Mistress Justice?' asked Basin, rubbing her back affectionately.

Justice lifted her damp hair out of her face to look at him. 'Do you actually have a glass, Basin?'

'Er, well . . . no.'

'Or any water?' she asked. The gnoblin boy hesitated. 'That isn't seawater,' she clarified. Mournfully, he shook his head. 'I appreciate the thought, though,' she told him kindly, rolling over to sit slumped on a thwart. When she looked up and saw where they were headed, though, her face turned even paler than before – which, for the record, made it look practically transparent.

The lifeboat had no sail, and its oars had got lost in the shipwreck, but a keen wind was blowing them quite rapidly across the surface of the sea towards a chain of high islands. Within a few minutes, they had drifted close to a grey rocky cliff, which rose to some unimaginable height above them.

'Where are we?' asked Frankie.

Justice looked at her appraisingly, as if trying to

judge how much she might frighten her with the answer she was about to give.

'We've been blown right off course,' she said. 'We're too far to the east, among the Islands of the Sky Wolves.'

'And are they incredibly friendly and helpful, despite their rather intimidating name?' asked Joel hopefully.

'No,' replied Justice, grimacing. 'They're not.'

Standing up unsteadily in the boat, Frankie looked a little more closely at the grey rocky surface of the cliff, which seemed unusually smooth, almost as if it had been polished to a deep, lustrous sheen. By now, it was close enough for her to reach out and run a hand over.

'This is a weird cliff,' she said, thereby winning the award for the most obvious and redundant sentence of the day, and it wasn't even breakfast time yet.

'The winds blow constantly across these islands,' said Justice, 'and polish the cliffs smooth. Feel the updraught?'

She held out a hand, and Frankie copied her. Immediately, she could feel her fingers being pushed upward. The wind, shooting in across the sea, hit the bottom of the cliff and – having nowhere else to go – was fired skyward. Thousands of years' worth of this had flattened and smoothed the cliff face, Frankie realized.

'The islands are full of these updraughts,' said Garyn from behind her. 'It's what the Sky Wolves use to fl-EEEERGH!'

His sentence trailed off into a strangled cry that seemed to vanish up into the air.

'Sorry?' said Frankie. 'It's what the Sky Wolves use to what, exactly? It sounded like you said "fleeeergh".' She looked round to question him further, but Garyn wasn't there.

'Frankie, look out!' cried Justice from the other side of the boat. 'We're under at-EEEEERGH!'

Frankie turned to ask what 'ateeeeergh' was, but Justice, too, had now disappeared. Frankie was beginning to fill in some blanks on her own, though, and wasn't happy about the picture that was forming.

'Joel, Basin!' She called out to the two boys who were also examining the cliff face. 'I think we'd better take cover. I think Garyn and Justice have been sn-EEEEEEEEAAAAAAUUUUUUURGH!'

What had happened to make Frankie add several unintended vowels to the end of her sentence? This had happened.

There was a soft thud in the boat behind her, then she was grabbed by something that passed swiftly under her arms and gripped her tightly, and she suddenly shot straight up in the air. It would have made you scream out quite a few vowels, too. The polished grey cliff plummeted past her eyes as if she was in a very fast and very modern lift with glass doors. She could hear an odd noise behind her – it sounded like the thrumming that a bird's feathers make when they catch the wind – but she was being held far too tightly to turn round and see who had snatched her, and the sudden surge upward had sucked the breath out of her so she was unable to say anything after that initial panicked shriek.

Frankie did manage to sneak a look downwards and was alarmed to see that the *Spindrift*'s lifeboat already looked like a tiny toy. She was shooting up at an incredible rate – it was exactly like one of those fairground rides that catapult you into the air, only without the prospect of candyfloss at the end of it. After a few more seconds, during which she was seriously considering doing some more screaming, there was a flash of green in front of her eyes as she passed a grassy clifftop. The ascent slowed and she

found herself drifting back to the ground rather gracefully to land beside Garyn and Justice, and right in the middle of a circle of the sort of people you really don't want to find yourself encircled by.

They were dressed in dark, oiled leather and bits of armour made out of burnished copper. They all had long, straggly hair with coloured feathers woven into the braids, and they were doing a very impressive piece of synchronized scowling. Basically, it's safe to say that they didn't look like they were about to break into a song-and-dance routine entitled 'Welcome to our Friendly Islands – Make Yourselves at Home'.

'FRANKIE!' came a cry from above. **'Look at me! Look at me! I'm flying!'**

Joel was now coming in to land, and for the first time his sister was able to see how she'd been lifted from the boat. A thick leather strap was fastened round Joel's chest, attaching him firmly to the front of yet another one of the weird bird-Viking-hybrid men and women who were now surrounding them. The bird-Viking's arms were spread out wide, and behind them she could see a large pair of wings fluttering in the wind as he skilfully touched down. Each of the man's hands was gripping a handle at the end of the wings, and when he released these handles, the wings folded neatly behind his back.

As Frankie watched, a final bird-person came shooting above the clifftop with Basin attached to her chest. He was squeaking in fear and excitement at such a high pitch that he sounded like an operatic bat. Frankie heard a click and realized the leather strap holding her in place had been released, and she turned a swift 180 degrees to confront this abductor and give them a fairly large piece of her mind.

The Viking-bird-hybrid person that was standing behind her was younger than the others, probably nineteen or twenty. He had dark, brooding eyes and looked rather like he belonged in one of the magazines her older cousins were always reading, probably in a feature called 'Island Hotties' or something. Like the others, his hair was bristling with feathers, though his seemed larger and more colourful – as if he'd called first dibs when it was feather-selecting time.

He was clearly in charge of the aerial abduction, and that made him a very handy target for the rage that was now building up inside Frankie like a kettle coming to the boil. A sleepless night in a storm, a terrifying shipwreck and now this. *I didn't want to come on this quest in the first place*, she thought to herself furiously. It was the last straw.

'What in the name of actual flip do you think you're doing?' she shouted furiously. 'You can't just go grabbing people off boats and flying away with them!'

'You are intruders on these islands,' said the befeathered Viking guy arrogantly.

'Oh, do me a favour, Hiccup!' she told him scornfully. 'We got blown here by the storm, obviously! I mean, look around you!'

Frankie did, at this point, look around her and was a little irritated to see that the panorama of the sea from the high cliff was absolutely breathtaking. Inland, the scrubby grass sloped downwards into green valleys studded with tall trees. She had been about to say something properly scathing about nobody in their right minds wanting to come to this barren rock, but the view kind of took the wind out of her sails. She rallied, though.

'As if anyone would want to come here voluntarily!' she shrieked. 'And get menaced by you bunch of unwashed pigeon fanciers!'

She was so mad that she actually shoved him in the middle of the round copper plate fastened across his chest. At this, the entire circle pulled out short curved swords from their belts and lowered themselves into a menacing, combatty-looking crouch. All except the man she'd been screaming at. He looked at her keenly, his eyes narrowing. And then, after a moment, he began to laugh.

'I like this one!' he declared. 'What do you call yourself, little firebrand?'

'I'm Frankie,' she told him, slightly mollified. She hated being called Princess, but firebrand, she felt, she might be able to get on board with. 'Pleased to meet you. Now can you please show us the way off your island? We're kind of on a schedule here.'

'No, Frankie Firebrand,' the man told her. 'You must be taken to the chief. The Sky Wolves tolerate no intruders. My father will decide your fate.'

'There isn't time!' said Frankie crossly, unable to stop a small inner glow building up at the fact that she now apparently had a cool, fantasy-land nickname. 'We're on a . . .' She stopped herself, aware that Joel, Garyn and Basin were all staring at her intently, wondering what word she was about to use.

Justice was taking deep breaths of fresh air and so not paying much attention.

'Fine,' she continued, catching Garyn's eye and giving him another little smiley shrug. 'We're on a *quest*,' she told the bird-Viking.

'Hoo-ha! Yes, we are! Ooh momma!' said a delighted Joel, doing a little capering dance until he came too close to one of the swords and stopped.

'A quest to rescue the Custodians of Parallelia and retrieve the lost Talismans,' said Frankie, scarcely able to believe the words now coming out of her mouth. This was most definitely not going in the 'What I did in my holidays' essay in September – she'd be a laughing stock.

Although, she thought to herself, looking round at the rest of the fellowship, *they're not laughing at me*.

Garyn was, in fact, grinning widely with an expression of pride and confidence that made her feel rather heroic and swordsperson-like.

'Anyway,' she announced loudly and sternly, 'we demand that you let us pass. The future of Parallelia is at stake if you delay us in our . . . our journey.'

'Just say quest,' coaxed Joel. 'You've said it now: there's no going back.'

'Our quest then,' she said, giving him a wink.

'Perhaps we should listen to them, Skendar.' A new voice suddenly piped up – and 'piped' is the appropriate word here. The voice did sound rather like someone playing a small pipe-like instrument of some kind, occasionally blowing too hard so it broke upward a couple of octaves.

Frankie looked about to see who their new ally was and was not particularly encouraged when she spotted him. He was a gangly youth of about her own age, dressed in the same leather and copper armour as their guards, but without the wings on his back. He was hovering nervously on the edge of the circle, looking like an uninvited guest at a Viking-themed fancy-dress party.

'Silence, little brother,' the leader said bossily. 'You are here to observe, not to interfere.'

'But she says Parallelia is in danger . . .' fluted the unwinged junior bird-person.

'ENOUGH!' His older brother held up a hand with the air of someone who's used to people paying attention when he says the word 'enough'. 'The intruders must face our father. It is my duty.'

'Come on, then, feather-head,' said Frankie

impatiently, rolling her eyes in the direction of Garyn with an expression that said *what's a quester to do?* 'Let's go and see your dad. Hopefully, he's got enough sense to listen to us. Every minute we waste talking to you lot is a minute closer to your precious Parallelia going *pfft*.'

• • •

The Sky Wolves live on the chain of high, almost inaccessible islands that jut out from the northern end of Calmwater Bay. These islands are whipped pretty much constantly by strong winds off the sea. And they are also home to Andrasta, the air-spirit of strength and speed, along with her talisman and her chosen custodian.

You already know about the restless yearning for power with which the presence of Fornax infects the area surrounding Tramont Castle. Andrasta's influence gives the Sky Wolves some rather special abilities – chiefly, the power to harness and ride the winds. Over the centuries, they have developed those rather clever wings. They make them skilfully from the light, flexible wood that grows in the island forests,

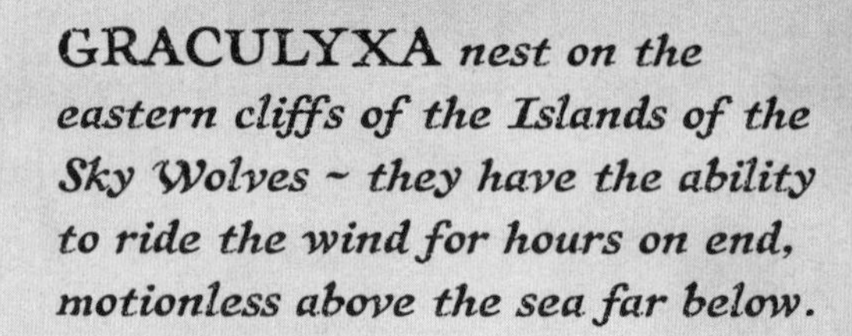

GRACULYXA *nest on the eastern cliffs of the Islands of the Sky Wolves ~ they have the ability to ride the wind for hours on end, motionless above the sea far below.*

GRACULYXA

Sky Wolves believe these birds are the souls of their dead ancestors.

The feathers woven into the Sky Wolves' hair must be plucked from a graculyx while in flight ~ this is a major test of flying ability, so the most able fliers will be adorned with numerous feathers. It also strikes me as rather unkind to fly about, plucking feathers from a creature you believe to be the spirit of one of your dead ancestors. I mean, what if it turned out to be your grandma?

Their feathers are white below and an array of different colours on top to camouflage them against the sea: green, blue, silver and creamy white. The silver feathers are the most prized and reserved for the island chiefs, their families and the most celebrated warriors and heroes.

and the feathers of a gigantic seabird called a Graculyx.

The Sky Wolves closed in on either side of the fellowship as they left the clifftop, swords still drawn. Despite the laughter of Skendar, the man who seemed to be in charge, it was clear that this little trip to his dad's house was not purely voluntary.

Justice and Garyn fell in behind Frankie, with Joel and Basin bringing up the rear. Frankie stomped along silently, furious at this hold-up. What if it meant her grandad's kidnappers got too far ahead? What if this ruined the entire quest?

We can forgive her for being a little moody at this point. Remember, she had just been shipwrecked and kidnapped within the space of a few hours, and she hadn't even had breakfast yet. She could have ended up on Chocolate Chip Cookie Island and she'd probably still have been fairly grumpy with the inhabitants until she'd eaten a few of them.

The path curved to the right to follow the valley floor through the tall, willowy trees. Birds sang above them, and occasionally they caught glimpses of small animals scuttling away through the undergrowth that resembled squirrels, but were striped orange and black like little tigers.

There was no time for wildlife-spotting, however. The Sky Wolves kept up a brisk pace, and before long they were being marched into a large clearing. A huge fire burned in a stone pit in the centre, and behind that there rose a tall wooden hall, its triangular roof level with the treetops. They were shoved roughly past the fire and straight into the dimness of the hall, which was lit only by what little sunlight could filter through the thatched roof.

While Frankie's eyes adjusted, she looked to either side. The walls were hung with huge tapestries showing Sky Wolves in flight. Giant birds seemed to feature a lot, too. They were now being herded into a line in front of a platform at the end of the hall, upon which stood two intricately carved wooden chairs. These had been placed in front of a tapestry that dominated the entire wall. It showed two huge pairs of embroidered wings, giving the impression that whoever sat in the chairs were monstrous birds of some kind. Finally able to make out a few more details in the gloom, Frankie peered ahead to see what kind of fowl they were dealing with.

The left-hand chair was empty. On the other sat a beard with a man attached to it. It's quite right to mention the beard first because he was a man who was extremely serious about his facial hair. It's very much the first thing Frankie noticed about him. It reached from his chin – obviously – all the way to the floor. And he wasn't slouching. Interlaced in this long grey beard were an enormous amount of feathers, and they were all a bright silver colour. (The rarest and most-prized graculyx feathers.) Above the beard was a pair of piercing blue eyes topped with white eyebrows so high and hairy that they looked not unlike feathers themselves. And completing the ensemble was a shiny bald head gleaming like an appetizing egg.

Frankie's mouth began to water. She was so hungry she was almost hallucinating. If you'd have given her a giant spoon at that point, she might well have attempted to eat the man in the chair, which would not have improved his mood one bit. And his mood was already very, very bad indeed.

'STRANGERS!' he roared as they stood nervously in front of him. **'Intruders! Invaders!'**

'Morning to you, too,' Frankie muttered to herself grumpily.

'We found these outsiders in a boat during our

morning patrol, Father,' boomed the Sky Wolf who had snatched Frankie. 'But –' he looked round the hut – 'where is my mother? Where's Chief Alika?'

Frankie followed his gaze, examining the Sky Wolves who were clustered round the outside of the hall. Now that her eyes had adjusted to the gloom, she could make out that many of them were red-eyed and frightened-looking. She thought back to the map of Parallelia and something clicked inside her brain. This led her to blurt out something that, she realized almost immediately, she really should have kept quiet about because it did make her sound ever so slightly suspicious.

'Your custodian has been kidnapped!' Frankie cried. There was an audible gasp from the assembled Sky Wolves. **'And what's more,'** she went on, **'your talisman has been stolen!'**

At this, there was angry murmuring. The old man on the throne let out a piercing howl, like the cry of some weird seabird. He pointed at her with a shaking finger. 'She knows!' he said, horrified. 'She knows . . . These outsiders are to blame! Where have you taken her?'

This was the point at which Frankie realized she

may have done better to keep quiet for a few moments.

The chief of the Sky Wolves had awoken that morning to discover his wife had disappeared, and the Sword of Andrasta that she guarded was gone as well. No sooner had he assembled his people to discuss the crime than a patrol led by his eldest son had brought in a group of strangers who knew all about the kidnapping. You can see how he jumped to the wrong conclusion.

Frankie held up her hands. 'No, look,' she said. 'It's only because of my grandfather . . .'

But everyone in the hall was now glaring at her furiously. It felt very much like the moment in this kind of story just before somebody shouts, 'Seize them!'

'SEIZE THEM!' bellowed the egg-headed chief, true to form.

'At once, Chief Aaghaad,' replied one of the guards.

And let's just pause here for a second and let that sink in, shall we? Because yes, the chief of the Sky Wolves really is called Aaghaad. As in, sounds like someone really posh saying 'Egghead'.

Now obviously Frankie was desperate to point this out immediately, but she was slightly preoccupied with a burly Sky Wolf grasping her arms and twisting them painfully behind her back.

'You're making a mistake!' roared Justice, frantically wrestling with her own guard in an attempt to reach her sword. 'You've got the wrong people! We're not the kidnappers!'

'We're the Fellowship of the Bacon Roll!' added Joel, which did have the effect of silencing everybody for a split second because nobody had the slightest clue what he was talking about. 'And this is our leader, Frankie Firebrand.'

'SEIZE THEM!' bellowed Chief Egghead – sorry, Chief Aaghaad – again adding a few more decibels for emphasis.

'You shouldn't seize us!' said Frankie desperately as she was dragged towards the door. 'You should do the opposite. You know – unseize us. Possibly, you know, offer us a light lunch of some kind before hearing our story! Because I think we're all on the same side here! We can rescue her!'

'Father!' came a tremulous voice from the side of the hall. 'We should listen to them!' Once again, Skendar's younger brother was speaking up in their favour.

The guards briefly halted in their seizing activity

as he stepped forward and stood beside the chief's bewinged chair. He looked extremely nervous – his lank hair was plastered to his forehead with sweat.

'I believe these strangers are telling the truth,' he said in presumably his bravest tone, which was not particularly brave.

'Silence!' the chief told him angrily. 'How dare you question me, Edwir? You who are not even of age yet? Your brother brings me the intruders that have taken our sacred talisman and you urge me to listen to them? You have much to learn, boy!'

'But this one says they can rescue her!' said the boy pleadingly, pointing at Frankie.

'A transparent lie! You will never achieve your wings if you do not learn – outsiders cannot be trusted! Now hold your tongue. Guards – take these intruders away until they are ready to talk. Throw them in the Nostril!'

'Throw us in the **WHAT** exactly?' wailed Frankie as the guards manhandled them out of the hall. The sunlight stung her eyes, but she was aware that Joel was being dragged along beside her. 'Don't worry,' she told him. 'We'll think of something.'

'Great,' he said brightly. 'What?'

'Working on that one,' she replied grimly as they were half led, half carried out of the main clearing and along a wide path towards the clifftop. But, before she could even start contemplating an escape plan, one of the Sky Wolves lifted a wooden hatch in the ground and, one by one, the fellowship were flung down the hole. The hatch was slammed shut and locked above them. They were trapped.

CHAPTER 14

Frankie sat up and looked around. She had landed on the soft sandy floor of a long, oval cave which sloped gradually downwards towards a round opening. Getting to her feet, she leaned on the smooth rock wall and peered down – and her stomach lurched at what she saw. The round hole was an opening in the cliff – and beyond it was a dizzying drop to the sea far below. A chilly wind blew her hair across her face, and she shivered.

'Well, I guess this is the Nostril, then,' said Garyn, struggling to his feet beside her. 'Amazing job, by the way, Frankie. Really impressive work. You knew that the Sky Wolves don't like outsiders and what do you do? Antagonize them and get us thrown in prison.

That's the quest finished. You realize that, don't you?'

Frankie bit her lip. She and Garyn had had their differences over the last few days, but this was the first time he'd spoken to her like that. She felt tears springing to her eyes.

'That's not going to help,' Justice told him, also standing up before placing a comforting hand on Frankie's shoulder. 'Let's work out where we are, and see if there's any way of getting out of here.'

'I wonder why they call it the Nostril,' said Joel, who was sitting glumly against the wall alongside Basin. 'Is it just because it's sort of round and empty, do you think?'

At that point, Frankie's hair was suddenly blown away from her face, and she realized. 'It's because the wind keeps changing direction,' she said. And she was right.

The constant flow of air up the cliff was creating a strange effect in the long, narrow cave. Every few seconds, the breeze inside started blowing the other way, giving the unnerving impression that they were, in fact, trapped inside the breathing nostril of some huge stone creature.

'Gross,' Frankie muttered to herself with a shudder.

She stumped across the sandy cave floor and plunked herself down not far from the entrance, unslinging her backpack to use as a cushion and glaring moodily out across the wide grey seascape beyond. As she sat back, something fell out of the top of the rucksack with a soft thunk. Reaching back without looking, she grabbed it – it was the old notebook that she'd found on her first night at Grandad's house and had been using as a journal.

The Journal of Frankie Best

So, here I am, trapped inside a giant stone nostril. I'm now apparently in charge of a fellowship who all think I'm rubbish because our quest has failed. We've been locked in a cave by a load of sky Vikings. And I've just checked – there's still absolutely no phone signal. In fact, it won't even turn on until we leave this weird place, which now seems unlikely to happen at all. Safe to say: Worst. Holiday. EVER. Even worse than that time in Spain when Mum had to sleep out on the balcony because her snoring was keeping us awake, and the neighbours started throwing pebbles at the windows because she was keeping THEM awake.

Talking of Mum and Dad – I wonder what they'll do when they get back to Grandad's house? Mrs Archer, the woolly-hat shop lady, will tell them where we went, I guess. And they obviously know all about Parallelia – they've been using it as the inspiration for their games for years. They must owe all these creatures a fortune in royalties. Will they try to rescue us? I can't imagine that. Dad complains if he has to do the big shop at the supermarket. And what's happening to Grandad while all this is going on? It looks like (and I can hardly bring myself to write this down) our mission to rescue him – all right, our quest – has failed. Even if we do manage to escape from this nose, there surely isn't time to overtake the kidnappers before they get to that castle they were going on about.

And you know what? I'm gutted the quest didn't succeed. I mean, not just because of being trapped in a cave and all that. I was actually getting into the idea of the whole fellowship thing. I'd almost got to the stage where I was seeing myself as Frankie Firebrand, fearless adventurer.

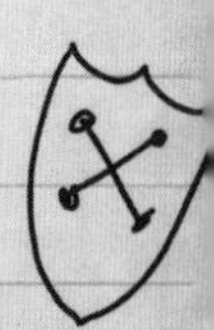

What's happening to me? A week ago, I would have thought that was the lamest thing ever. And I'm DEFINITELY never going to tell any of my friends about this. If they ask why I wasn't on my phone for a week, I'll just tell them I got run over, or abducted by aliens or something.

You know what, though? It just hit me, writing that down – *why* can't I tell my friends about this? Because they'll laugh at me? Like they did when they found out my parents created *Spingle's Quest*? Because it strikes me that, if that's the case, then maybe they're not really . . .

Suddenly the page swam in front of Frankie's eyes and her head reeled. She realized that, after a sleepless night on board the *Spindrift*, coupled with the dramatic events of that morning, she was so exhausted that she could barely think straight. Resigned, for now, to being trapped in the Nostril for the foreseeable future, she let the notebook slip from her hands, curled up on the sandy floor and within seconds she was fast asleep.

When Frankie woke up, she felt a lot less tired, but a huge amount hungrier. Dinner on the ship now seemed like a week ago. But there was no sign of any food, and the wooden hatch above them was too high to reach. She tried bellowing 'Guard!' a few times, because that was what people tended to do in this situation in the stories she'd read, but nobody replied. In the end, she gave up, and joined the rest of the Fellowship of the Bacon Roll, who were sitting in a circle, trying to work out their next move.

'We're trying to figure out who this Haggister is who's stealing the Talismans,' said Garyn. 'Your little brother has some interesting ideas about it.'

'I was just explaining my Theory of Baddies,' Joel told Frankie, and she sighed. He had spent a great deal of time expounding this theory to her, and she was extremely familiar with it.

Joel's Theory of Baddies goes like this: there are three main types of baddie. You've got your Type A, which is someone who's evil in a non-changeable, elemental kind of way. Evil spirits, devils, dark lords, that sort of deal. Then there's your Type B baddie, which is someone a bit more morally complicated – who maybe started off good, but got turned bad. Think Darth Vader. But, Joel claims, the most dangerous and hard-to-defeat baddie is Type C, which he refers to as the 'Moist-Palmed Lurker'. That kind sits on the sidelines, plotting away, and you don't find out they're a wrong'un until they make their move.

'And I think we must be dealing with Type C here,' Joel was now telling the others. 'If there was a Type A operating in Parallelia, you'd all know about it. And a Type B couldn't have gone undetected, not with Justices on the prowl.'

Justice nodded sagely at this, waving her Moral Compass for emphasis.

'So there must be a Type C about,' Joel reasoned.

'And whoever they are,' Frankie added, 'they're

putting the warrior's armour back together.'

'It's a classic Type C move,' said Joel. 'Seizing all the power in such a sneaky way, and not caring if they completely trash Parallelia in the process.'

'So, if we manage to escape from this nose, we can still follow the Moral Compass until we find them,' added Frankie, 'stop them, and return the Talismans and custodians to their proper places.' After her nap, she was feeling a little more hopeful that the quest might not yet be over.

'Plus rescue Grandad into the bargain,' Joel reminded her.

'Well, obviously rescue Grandad,' she said in a wounded tone. 'Like I'd forget that. It's the whole reason we're here.'

'I seem to remember you saying something about just getting your grandad and going straight home. Who cares what kind of stupid storybook nonsense is going on in Magical Pixie Bunnyland?' said Garyn, grinning at her rather infuriatingly. 'You seem to have changed your tune slightly over the last few days.'

'OK, you got me.' Frankie held up her hands in defeat. 'I mean, we may as well save the Magical

Fairytale Kingdom while we're here, eh? As we're going in that direction anyway.'

'It really is a quest now,' murmured Joel.

'Well, it will be if we ever manage to get out of this Nostril place,' said his sister. 'I certainly can't see a way out – not unless we suddenly learn how to fly, that is.'

At that exact moment, there was a fluttering of wings from the end of the cave. A dark shape blocked the opening and there was a scuffling of feet as the figure made an extremely poor landing, ending up flat on its face in the sand.

Unthinkingly, Frankie dashed forward to help the visitor up, and she was startled to see that it was the weedy-looking kid who'd stuck up for them earlier. He was wearing a pair of Sky-Wolf wings that looked far too big for him and, if his landing was anything to go by, he was definitely not an expert at using them.

'Were you telling the truth?' asked the boy without preamble. 'Has my father imprisoned the wrong people? Can you really rescue my mother?'

'Might I just turn the questions round and ask: have you brought anything to eat with you?' said Frankie. 'Because I am far, far too starving to think about rescuing anybody right now. The only thing on my mind is having a nice, relaxing loss of consciousness due to lack of food.'

The boy scrabbled on his back for a leather bag, which he handed to her.

'I thought you might be hungry,' he said as Frankie opened it with frantic speed, beckoning the rest of the fellowship over.

She pulled out some strips of dried meat – which she strongly suspected might be tiger-squirrel – but she was too hungry to care. Within seconds, the Nostril was full of the sound of very satisfied chewing.

'So, what's your name again?' asked Frankie through a mouthful of possibly-squirrel. 'Edwin or something, wasn't it?'

'Edwir,' the boy replied. 'Edwir Valkin. I'm the chief's youngest son. My older brother is Skendar. The one whose patrol captured you.'

'Yeah, the one with the cheekbones?' said Frankie. 'We didn't really hit it off. Though he did call me Frankie Firebrand, which might well become my new handle.' The boy looked bewildered. 'Never mind,' she told him. 'So you actually believe us, huh?'

'I do,' the boy said earnestly. 'I know my father doesn't trust my judgement, in this or anything . . .' Frankie sensed there was a whole family history going on here. 'But I think that if you'd really kidnapped my mother and stolen the Talisman,' he went on, 'then you wouldn't have allowed Skendar's patrol to capture you.'

Justice stepped forward. 'Do you know who I am?' she asked Edwir quietly.

'You're a Justice,' he said. 'We don't normally see Justices on the islands.'

'That's right,' she said. 'The Sky Wolves are a proud people. They don't like to admit that someone else can solve their problems for them. But look.' She pulled out the Moral Compass, which was pointing towards the back of the cave. 'This tells me that Parallelia is in danger, and your mother's part of that.' The compass tapped and tinged urgently. 'It says time is running short.'

'You're so right,' added Frankie, a knot of anxiety in her stomach. 'Mum and Dad will be back at the weekend, and if Grandad's not there I don't know what they're going to say.'

'So, will you help us?' asked Justice. 'I swear to you

that if you set us free we will make sure your mother is returned to you.'

'I will,' said Edwir solemnly, straightening his shoulders. 'I'll gather some of my friends, and we can take you and your companions down the Thunderdell Stair.'

'I don't know what that is, but if it's the exit from Bird Person Island then I'm very much feeling it,' Frankie told him. Once again, he looked at her in puzzlement.

'She speaks rather strangely,' Justice explained, 'but she is thanking you for your assistance.'

'I shall return,' promised Edwir. And he marched to the edge of the Nostril and – rather awkwardly, it had to be said – launched himself back out into the sky.

• • •

On a deserted beach not far from the bustling, beautiful port of Splendidness (which does not appear in this story), a boat had been pulled up on to the sand.

'Get the custodians, quickly!' Haggister was

issuing orders to the Mort brothers, who each grabbed one of the wooden cages from the prow and hoisted them up on their backs.

All four cages were now full – the final one containing a hawk-faced woman with numerous bright feathers woven into her long hair. Alika, the Custodian of the Islands, was not used to captivity. She was a proud, fierce warrior and, since she had been snatched from her chambers by a huge gnoblin in the early hours of the morning, she had not stopped trying to escape. At this point, she was actually attempting to chew through one of the leather straps holding the cage together.

'Make haste!' Haggister was urging his villainous crew to greater efforts.

Slytely Good, his greasy hair straggling over his face, was loading a wooden case containing the four Talismans on to the side of Gammort's backpack.

'We're ready,' he told Haggister as he tied the final strap securely. 'But shouldn't I wait here and ensure we're not being followed?'

'Nothing could have survived that storm, hmm,' Haggister replied, humming his trademark tune briefly as he cast a glance back over the waters of the bay. Angry-looking black clouds were still rolling across, far out over the water.

'If anything's happened to my grandkids,' warned the occupant of one of the other cages, his purple dressing gown now looking rather bedraggled after its sea voyage, 'your life is not going to be worth living.'

'Once I gather all five Talismans in the sacred chamber,' Haggister countered, 'my life is going to be very much worth living, thank you very much, Custodian. And, what's more, the Protections of Parallelia are about to, hmm, disappear. The future belongs to people like us – so you'd better get used to that idea, you old relic.'

Grandad banged at the cage door with his palms in fury. Chief Alika kept on chewing. But it was no use. They were powerless as the Mort brothers broke into a lumbering jog. Before nightfall they would be in Tramont Castle, where Haggister would put his plan into action. Time was running very, very short.

(This is not strictly relevant to the story, but on another beach, not terribly far away, Captain Fry and his crew were just washing up in the *Spindrift*'s other lifeboats. These were larger boats and were therefore also able to accommodate the ship's rats. Just so you know. In case you were worrying.)

• • •

As the sky outside the opening at the end of the Nostril began to darken to the rich dark blue of late afternoon, the wooden hatch in the ceiling opened and a rope ladder came jiggling down.

'Quick!' said Edwir's voice from the world above. 'We've distracted the guards, but you have to hurry!'

The Fellowship of the Bacon Roll rushed to their feet, all ten of them, and began to climb.

As Frankie's head popped up through the hatchway, she had the strange impression that their capture from that very morning was being re-enacted by a school drama club. They were, once again, surrounded by a circle of Sky Wolves. But, whereas their captors earlier on had been proud and burly, this lot were teenage and gawky.

'We're here to rescue you,' said Edwir, who was holding the hatch open – but Frankie couldn't help thinking that this was a phrase that sounded best being panted out by some cool hero rather than quavered at her in the just-breaking voice of a weedy adolescent.

Oh well, she thought. *I guess sometimes you've just got to take what rescues you're offered without getting too picky about it.*

Edwir and his spindly band led the fellowship quickly along the clifftop and down a path through the woods. They followed this for an hour or more, as tiger-squirrels darted among the trees and made Frankie feel oddly guilty about her lunch. Then they came to a narrow rope bridge strung with planks. It led to another island not far away, but spanned a gap of at least twenty metres. The sea, far below, roared and churned through the narrow passage, and the wind screamed up the smooth surface of the cliffs.

'Is this the Thunderdell Stair?' shouted Frankie above the shrieking of the wind.

'Of course not!' replied Edwir. 'This is a bridge. The stair is at the other end of that island. Quickly! When my father discovers what I've done, he'll send his guards after us. We've no time to lose!'

It's truly amazing what being chased will do to encourage you to cross a rickety bridge over a terrifying chasm. Frankie hardly thought about it as, grabbing Joel by the hand, she led the rest of the fellowship across. Basin – who had never been so high up in his life before – accompanied their crossing with a selection of high-pitched noises, but they all made it to the other side safely.

'Well, that wasn't too bad,' said Frankie. 'If we can cope with the scary bridge, this staircase of yours can't be much worse. Right?'

Wrong, as it turned out. When – just as the sun was about to set – they reached the other end of the island and Frankie got her first look at the Thunderdell Stair, she actually took a few steps backwards in pure shock. It was so jaw-clenchingly, brain-fizzingly, eyebrow-hoistingly incredible that it really needs its own chapter title . . .

CHAPTER 15

The Fellowship of the Bacon Roll actually heard the Thunderdell Stair long before they got their first look at it. As soon as they were across the rope bridge, a rumbling began to fill their ears – a deep, constant roaring like a distant peal of thunder that never ended. This island was much more barren than the others – mostly bare grey rock and a few stunted bushes that all looked fairly annoyed that their seeds had been stupid enough to land here instead of in a nice sheltered valley.

The noise grew as they followed a vague path across the grass and, by the time they reached the stair itself, it was so loud it seemed to make the actual air inside Frankie's ears shake. But at that point she hardly even noticed because she was too busy saying, **'WOW!'** at the top of her voice. Your first sight of the Thunderdell Stair isn't a moment you forget in a hurry. Or, indeed, ever.

Stretching out in front of her, leading away towards the distant coastline on the right-hand side, was a series of smaller islands, each decreasing in size and height, and looking for all the world like a staircase used by some legendary giant. Hence the name, obviously. They don't just make up these silly titles for no reason, you know.

So, as we're already aware, the Islands of the Sky Wolves are constantly whipped by strong winds off the sea. Well, all these winds converge on one single point, and that point is the Thunderdell Stair. In between each of the smaller islands – in between each step of the staircase if you like – there was a whooshing updraught of air. The high winds had whipped up the sea as well, so here and there Frankie and her companions could see a spout of white spray shooting up. Far below them – and it really was properly far below, far enough to make your legs do that weird thing where they go all fizzy – the sea boiled and churned as the wind lashed it into a series of eddies, whirlpools and deadly-looking riptides.

Beyond the Thunderdell Stair, the northern part of Parallelia was spread out beneath them. Frankie was so high up it actually felt like she was looking at the map rolled up in her backpack. To her left, a range of breath-snatchingly high mountains marched away into the far distance. They were so massive they actually seemed part of the sky unless you really concentrated. A little closer, but still indistinct, she could see a sprawling city beneath the three closest peaks. And these peaks she remembered clearly from the map and was even able to name them as she drank in the view.

On the left, a spike of purest white, dazzling in the early-evening sun: the Sprudelhorn. Next to it, behind the clustered roofs and towers of the city, was the jagged black mass of Mount Perspective – the volcano that threatened to destroy the area at any moment. And to the right of both of those, lower but somehow more mysterious, a much smoother green mountain, its top completely obscured by a mass of thick cloud and its left-hand side coated in thick forest: Silknaw Pike.

Much closer, Frankie could follow the line of the

coast away to the left and make out a cluster of bright white buildings spilling down the slope to fill a wide sandy bay. That must be Splendidness, she realized – the place the *Spindrift* had been supposed to dock. *Well*, she thought, *at least I saw it from a distance*. And it did look very pretty.

'Wow!' she said again. She'd said it already, but felt it was a point worth repeating. It was a wow-inducing kind of view. Beside her, Justice was also peering over the edge, once again turning a fetching green colour.

'Not many outsiders ever see this view,' said Edwir. 'And none has ever been permitted to descend the Thunderdell Stair. It is sacred to our people – a test of strength and skill that all of us must face when we come of age.'

'Hold up, hang on, wait just a squirrel-biltong-chewing minute here,' said Frankie. 'I distinctly remember your dad, Egghead . . .'

'Aaghaad!' one of the other youths corrected her proudly.

'Whatever,' dismissed Frankie. 'I remember him quite clearly saying that you haven't come of age yet.'

'Ah yes,' said Edwir a little shiftily. 'Well, that's

technically true. But I've done a lot of practising on the other cliffs, you see. We all have. And my mother's safety is at stake! We're definitely ready.'

Now it was Garyn's turn to step forward. 'Do you mean to tell us that you've never actually done this before?' he demanded. Edwir shook his head.

'None of you?' He rounded on the rest of the gang, who were hanging their heads in a slightly embarrassed fashion. 'Whose wings are those?' the knelf asked.

Edwir blushed a deep scarlet. 'They're, um . . . my dad's?'

And now Frankie realized why the wings strapped to the young Sky Wolf's back appeared oversized and wrong somehow. They didn't belong to him. Suddenly he looked as out of place as a teen who'd borrowed their parents' posh car, but didn't really know how to drive it.

'Well, I think we have to trust him.'

Frankie looked round in surprise. Joel was standing by her shoulder, hands on hips in a very dramatic pose.

'I think he can do it,' said her brother. 'It's just like that part in *Spingle's Quest Three* – remember? When Spingle needs to collect the final jewel, and he recalls the words of Wombo the Wise Old Warlock who told him to trust in his own abilities? And he leaps over the Chasm of Fear?'

At this point, Frankie's brain instructed her mouth to utter the phrase, 'For the last time, Joel, this is **NOT SPINGLE'S QUEST!**'

But her brain was somewhat startled to hear that her mouth was already speaking on its own.

'Oh YEAH!' it was saying. **'That was my favourite bit!'**

Joel looked rather shell-shocked at this. 'So, shall we do it, then?' he asked. 'Shall we cross the Chasm of Fear?'

Frankie Best made a decision. After all, what was their alternative? Go back and shut themselves up in the Nostril and wait for Chief Egghead to see sense? That would be far too late – if indeed it ever happened. As she pondered, she realized another thing. Four faces were turned expectantly towards her: Joel, Basin, Garyn and even Justice. The rest of the Fellowship of the Bacon Roll were waiting for her to take the lead.

'Fine,' said Frankie. 'If you think you can do it – I believe you. Strap on your overlarge wings, youngling. Let's ride that stair.' It wasn't a phrase she'd been expecting to ever come out with in her life, but this had been a very unexpected week so far.

'Yay!' said Edwir, punching the air and doing a little jump before remembering he was supposed to be all grown up and serious. He gave a small cough. 'Right,' he said, 'Frankie Firebrand, you come with me.'

Mentally resigning herself to whatever was about to happen – which, in the end, is the only way to really do adventures properly – she stepped over to stand in front of him.

'Ready?' he asked, fastening the leather strap from his harness tightly round her middle and grasping the wooden handles on the end of his wings.

'I mean, "ready" is probably an overstatement,' said Frankie, scrunching up her face doubtfully. Beside her, she could see Joel getting strapped to the front of a tall girl with flaming red hair. 'Careful with him, OK?' she said anxiously.

The girl gave her a hawkish grin, which Frankie somehow couldn't help returning. Danger of imminent splattage aside, this was all pretty exciting.

'THREE!' yelled Edwir, taking a couple of steps

backwards. Frankie could feel his arms tense as he lifted her clear of the ground, ready for take off.

'See you at the end!' she called to Joel, smiling at him encouragingly. 'Don't forget to smile for the camera. Scream if you wanna go faster.'

'TWO!'

The red-headed girl with Joel firmly strapped to her front was peering keenly down the stair, apparently gauging the best moment to take off. She flexed her wings, first to one side and then the other, planning how she would steer sharply left and right to avoid the columns of crashing seawater.

'Actually, on second thoughts –' said Frankie nervously.

'ONE!'

The Thunderdell Stair is over a mile long, and descends approximately seven hundred metres from the Islands of the Sky Wolves to the beach below. Those are the statistics for you. Strong winds make it impossible to land on the Stair itself, so you need to fly carefully above the small islands, banking to dodge treacherous air currents and waterspouts as you hurtle forward and downwards at incredible speed. Put it this way – it's impossible not to go, **'AAAARRRRGGGGHHHH!'** at the top of your voice.

'AAAARRRRGGGGHHHH!' bellowed Frankie at the top of her voice as Edwir, shouting, **'FOR CHIEF ALIKA!'**, sprinted to the edge of the cliff and dived off.

Think of the most exciting theme-park ride you've ever been on. Now multiply that feeling by twelve. Then double it. You're still not close to what it's like to soar crazily down the Thunderdell Stair, veering round gigantic spurts of water and being carried sharply upward on sudden freezing updraughts, with the constant thunder of the angry sea filling your head and your eyes watering from the incredible speed. Until you've done that, you really don't know what excitement or fear are. Until you brave the Stair, you've only been experiencing fear lite, and fifty-per-cent excitement, maximum.

Frankie wasn't able to time her flight – her phone still being tucked in her pocket with its black screen – but, if she had, she'd have been able to work out that she was going at something like fifty miles an hour. Which is a reasonable speed in a car, but feels a great deal faster when you're suspended in mid-air, strapped to a teenage flying novice who's doing this for the first time.

But Edwir had been right – he steered capably round the waterspouts and finally, as they dropped lower and lower, the thundering of the waves was left behind them, and the roaring of the wind left above, so when they landed gently on to the beach there was a sense of calm and quiet that was almost eerie. It was partly because Frankie's ears had popped with the rapid descent, and as Edwir released her from the harness she quickly did that hold-your-nose-and-blow trick to clear them.

''Tis **GRRRREEEEEEEAT!**' Basin had also come in to land, attached to another of Edwir's friends. 'Quests is the best,' he squeaked excitedly. 'I do shall be going on loads more when this 'un's finished. I don't think I've not never had this much fun since . . .' He scrumpled up his plump face. 'Actually, I don't think I never did have fun before.'

Justice, who'd landed on the other side of him, reached out and patted his shoulder.

'If this was a theme-park ride,' shouted Joel from somewhere above them, 'I would literally queue up for it for a week. And when I got off it I'd happily join the back of the queue again and wait for a second week just to have another go.' And he, too, floated in to land on the soft sand of the beach, Garyn beside him.

Edwir had stepped a few paces away and was looking back up at the islands that were his home. He wiped a hand across his eyes.

'Well, I guess you just came of age,' said Frankie, walking over and holding out a hand to shake.

'I defied my father,' said Edwir shakily.

'Well,' said Frankie reasonably, 'maybe that's what coming of age means. Anyway, thanks.'

'We shall remain here,' the young Sky Wolf told her. 'If you are pursued, we can make sure the guards go in the wrong direction. And if you could send my mother home, and the Sword of Andrasta, that would be massively helpful, actually. I've staked quite a lot on trusting you. I mean, if I was wrong, and you don't succeed, I'll be banished. I mean, we all will,' he said with a sniff.

'Hey, hey,' Frankie said soothingly. 'Don't worry. We've got this.'

'She's right,' said Justice, coming over to stand

beside Frankie, with her hand on the hilt of her sword. 'Frankie will lead us in the right direction – don't worry. We'll stop whatever plan this Haggister has cooked up, and send back your chief along with her talisman.'

'You know what? I believe you.' Edwir shook Frankie's hand, which was fortunate because she was getting slightly embarrassed at how long she'd been holding it out for. 'For now, farewell, travellers. I wish you well in your quest.'

'It's not a . . .' began Frankie, but then stopped and grinned to herself. 'Thanks,' she said simply. 'See you again, yeah? We'll come for a proper visit – you can show us how your flying's coming on.'

'Agreed.' And Edwir led his friends away up a nearby dune to lie in wait for any Sky Wolves that might follow them down from the island chain.

The Fellowship of the Bacon Roll made for the series of taller dunes visible ahead, making it heavy going across the wet sand. As she trudged, Frankie glanced backwards to see the Thunderdell Stair illuminated by a flaming sunset. The plumes of spray were lit up like fireworks by the rays of the setting sun, and the series of island steps were burnished a rich red.

At the top of the beach, they laboured up a sandy slope and threw themselves down in a hollow. It was fringed with that sharp grass that grows on sand dunes and hates human ankles, but it was out of the breeze, and the sand was soft and warmed by the heat of the sun.

Frankie flopped down beside Joel. 'Are you OK?' she asked.

'Seriously?' he asked.

'Yeah. I'm your big sister, remember? Checking up on you . . . it's kind of my job.'

Joel looked surprised but not displeased. 'I'm good, Frankie,' he said, giving her arm a pat. 'Thanks. Now let's get some rest. Your fellowship has a long way to go tomorrow.'

'Whoa, whoa, whoa.' Those words had knotted up her insides as tightly as the *Spindrift*'s rigging. 'This is no way my fellowship! Garyn's the guide. Justice is the muscle. Basin's the catering consultant. You're the weird fantasy kingdom expert, complete with book of fantastic beasts. I'm last in the queue!'

'Didn't you notice?' said Joel, already sounding like he was on the very edge of sleep. 'On the Islands of the Sky Wolves, who did all the talking? Who did

Edwir come to help? Who stood up to the chief?'

'Come on,' his sister said disbelievingly, although she was too tired to really argue. Frankie could feel delicious exhaustion wrapping round her shoulders like a duvet as the twilight in the sandy hollow deepened. Garyn was already fast asleep, she could see, and Justice had taken a blanket from her bag and was tucking it tenderly round Basin.

'You'll realize it before it's too late,' murmured Joel.

Above them, the stars had begun to blink on, bright and crystal clear in the unpolluted Parallelian sky.

• • •

It's possible to fall asleep in a sand dune if you're tired enough. If you're really, properly exhausted, it's even possible to find it relatively comfortable. But, whatever state you fall asleep in, you will – and this is guaranteed – wake up with a) sand in places you don't want sand and b) a cricked neck.

'OW!' said Frankie as she sat up, massaging the top of her back. Justice, not far away, was doing a strange hopping dance, shaking sand out of one of her tall grey boots.

'Morning,' said Garyn, who was crouched down, peering over the edge of the hollow. 'Hungry?'

'Starving,' she told him, mental bacon sandwiches sizzling inside her head. But Garyn rummaged in his bag, producing some of the oatcakes they'd been given at the Wandering Walrus.

'Just the continental breakfast today, then?' she said, trying not to look too disappointed as she accepted a couple of them.

'No time,' he replied. 'It's a long day's march to Tramont.'

Frankie's stomach turned over with a sickening first-day-at-school feeling. This was the day the whole quest had been leading up to, she realized.

'Besides, we can't risk a fire here,' the knelf added. 'We're right on the edge of the Dunelands of the Sand Witches. They're not fond of outsiders. Pack up your stuff and we'll get moving.'

Have you ever walked a long distance over sand dunes? If you haven't, there's one crucial detail you need to know: it's murder on the old knees. For hours, the Fellowship of the Bacon Roll plodded through the soft pale sand, which quickly found its way inside their boots and, indeed, everywhere else.

Once, as they clambered over the top of a steep rise, Justice (who was leading the way) was confronted with a strange creature. It looked not unlike a large rabbit, with foxy reddish-brown fur, and it was standing uncertainly right in the middle of the path. Its eyes were wide with fright, but it didn't run away. Instead, it kept making little darts to the left and the right, emitting an alarmed chittering.

'It's just a dither,' Justice explained, gently nudging it with her foot to the side of the path, where it stayed, panting and looking at them with frightened eyes as they filed past.

DITHER ~ *the most indecisive animal I have ever encountered. When stressed, a dither is completely unable to work out in which direction it should flee.*

DITHER

They would definitely have been hunted to extinction many years ago if they didn't taste quite so revolting when cooked. Kind of like parsnips mixed with burnt rubber.

Dithers can be tamed and kept as pets, but I cannot for the life of me understand why anyone would want to.

Garyn kept casting nervous looks to either side as they skirted the edge of the Dunelands. 'He's worried one of the Sand Witches will catch us,' Joel whispered to Frankie.

'I wonder what they're like,' his sister mused.

'I wonder what they're called,' added Joel. 'Do you think they have names like Cheesan Pickle? Or Bee El Ti?' He let out a small chuckle.

'Hang on, hang on.' Frankie stopped in the sand. 'Are you making jokes about Parallelia now? Because that's supposed to be my job, you know.'

'Come on, keep moving, you two,' Garyn urged in a stage whisper, beckoning to them.

'Yeah, come on,' said Joel. 'Let's get going before we're kidnapped by the evil witch, Hamman Cheez.'

'Or their infamous leader, Eg Mayo . . .'

'Or Bim Bam Bip Boop!' Basin trotted up beside them, panting.

'That one doesn't work, Basin,' Frankie told him. 'It's got to be a sandwich filling or the joke's not funny.'

'What be a sandwich fillin'?'

'I'll explain as we go,' she said kindly. 'Come on, last one to Tramont's a mouldy Bethcar pear.'

• • •

Not far away, in her bedchamber, Princess Prince was looking out of the window across the proud city of Tramont and combing her long and very princessy hair when there was a knock at her door. She answered it to see a footman standing outside. She didn't recognize him, but then again Princess Prince didn't make a habit of memorizing the faces of her staff.

This man was rather small and stooped, with long hair that looked as though it could do with a good wash. 'Princess, you must come quickly!' he said dramatically. 'Your presence is required in the Chamber of the Talisman. A terrible crime has been committed that threatens the whole of Parallelia!'

Princess Prince was extremely alarmed to hear this. She deeply loved the Kingdom of Parallelia, which was why the Guardian Spirit had selected her to be a custodian in the first place. Quickly, she followed the footman along the twisting passageways of Tramont Castle as he scurried along ahead of her at a rapid trot.

'What on earth has happened? Am I in danger?' she called after him as they ran.

'A custodian is always in danger, Your Highness,' he replied. 'You must trust nobody.'

But – again unfortunately – Princess Prince was not aware of Joel's Rule One. (Which, if you had forgotten it from earlier, is this: anyone who tells you to trust nobody will turn out to be a baddie and will later follow it up with the phrase, 'I did warn you to trust nobody.')

When Princess Prince arrived at the gloomy

corridor that led to the chamber where the warrior's breastplate was stored, she was slightly surprised to see a man whom she vaguely recognized as the silver polisher waiting beside the door.

Oh well, she thought, *perhaps it's due for a clean.* And she placed her hand on the door without a lock or a handle, opening the way to the cave beneath the volcano.

'So what's the crime?' she asked the footman.

'Someone's been kidnapped,' he replied.

'Oh no, that's terrible!' said Princess Prince. 'Who?'

'You' snarled the silver polisher, as four huge, hulking shapes appeared in the passageway behind him.

Sneering, the greasy-haired footman said, 'I did warn you to trust nobody,' as they closed in on her.

CHAPTER 16

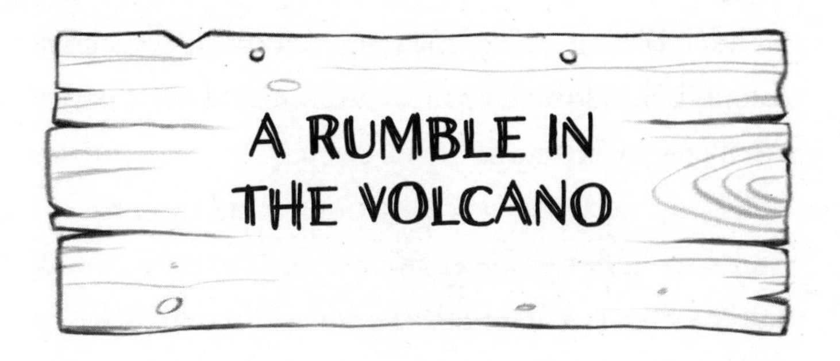

Tramont, the largest city in Parallelia, is a fascinating place, and in many ways it's a pity that on this visit Frankie didn't really get to appreciate it. She couldn't even pause to take in the stunning view spread out before the fellowship as they reached the edge of the dunes and got their first proper look.

The huge city wall curved away to their left, and beyond it they could see the afternoon sun bouncing off the calm waters of Lake Gah. The white spike of the Sprudelhorn rose from the lake shore, and far beyond that lay the green haze of an enormous forest. But that's the thing about quests – there often isn't time to stop and drink in the view, even when it's as impressive as that one. They were looking out for only one thing – the castle – and fortunately it wasn't hard to spot.

The looming black mass of Mount Perspective rose up behind the city of Tramont, and built partly into its rocky frontage was a castle.

'Whoa,' said Joel, reaching out a hand to grasp his sister's shoulder as he stumbled on the path. 'Now that is a classic villain lair if ever I saw one. Spooky black-walled castle actually set into a volcano? I mean, talk about over-egging your baddie pudding.'

Justice was consulting the Moral Compass, which was tinging and clicking frantically as she held it up in front of her face. 'Your grandfather is in that castle,' she declared.

'No kidding?' Frankie asked her. 'Seriously? He's in there, the big black castle sticking out of the volcano? And here's me thinking he'd been taken to the tranquil woodland clearing of Bunnykins Dell to dance with some pixies.'

Justice looked at her blankly – people in her profession don't really do a lot of sarcasm. They're more in the 'constantly fighting injustice while wearing an expression of grim determination' line of work.

'Let's go,' said Justice, leading the way towards

Tramont with an expression of grim determination.

Frankie followed and, despite her apprehension about what they might find inside the castle, she found her chest filling with a rising swell of excitement.

Imagine for a second how cool it must feel to be leading your very own fellowship of fantasy characters across the sand dunes towards a scary castle. Sure, they were about to face a villain who was trying to take control of some incredibly powerful magical talismans, which, if he succeeded, could turn each of them into a small smear on the castle walls. But it's hard to stay frightened when you're stampeding down a slope with a warrior and a knelf who are sworn to help you execute a daring rescue on either side of you. If you ever get the chance, it's well worth giving it a go.

Tramont's an intriguing city, but on their mad dash through the streets, the Fellowship of the Bacon Roll had missed every single one of its amazing tourist attractions. Here's a quick rundown, though, in case you find yourself there one day.

In the Downleft district, you'll find the huge Ready-or-not Gardens, which have been specially constructed to play hide-and-seek in. They're awesome. If ancient buildings are more your thing, there's the Ice Catacombs that were dug right underneath the lower slopes of the Sprudelhorn and have carvings dating back to before the founding of Parallelia, plus Slushie Falls, the only known half-frozen waterfall. You've got the Soup Market – Justice's least favourite place to eat in the whole city – and the Caw Centre where you can send a crow with your message to any part of Parallelia. Oh, and there's a place in Upleft that does the BEST milkshakes.

But for Frankie and her friends there was no time for sightseeing. It was rescue-mission-a-gogo and, that being the case, the stately streets of lower Tramont passed by in a kind of blur. They kept on climbing as the houses on either side became smaller and more soot-stained, until they reached the huge, open piazza that stands in front of the black stone castle.

If you do ever hit the tourist trail in the Parallelian capital, Lava Plaza is definitely worth a visit – probably just before you hit the milkshake shop. It's paved with pure black stones and backed by the glowering bulk of the castle and the volcano above it, which makes it sound kind of gothic.

But in front of Tramont Castle there's a very, very deep moat, and at the bottom of the moat is a sluggish stream of bright red lava. This lava has been channelled through the rock beneath the square as well, so not only does Lava Plaza have some very efficient underfloor heating, it also has a series of fountains that shoot streams of glowing lava into the air every few minutes. They don't even need those warning signs saying:

because, if you tried to swim in these fountains, you'd be deep-fried before you could say, 'Ow, that's hot!'

The piazza was crowded, which is nothing unusual.

But whereas you'd normally find the good people of Tramont admiring the fountains, second-guessing the price of one another's sumptuous outfits or gazing up at the cone of Mount Perspective and wondering whether today would, finally, be the day it erupted and wiped them all out, they were all running about like ants who'd accidentally sucked up a really strong coffee. The square was full of noise and chatter.

'THE PRINCESS HAS BEEN KIDNAPPED!' wailed a man in a richly embroidered cloak to his friend.

'THE PRINCESS HAS BEEN KIDNAPPED?' said the friend with a gasp.

'THE PRINCESS HAS BEEN KIDNAPPED?' screeched a woman who'd been running past at the time and overheard them.

'THE PRINCESS HAS BEEN KIDNAPPED!' confirmed embroidered-cloak guy breathlessly.

'THE PRINCESS HAS BEEN KIDNAPPED!' the woman howled like a siren as she dashed off across the piazza in a panic, prompting a lot of other people to also start saying, **'THE PRINCESS HAS BEEN KIDNAPPED!'** to each other.

Hey, I said the square was full of noise and chatter.

I didn't make any promises about how high-quality that chatter was going to be.

Frankie and her friends weren't the only ones to arrive in Lava Plaza at that exact moment. As they stood looking at the milling crowds among the red-hot fountains, four other people also came sprinting up and stopped dead. All four were dressed identically, in long grey cloaks and grey boots. Each of them carried a sword and held a small metal compass on an outstretched palm.

Justice greeted them politely: '**Justice**,' she said, nodding to the first grey-cloaked figure, and then, '**Justice, Justice, Justice**,' to the other three.

'**Justice**.' The first Justice, a grizzle-haired man, acknowledged her greeting with a curt nod.

'**Justice**,' replied the second, a young woman whose sword had an ornately carved pommel.

'**Justice**,' the third Justice also said formally as she dropped into a low bow.

'**Justice**,' said the final Justice from behind his rather dashing bandit-style neckerchief.

'Can someone please say something that isn't "**Justice**" or "**THE PRINCESS HAS BEEN KIDNAPPED**"?' pleaded Frankie.

'THE PRINCESS HAS BEEN KIDNAPPED?' repeated the Justice with the fancy sword, looking shocked and turning questioningly to her neighbour.

'Justice!' Frankie screamed at her briefly and she held up a hand in apology.

'I rather think we're all here for the same reason,' said our own Justice, holding out her Moral Compass. The others did the same – all five compasses were now pointing directly at the castle.

'I've been tracking an injustice that was committed in Bethcar,' said the grizzled man. 'A kidnapping and robbery at the lighthouse.'

'My compass tells me the Custodian of Tygermere is being held here against his will,' added another.

'We're all here because of stolen talismans and kidnapped custodians?' asked Justice. As one, the other four nodded. 'We know the perpetrator,' she told them. 'It's a man called Haggister.'

'So, shall we get in there and stop him?' suggested Frankie politely, feeling that they'd spent quite enough time bringing the new Justices up to speed.

'Let's go!' said fancy-sword Justice. 'The princess is in danger!'

'Clear the way, please! Clear the way for

the Justices of Parallelia!' cried Justice (original version), and the crowd parted before her like a flock of chattering birds.

Everyone stared at the fellowship as they marched across Lava Plaza with the five Justices up front. Frankie was fully anticipating some fancy swordfighting when they got to the castle guards, and possibly at one point one of them falling into the molten moat with a startled **'AIEEEEEE!'**, but as it turned out that wasn't necessary.

One of the fundamental rules of Parallelia is that Justices are allowed to go absolutely anywhere their Moral Compasses direct them – princes and princesses don't get any special protection. So the Justices simply showed their compasses to the guards at the head of the massive black stone bridge and the Fellowship of the Bacon Roll were waved across like celebrities with passes saying:

CASTLE –
ACCESS ALL AREAS.

On the other side of the bridge, the doors of ancient scorched wood were swung open and they dashed inside.

Navigating the winding corridors of Tramont Castle wasn't easy, even with five separate Moral Compasses to guide the way. A couple of times they hit a dead end or realized they were on the wrong floor, but eventually they found themselves on the lower levels.

Frankie had always thought of castles as being cold places – because, to be fair, they almost always are. But Tramont Castle, being built into the side of a volcano, was boiling. Each time she went down a set of stairs, the air got warmer, thicker and slightly more eggy-smelling. Finally, as they all tumbled into a wide stone chamber on the very lowest level, it felt – and smelled – like they had entered a large oven where someone had left an omelette unattended since last Wednesday.

There were two very excellent reasons why this particular underground chamber smelled so bad. Reason one was the general sulphurous reek that you get beneath a volcano. Reason two was the fact that the chamber wasn't empty. Four huge gnoblins were sitting in it, and they had spent the past week running across Parallelia with heavy cages on their backs. At no point had they stopped to freshen up.

If Frankie, Joel and Garyn had completed their quest alone, this might well have been the last page of the book, and a short, gooey and painful ending to boot. But, of course, they weren't alone. They were the Fellowship of the Bacon Roll – now with added Justices – and they were in full rescue mode. There was a hugely pleasing **schiiiinnnnnkkkkk** as all five Justices drew their swords and spread out across the stone chamber.

'Stand aside!' ordered Justice One.

'GAR!' snarled Titch, pulling a thick wooden club from his belt.

Justice One wasn't expecting anything less, to be honest. I mean, think about it – very rarely does someone in this kind of story bellow, **'Stand aside!'** and the other people just go, 'Oh sure. Sorry, didn't realize I was in your way.'

The four newest

Justices and the four Mort brothers closed in combat, and the underground chamber was soon full of the sound of cold steel hitting wooden clubs. It's a fairly hard noise to describe, actually. Imagine filling a wooden barrel with cutlery and rolling it down a hill – kind of like that.

'Go!' panted fancy-sword Justice, executing a neat pirouette and parrying a blow from Hackmort that would have been relatively career-ending if it had connected. 'Save the custodians! We'll hold them off!'

Nodding, Frankie led the rest of the fellowship out of the chamber and away through the maze of passages.

Shortly after passing a sign that rather bafflingly read:

they arrived at a gigantic wooden door with no handle. At this point, the Moral Compass was tinging and clicking madly, as if it was trying to shout, 'In there! In there!' at the top of its tiny metallic voice.

Without thinking, Frankie placed the flat of her hand on the door and shoved it open. Ignoring some kind of question from Joel behind her about custodians and portals, she led the fellowship into the huge chamber beneath the mountain.

Frankie didn't immediately take in the statue of the warrior, or the huge, cathedral-like edifice of black rock opposite. She was only looking at one thing – the white-haired, pyjama'd and dressing-gownerized figure of her grandfather, who was tied to a stone chair on the other side of the cavern.

'Grandad!' she shouted. 'We're here to rescue you!' and his face, which had been stretched with surprise, broke into a wide grin of such calm confidence that Frankie felt her eyes pricking with tears.

Someone wasn't quite so pleased to see them, though. He was a tall man in a dusty black outfit who was standing on the plinth in the very centre of the chamber, beside the statue.

'How on earth did you get in?' said Haggister venomously.

He had been placing the silver helmet on the statue's head. It was, Frankie could now see, already wearing a brightly polished breastplate and a pair of metal boots stood between its legs. A bright silver sword had been placed across that statue's raised hands and a shining blue shield buckled to the left arm.

Justice stepped forward. 'I am a Justice of Parallelia,' she said, her voice filling the enormous chamber. 'You have been detected as the source of an injustice. As such, you are required to make amends or face punishment. The Kingdom is the King.'

'The Kingdom is the King,' repeated the five custodians in their stone chairs.

'Not any more,' snarled Haggister, his long face twisted into a peculiar smile. 'Finally, hmm, Parallelia is about to get a real king.' And he jammed the helmet down on to the stone head.

Immediately, the chamber was filled with a new sound, a deep ringing as if it was inside a gigantic bell. The warrior's armour began to glow with a strange reddish light, and the bright ruby in the centre of the breastplate pulsed like a heartbeat.

'THE TALISMANS ARE ASSEMBLED!' screeched Haggister, turning to face the cliff of red-hot rocks behind him, which were formed into the shape of a face – a face wearing an expression of greedy triumph. 'The five custodians are assembled. Guardian Spirits of Parallelia, I command you! Imbue this suit of armour with its full power!'

'Imbue?' Frankie asked Joel, who was standing beside her.

'It means to fill or infuse,' he said helpfully.

'I COMMAND YOU!' yelled Haggister again. Now, so close to his goal, he had stopped his strange humming. Instead, his voice was loud and confident. Behind him, on the statue, the boots, breastplate, shield and sword now all looked as if they'd been heated up in a furnace.

'I claim the armour of the warrior!' he cried and, at once, the four shimmering sections of armour disappeared, reappearing on him. 'I am all-powerful!' Haggister gloated, seeming to expand to fill the flaming breastplate, his hand tightening on the hilt of the fiery sword.

'I can't help thinking that you're missing

something!' Frankie shouted up at him.

With a clank, the armoured Haggister clomped over to the edge of the stone platform to stare scornfully down at her.

'Puny child,' he said with a sneer. 'Nothing is missing. You and your pathetic friends have arrived too late to stop me. I control the armour of the warrior. I control the Guardian Spirits of Parallelia. I am unstoppable.'

'Ah.' Frankie held up a finger. 'Well, technically, all five points you made there are completely and utterly wrong.'

'What do you mean?' said Haggister, as doubt flared in the back of his eyes like faraway fireworks.

In reply, Frankie Best simply angled her finger downwards slightly to point behind him. Haggister turned his head to look at the black stone statue of the warrior, and his eyes widened. The statue was still wearing the helmet, which was its usual bright shining silver with none of that unearthly red glow.

'How is this possible?' Haggister grabbed the helmet and smooshed it down on to his head in what looked like quite a painful way. It wobbled around ridiculously, falling forward over his eyes.

'Yeah – doesn't fit you, does it?' said Frankie. By now, the rest of the Fellowship of the Bacon Roll had gathered in a group behind her. 'And you know why? Because it doesn't belong to you.'

'Frankie,' said Garyn from behind her, 'would you mind letting the rest of us know what exactly is going on? Please?'

'It's Joel's Rule Two! All villains have a weak point,' she said as the armoured man on the plinth looked down on her with growing fury. 'Haggister's plan, like all evil plans – without exception – had one fatal flaw.'

She stepped away from the group and turned back to face them, spreading her hands out wide. It's very difficult to resist the temptation to showboat just a tiny little bit when you have all the answers and you're about to spring a dirty great reveal on the rest of your fellowship.

'His plan,' she continued, 'was to gather all five Talismans and all five custodians here in this chamber. That would let him reactivate the warrior's armour and become some kind of all-powerful super-villain. He's obviously been encouraged to do it by Fornax, who incidentally is just using him as a puppet and plans to double-cross him as soon as the ritual is over. But that needn't concern us right now.'

There was a deep rumble that shook the chamber.

'You, erm, mentioned a flaw in the plan?' said Garyn hesitantly. 'Because, from where I'm standing, he does seem to have assembled all five Talismans . . .' He gestured towards Haggister in the warrior's glowing armour. 'He also appears to have turned into some fairly powerful kind of super-villain.'

'Ah,' said Frankie, trying to sound as un-smug as possible, but, let's be honest, probably failing, 'you've missed something out.'

'The custodians?' queried Garyn, looking round the chamber in confusion. 'But . . . they're right here, Frankie. Look.'

Fastened to the stone chair nearest to them was someone who was, quite obviously, Chief Alika of the Sky Wolves, the Island Custodian, clad in the same leather and copper as Edwir. Further away, Frankie could see a tall woman in a sea-blue gown who must surely be the Custodian of Bethcar. Princess Prince, the Custodian of Tramont, who looked completely furious, was in the chair next to her, struggling against her bonds. Further round the enormous circle was a man in simple brown clothes who was regarding her with wise eyes – the Custodian of Tygermere from the farmlands and orchards to the west of Parallelia.

And, finally, directly opposite them was the smiling face of her grandad, still looking at her with that quiet confidence.

He knows, thought Frankie. *He knows I've worked it out.*

'There aren't five custodians in these chairs,' she told Garyn, and as she spoke she could feel Haggister's fury building up behind her like an electrical storm. 'Because my grandad over there –' she pointed – 'is not the Custodian of Angel Woods.'

'He's . . . he's not?' said Garyn blankly.

'Nope,' replied Frankie Best calmly. 'I am.'

CHAPTER 17

THE CUSTODIAN OF ANGEL WOODS

The Journal of Frankie Best

I know, right? Quite the curve ball at this point in the story.

I'd been doing a lot of thinking, you see, over the last couple of days. And I'd finally worked a few things out. Firstly – and this is the really shocking one, so brace yourselves.

Are you ready?

I don't actually hate quests that much after all. Phew. Feels weird to be writing that down, but I thought it was best to get the real shocker out of the way first.

Secondly, I had realized that Joel, Garyn, Justice and Basin had become, like, my best friends in the world. They didn't judge me in the way my friends at school did. They were my gang, my crew . . . my fellowship. I mean, I know Joel was already my brother, but I think it's safe to say that it was only during our quest across Parallelia that he became my friend as well.

Ah yes, and another thing I'd realized about Joel. When we arrived at Grandad's house, I'd just been looking at him as my infuriating, super-nerdy little brother. But the further we went through Parallelia the more I realized something. His enormous wealth of nerdy knowledge was actually useful there. I mean, he called it right when he warned me not to trust that creepy guy Slytely Good, remember? He tried to get me to realize that there actually *were* a few clues from *Spingle's Quest* that we could use. And finally, when we were in that awful chamber under the volcano, I decided to do something I hadn't done properly for a good few months. I decided to listen to my little brother.

What was it Joel had said, all the way back in Grandad's house? *Why did the door open when you told it to?* At the time, I'd just brushed that question off, but it had been buzzing round my head like a gnat for the whole journey. How *had* I opened up the Mirror Door? Then, when I pushed open the entrance to the volcano chamber, it finally hit me. I'd been selected as the new custodian! Parallelia had chosen me, right back at the start of the story. At the very moment I'd pushed that wooden panel in Grandad's house, the spirit of Ilvatar had made me the new Custodian of Angel Woods. That's why I'd been able to open the secret door.

I know what you're thinking. *That's mad.* And also why didn't it choose that tireless little wizard-botherer Joel instead of me? Fair question. And it's the first thing he wondered, too, when I did my 'big reveal' moment inside Tramont Castle.

'You're . . . one of the Custodians of Parallelia?' asked Joel, open-mouthed.

'Yup,' his sister confirmed. 'How do you think we got in here? Remember that big door without a lock or a handle just back there? Who opened it?'

As they all pondered this question, Frankie saw the jaws of the fellowship collectively drop as the realization hit them.

'That is **SO UNFAIR!**' wailed Joel. 'You don't even **LIKE** Parallelia! You think all this stuff is stupid!'

'Hey.' She comforted him with a pat on the shoulder. 'It's really growing on me.'

'You worked it out, then?' Grandad asked from across the chamber.

Joel gasped. 'You knew!'

'Of course I did!' he said, grinning infuriatingly at Haggister. 'I've known all the time this idiot's been carting me across Parallelia that I was no longer the custodian. I realized as soon as I saw you two in the attic that the spirit Ilvatar had decided to pass on the torch.'

'Rule Two,' recalled Frankie, placing a hand on Joel's shoulder again. 'Every bad guy has a weak point. And, by extension, every evil plan has a flaw.'

'That can be Rule Two B,' her brother said.

'I hesitate to interrupt this touching family moment,' said Haggister from above them. 'But haven't you realized that your, hmm, plan also has a flaw in it?'

'Ah,' said Frankie Best, 'I was slightly worried you might say that. What?'

'You may have prevented me from activating the full suit of armour,' Haggister continued, 'but I still have the breastplate, the boots, the shield and the sword. What's to stop me wiping out all your pathetic friends, and your grandfather, before forcing you into the chair and completing the ritual?'

'Well,' said Frankie, 'you do raise a good point – there's no doubt about it.'

'However,' said Justice, 'there is a slight problem. You see, to get to Frankie, you'll have to come through me.' And she drew her sword and crouched into a very mean-looking combat stance.

'And me!' added Garyn.

Frankie had never really thought to question the knelf about his combat abilities, trusting that Justice would deal with the swishy-sword stuff when the time came. But Garyn had produced a short, bejewelled and very sharp-looking sword from his probably-magic backpack. And now, leaving the backpack propped up against one of the stone chairs, he did a completely unnecessary double front somersault, brandishing the sword at the same time, and slashing the air with it, as well as throwing in a knelvish war cry.

'And me!' shouted Basin in his squeaky voice, pushing past Joel. He had managed to get hold of a spoon from somewhere and was waving it threateningly.

'Because she's not just Frankie Best,' said Joel proudly, standing beside his sister. 'She's Frankie Firebrand, Custodian of Angel Woods and leader of the Fellowship of the Bacon Roll.'

Frankie couldn't help blushing at this and, despite the hugely powerful villain who was about to try and smoosh them all into conveniently sized pieces, she could feel a smile forcing its way on to her face.

With a huge clatter, Haggister leaped from the plinth and stood facing the two warriors and the spoon-wielding gnoblin. The rest of the fellowship very sensibly dived for cover, with Frankie grabbing Basin and dragging him, along with Joel, beside a stone chair.

'We've reached the final level! Joel was gabbling excitedly. **'BOSS FIGHT! BOSS FIGHT!'**

'Stop shouting "boss fight"!' Frankie scolded him. 'This isn't a game, remember?'

There was a resounding clang as Haggister swung the red-glowing Sword of Andrasta. Justice parried the stroke but, peeping from behind the chair, Frankie saw her stagger from the force of the blow.

'They're buying us some time,' she told Joel and Basin. 'Let's use it to release the other custodians. You two, go left – untie Chief Alika and the lady in blue over there, then keep going! The more custodians we release, the less chance Haggister has of completing the ritual! It's the only way to save Parallelia!'

'And we're also going to rescue Grandad, right?' Joel wanted to be certain.

'That's why we came here in the first place, remember?' she replied, grinning. 'So let's do it, and we can all go home!'

Chances are you've never spent a week tracking a kidnapped grandparent through a Magical Fairytale Kingdom. But, if you have, you'll know that it's kind of hard to know what to say to them when you actually reach them. A simple 'hello there' would be a bit of an anticlimax, but equally you don't want to go too far the other way and make a big long speech – especially if there's a hugely powerful maniac slashing at your friends with an enormous sword a few metres away. In the end, Frankie settled for the classic 'Are you OK?' as she rushed to the stone chair and began struggling with the thick knots that bound him.

'I'm a bit more than OK, petal,' said Grandad, pulling one hand free and shaking it to bring the feeling back. 'I'm so proud of you I could pop like a happy balloon. Both of you. You've come all the way through Parallelia! Oh my, I can't wait to hear the story.'

Frankie glanced across the stone chamber to see that Joel and Basin had already freed Chief Alika and the Sky-Wolf warrior was now rushing to help the Custodian of Tygermere, the silver feathers in her long hair catching the reddish light. Closer to her, Garyn and Justice were still locked in combat with Haggister, but they were clearly coming off worse. As she watched, the knelf caught a glancing blow from the Sword of Andrasta, which dinged off his own weapon and sent him flying through the air to crash into the rocky cavern wall. Justice held her sword aloft as Haggister clomped towards her.

Frankie and Grandad were backing gingerly away towards the high carved archways at the back of the chamber when Joel scurried along the wall to join them, leaving Chief Alika to protect Basin and the Custodians of Tygermere and Bethcar. The tall Sky-Wolf woman herded them into a shallow alcove and stood in front of them, arms folded and with a face that said 'don't even think about trying to get past me'.

'You said it was the cat making a noise,' said Joel to their grandfather accusingly as he approached. 'When it was actually an escaped tree pook.'

'Ah yes, sorry about that.' The old man looked sheepish. 'I'll explain everything, Joel. I promise.'

'Perhaps later,' said his granddaughter, glancing back over her shoulder. 'We have a more pressing problem right now – how to escape from the hugely powerful armoured maniac. I don't suppose there's another one of your rules that might help us out here?'

'Well, Rule Three,' Joel replied, 'is – always check for secret doors.'

'Secret doors?' Frankie's eyes were caught by the line of dark archways set into the rear wall of the Chamber of the Talisman.

'Yes, secret doors, like in –'

'*Spingle's Quest Two*, when you're trapped in Darzil's cavern and you need to push the statue to reveal the hidden passageway?' said Frankie before he could finish.

'Frankie –' he tutted mockingly – 'this is not *Spingle's Quest*, you know.'

'Shut up.' She cuffed him affectionately on the shoulder. 'Start checking the walls! Just stay out of reach of those swords.'

Behind them, Justice was leaping and vaulting from the now-empty stone chairs, attacking Haggister from all angles. But the magical armour kept him protected, her blows glancing off the breastplate and shield harmlessly.

Frankie wished fervently that she could just stop for a few minutes and watch what was undoubtedly one of the most amazing swordfights ever staged, in any world. But there wasn't time.

'Secret door, secret door,' she said, scuttling in a crouch towards the dark archways – was one of these a possible way out?

Justice clearly wouldn't be able to hold Haggister off forever, armed as he was with four powerful magical weapons. Several possible outcomes were now seeming likely, and almost all of them involved being hit with a really big sword, which wasn't how Frankie normally enjoyed spending her evenings.

At that point, something very unexpected happened. Really, really, *really* unexpected. If a troop of beefy warriors had burst through the roof, riding dragons, that would have been a bit unexpected, but after the week she'd just been through Frankie would almost certainly have taken it in her stride. But the thing that happened – and which massively took her by surprise – was this: her phone buzzed in her back pocket. It had been stuck there, dull and lifeless, for the entire week, but now – here, in the scary carved volcanic chamber – it had mysteriously turned itself on.

Frankie thought furiously. What was it that Garyn had said to her, all those days ago, as they'd set out into Angel Woods?

Magic from your world won't work once you're more than a short way past the portal. Just as magic from

Parallelia won't work if we travel the other way.

Where had that portal been located? Close to the resting place of one of the Talismans. Was there, she wondered, just possibly, a portal close to every Talisman? And was the phone suddenly working because it was now right beside another one of these portals?

'Oy!' shouted Frankie suddenly, leaping to her feet and sprinting across the chamber towards Haggister. 'You! Phlegm-face! Tripe-ears! You great big knock-kneed, jelly-elbowed, mushroom-nosed failure!'

Give her a break: she was just desperate to get his attention. She wasn't looking to win any prizes for Most Brilliant Insult. And it worked.

Haggister had managed to catch Justice with a glancing blow using the edge of the Shield of Ran, and she'd stumbled. He was now looming over her grey-cloaked figure, sword raised to deliver a blow that could well have been more than a little nasty. But, seeing this girl who had ruined all his plans capering about within his grasp, he paused and regarded her with his dark, mean-looking little eyes.

'You want to capture a custodian?' she bawled at him, hopping from foot to foot, putting her thumbs in her ears and doing that wiggly-fingered taunt that toddlers do. **'WELL, COME AND GET ME! LAST CHANCE! CATCH ME IF YOU CAN!'**

With a roar, Haggister abandoned Justice and made a grab for Frankie. She danced out of range – Year Five ballet classes finally paying off here – and ran pell-mell for the black archway in the wall.

'Get Justice, get Garyn and follow us – quick as you can!' she said breathlessly to Joel and Grandad as she sprinted past. 'And bring rope! Lots of rope!'

She couldn't pause to take questions at this point because Haggister was showing a quite worrying turn of speed. He was, after all, wearing a pair of magic boots. By the time Frankie reached the arch in the carved rock wall and plunged through, he was so close to her that she actually felt his hand brush the heel of her own boot. But he didn't manage to get a proper grip and she dashed off down the passageway like a cheetah that just realized it had left the iron on.

The black archway led to a narrow stone tunnel that sloped slightly upward. It was floored with the same shiny volcanic rock as the chamber – and there's a reason they don't make athletics tracks out of that material: it's extremely difficult to run on. Frankie's toes got stubbed so many times that it felt like they were being hammered backwards into her feet like nails.

But she kept on running, ignoring the fact that her lungs were, apparently, filling up with hot sand and her legs were rapidly transforming into floppy tubes of luncheon meat. Far, far ahead of her was a distant crack of light, and the Custodian of Angel Woods fixed her eyes upon it and raced ahead with every morsel of strength she had left, feeling the air rushing past her face begin to gradually, subtly, change its taste.

At any moment, she expected to feel Haggister's hand grab her by the shoulder, or Andrasta's Sword hit her, which would be considerably worse. But neither of these things happened. Because Frankie had been right. The doorway beneath the mountain did indeed lead to a portal back to her own world. And, once he passed through this invisible barrier in the air, the magic that had made Haggister super-powerful abruptly failed.

There was a clatter and a clanging that sounded like the contents of the kitchenware section of a large department store being tipped out of a third-floor window. Frankie stopped running, which took a few steps because she'd built up a fairly impressive momentum, and looked behind her.

Haggister was splayed out on the tunnel floor, which was now lit by faint sunlight from ahead. The boots had detached themselves and rolled away from his feet, no longer glowing red but looking very old and rather tarnished. Andrasta's Sword and the Shield of Ran had dropped from his outstretched hands and clattered to the stone floor, and here in this world they simply looked like ancient relics – rusty and rather rubbish. Quite as useless as her own very high-tech, though somewhat clunky, phone had been inside Parallelia.

'Feeling a bit unmagical all of a sudden, are we?' asked Frankie, walking back to stand over him. 'Welcome to my world.'

Haggister snarled. **'What . . . hmm . . . what wizardry is this?'** he said, humming a short snatch of his odd little tune again as he struggled to rise. He was, however, suddenly unable to move beneath the weight of the gigantic Breastplate of Fornax which, like the other Talismans, was now nothing more than a rusted and dinted piece of old metal.

'Oh, no wizardry in particular,' Frankie replied, holding up the phone clasped in her right hand, the screen already filled with messages and notifications. 'Just good old-fashioned cellular data. Though it probably looks pretty magical to you.'

Haggister was staring sullenly at the phone screen. A fraction of a second too late, Frankie saw his eyes dart to the right and an expression of sly triumph flickered across his face. She tensed herself to turn round, but before she could move she was grabbed firmly from behind. Out of the corner of her eye, she could see the end of the brightly polished dagger that was being held at her neck.

The crunching of running feet sounded from down the slope, and the rest of the fellowship came rushing up the passageway.

'Well, this feels odd,' Justice was saying to the others, sniffing the air. 'Where are we?' But she stopped in her tracks when she saw what was ahead of them, reaching out a hand to hold the others back, too.

Haggister lay on the tunnel floor, pinned down by the tarnished and dull breastplate. Just beyond him was Frankie, being held firmly by Slytely Good. The lank-haired, rat-faced little man was pressing his long dagger to her throat.

'Come no further!' he said menacingly. 'Or your leader here is going to meet with a very nasty little surprise.'

'DON'T YOU DARE HURT HER!' yelled Garyn furiously, struggling to get past Justice's arm.

'Oh, nobody needs to get hurt,' Slytely Good reassured him in an oily tone. 'Not if you do exactly as I say, that is. You're going to help me take Haggister here, and the armour, back to the Chamber of the Talisman. And then, who knows? I might just decide to become the all-powerful ruler myself.'

'YOU TREACHEROUS VILLAIN!' screamed Haggister furiously.

'Who did you think you were hiring, a dance teacher?' asked Good mockingly.

But it's never a good idea to break off from your evil plan for the purposes of sarcasm. It gives your opponent time to make their move, you see. And Frankie Best chose this moment to make hers. She decided to fight back with the only weapon she had to hand. A weapon she did, in fact, have literally *in* her hand at that exact moment.

Frankie brought her right hand, which was holding her phone, swinging sharply upward. And, for the first time ever, she was pleased that her phone was larger and clunkier than average. She'd complained to her mum and dad endlessly and pleaded with them to get her a newer, smaller, lighter model. But there in the underground passageway she was heartily glad they'd refused to let her upgrade, as the chunky black handset slammed into Slytely Good's sneering face, sending him reeling backwards, and his knife clattering harmlessly to the stone floor.

Garyn sprinted forward and dived on top of Good, kicking the dagger well out of reach as he did so. Justice stalked calmly up to Haggister and stood over him. 'As I was saying previously,' she said slowly and deliberately, 'I am a Justice of Parallelia. You have been detected as the source of an injustice. As such, you are required to make amends or face punishment. The Kingdom is the King.'

'The Kingdom is the King,' repeated the entire Fellowship of the Bacon Roll.

CHAPTER 18

THERE AND BACK AGAIN

I said right at the start this is not a story about some mystical quest through a magical land. Or about fantastical creatures, or elves, or witches, or any of that rubbish.

Well, all of that was kind of true. Because, although all of those things did crop up in the end, they weren't really what the tale was about. It was really about me and my brother. About my grandfather and his own daughter. And about some lessons I learned during a very, very strange journey.

Most of all, I remember mentioning right back at the beginning that it is not a story about a princess.

Ah. Yes. Well. That might not have been entirely true.

There's just time to tell you about it before we finish.

Frankie Best

Back in the Chamber of the Talisman beneath the volcano, the Fellowship of the Bacon Roll gathered together for one final time. Four of them were holding it together quite impressively, considering the emotional weight of the moment. Basin, however, was bawling uncontrollably.

'I never wants the adventure to end!' he wailed. 'I *likes* adventures!'

Justice tried to soothe him. 'Fear not,' she said. 'You and I are travelling back to Tygermere with the custodian and Celidon's Boots. There'll be plenty more adventuring before we get there, I guarantee it.'

'And, when we arrive, a huge feast to celebrate my

rescue,' promised Jon Topham, the Custodian of Tygermere, clapping a work-hardened hand on the little gnoblin's shoulder. Basin's eyes shone with excitement.

Princess Prince, who had just finished fastening the Breastplate of Fornax back on to the statue in the centre of the chamber, stepped forward. 'We'll be a bit more careful about who is granted access to this chamber in future,' she said grimly, nodding at the trussed-up Haggister, who had been dumped in one of the stone chairs. 'Getting too close to power can be a dangerous thing, it seems. And we must make sure we properly express our gratitude to you,' she told Frankie, 'fellow custodian.'

'Ah yes,' said the Custodian of Angel Woods. 'Still getting used to that, to be honest. Can we pick it up in a few weeks?'

'Of course,' the princess replied. 'You must be anxious to return Ilvatar's Helm to Angel Woods.'

'Yes, that,' said Frankie nervously. 'And also quite anxious to get Grandad home before Mum and Dad get back in a few hours' time.'

'Crikey!' exclaimed Grandad, who had been deep in conversation with Chief Alika on the other side of the chamber. 'You're right! We need to get back! She's going to be furious enough with me as it is when she discovers you stumbled into Parallelia. And –' he clutched his head in despair – 'that you're now one of the custodians. I'm going to need a cup of tea.'

'So, how do we get back?' Frankie asked Garyn. 'You're the guide.'

'I've been thinking about that,' he said excitedly. 'Just outside Tramont, if we skirt the northern shores of Lake Gah, we can reach the foothills that lead to the Lost Pass. There lives a most miraculous creature, the land sprinter. With its long legs, it can travel great distances without tiring. If we manage to capture and tame four land sprinters, we might just be able to cross the Central Plain, find our way across the Insurmountable Slodge and reach the portal in Angel Woods before your parents get back.'

'YEEE-E-E-EEEE-SSSSS,' she told the knelf. 'Or, alternatively, we could go through that portal over there, find a phone and call your mum, who can come and pick us up.'

'Oh yes.' He blushed slightly. 'I hadn't actually thought of that. Good plan.'

'I still don't understand much of your speech,' said Justice, frowning, 'but it sounds to me like this is the breaking of our fellowship.'

Frankie felt an unexpected sob fighting to escape and sternly ordered it to stay in captivity. Now she was Custodian of Angel Woods she felt she had to maintain a certain dignity. Joel, however, had tears running down his cheeks as he hugged Justice and then Basin.

'You'll come and visit, won't you?' he begged. 'Now you know where the portal is.'

'We've only got a few weeks left as Sentinels, but you should try to come and see my mum's shop if there's time,' Garyn told the little gnoblin. 'There's loads of interesting food for you to try there. You think that Bethcar pear was good – wait till you have a Twix!' Basin looked perplexed but fascinated.

'What will you do next?' Frankie asked Justice.

'Once we've returned the Talisman?' said the woman in grey. 'Keep on following my Moral Compass, of course. Who knows where it will lead me? Hopefully, away from too much soup,' she said, grimacing. 'And, I very much hope, back towards you some day soon.'

There seemed little more to say as the leader of the fellowship and her brave protector embraced.

'Our thanks, Frankie Firebrand,' said Chief Alika, approaching along with the Custodian of Bethcar. 'You will always be welcome on our islands.' Solemnly she removed a single silver feather from her braids and fastened it in Frankie's hair. The two custodians gave a long, low bow.

'Right – come on, then,' said Grandad finally. 'Or your mum really will have my guts for garters. Plus, nobody will have watered my marrows for the past I-don't-know-how long.'

• • •

Frankie, Joel, Grandad and Garyn ducked through the archway at the back of the cavern and travelled through the portal once more. Passing the place where Frankie had defeated both Haggister and Slytely Good, they carried on as the air got fresher and the stone underfoot rougher and less volcanic.

When they finally reached the very end and scrambled out of a narrow opening in the rock, there was no glowering volcano towering up behind them.

They had emerged at the back of a row of three low hills, nothing like the mountains of Parallelia. It seemed more like a pale echo of the land they had left behind, and Frankie felt a sudden undeniable pang of homesickness, a yearning to see Bethcar or the Dunelands again. She missed Justice and Basin already – and longed to be there when Edwir's mother came home to reveal he'd been right to trust them.

But there would be time for wistfulness later. For now, she had to put her wist on ice. They had a helmet to return. Half an hour down a grassy footpath led them to a small roadside pub, and Garyn disappeared inside to use the phone. Grandad brought cold drinks out and they settled down on a wooden picnic table to wait.

Frankie smiled at a chalkboard by the door advertising the soup of the day, imagining Justice and Basin beginning their long journey on foot. Somehow she was sure Justice wouldn't be dealing with many more petty cases of cheating at dice – not now she'd rescued the entire kingdom.

Considering how long it had taken them to travel across Parallelia, it seemed a surprisingly short amount of time until a rattling and clanking announced the arrival of Mrs Archer in a small and rather battered-looking car. She steered wildly into the pub car park, almost knocking over one of the gateposts in the process.

'Here you all are, here you all are,' she puffed, bustling over to them with the flaps of her woolly hat bobbing up and down. 'Oh, you've got fizzy drinks – how marvellous! Custodian! There you are! All rescued. How splendid!'

'Actually,' said Grandad, rising to his feet to formally welcome the knelf lady, 'I'm not the custodian any more.'

Mrs Archer gasped. 'The responsibility has been passed?' she said. 'When is the new custodian arriving? Who did the spirits choose?'

'She's arrived already,' Grandad replied. The knelf looked around in confusion, before noticing that everyone else was looking significantly at Frankie, who was blushing a little.

'It's you?' said Mrs Archer in surprise. 'You're taking over as custodian? Oh, that's wonderful! We'll just have time to show you the ropes before we leave.'

'Leave?' Frankie's happiness drained out of her like bathwater. She looked at Garyn questioningly.

'I told you on the first day, remember?' he said, looking regretful. 'Mum and I have almost served our five years as Sentinels. We'll go home to Artleknock in a few weeks' time. But don't worry.' He reached out and grabbed her hand. 'You remember where it is, right? Just down the hill? You can stop for a proper visit next time.'

There was a slightly awkward silence until Grandad broke it. 'Shall we talk more on the way?' he suggested. 'Only I really think it's a very sensible idea to get home before your mum and dad arrive back.'

Thanks to Mrs Archer's somewhat erratic driving style, however, that did not happen. When they pulled up outside Grandad's house, their parents' car was already there. Frankie and Joel's mum was in the front garden, peering through a window, having evidently been banging on the front door for some time.

'Dad!' she was shouting. 'Dad! Where are you? I knew we shouldn't have left them here. Any sign in the back garden?'

'Don't worry, Kate,' came a voice from the side of the house as Frankie's dad appeared.

At the noise of Mrs Archer's car grinding to a halt with the sound of tortured gears, both parents turned.

'There they are, you see,' said Dad, relief flooding his frame. 'Looks like they've been out for a nice . . . outing . . . somewhere . . .' He trailed off as the occupants of the car spilled out and approached.

Frankie and Joel were both filthy – smeared with mud and volcanic ash, wearing stained tunics and, in Joel's case, a tattered cloak. To complete the effect, Frankie was carrying a large silvery helmet. Behind them came Grandad, still in pyjamas, dressing gown and large black army boots. And on the other side of the car were two extremely peculiar characters in large knitted hats with ear flaps.

As Mum and Dad watched, Mrs Archer pulled off her hat and waved it cheerily, revealing her large pointed ears.

'*Oo-ooh!*' she trilled. 'You must be Mr and Mrs Best. If you're hungry after your trip, do pop over to the shop. I've got all the noodle flavours – there's a new spare rib one I'm dying to try!' She dried up slightly as Frankie and Joel's parents continued to glare at her and Grandad in complete fury. 'Well, I'll leave you to have a nice family catch-up, then,' she said awkwardly. 'Come on, Garyn.' Both knelves began to edge away towards the village green.

'See you later, then, Frankie,' said Garyn.

''K.' She made a face at him that meant *this is gonna be bad*.

He made one back that meant *don't worry, you're Frankie Firebrand, you've got this*.

'Thanks,' she replied quietly as Garyn and his mum finally shuffled out of sight behind a tree.

'Dad,' said their mum in a very strained voice, 'can we have a quick word in the house, do you think?'

'Lovely idea,' said Grandad, tugging nervously at the collar of his pyjama jacket. 'Let's go in and have a cup of tea, shall we? The key's under the gnome.'

It's incredibly awkward listening to somebody else's family arguments, so there's no need to give you the whole rundown of what was said in Grandad's hallway over the next hour. The argument started almost as soon as they got inside. Not immediately, because Joel insisted on stepping over the threshold several times and saying, 'Well, I'm back,' in different tones of voice until he was completely satisfied with his delivery. But, after that, their mum launched into what is probably best summarized as her 'you are a bad babysitter and also a bad father and grandfather for the following reasons' monologue.

'You know that place is dangerous, Dad!' She was still raging some forty minutes later. 'When I was growing up, you never had time to do anything with us because you were always catching some stupid creature or sorting out some problem in Parallelia! We swore to keep the kids away from all that!'

'Well, what if we didn't want to be kept away from it?' blurted Frankie, who'd been loitering near the kitchen doorway pretending not to listen. 'What if we might have wanted some wonder, and some adventure, and a little bit of magic? You certainly didn't mind pinching all the best stuff from Parallelia and putting it in your games, did you?'

'Oh, you spotted that, did you?' said her dad from behind her, his eyes shining. 'Which bits did you like the best? The Owl Forest or the . . .' He stopped talking and gave an embarrassed cough, noticing their mum looking at him furiously. 'I'll, erm, make another pot of tea,' he suggested meekly.

'We would have liked to visit Grandad more, you know,' Frankie said more gently. 'Even if you didn't want us getting involved with Parallelia. I think he's been pretty lonely.'

Abruptly, her mum sat down on the stairs, pressing a hand to her face.

'Listen, Mum,' Frankie said, sitting down beside her and squeezing her leg affectionately, 'I know you were trying to look out for us. You chose not to show us Parallelia, and I can understand that. But things just haven't worked out that way, OK? Parallelia ended up choosing *me*.'

'She was pretty amazing, actually, Mum,' said Joel quietly. 'I mean, she kind of saved the whole kingdom. She's, like, an actual hero and stuff.'

'I thought I was doing the right thing,' Mum said tearfully, 'but maybe I should have had a bit more faith in you both.' She blew her nose on a tissue and smiled up at them. 'Well, in all of you, actually,' she added, giving Grandad a meek smile.

'We'll tell you the whole story later, all right?' said Frankie. She held up the silver helmet, which she was still grasping firmly. 'But we've got a little job to do first. Joel, Grandad – shall we?'

• • •

At the very top of Angel Woods there is a tranquil glade in the forest. Five stone towers surround one of the resting places of the five Talismans of Parallelia. And one day, just as twilight was deepening from gold to a rich purple, the Custodian of Angel Woods came with her brother and her grandfather.

She was bearing Ilvatar's Helm, which she had rescued at the climax of a daring quest. And, as the others looked on, the custodian returned the silver helmet to the top of the warrior's statue.

'**Don't fall off!**' said Joel as Frankie teetered on tiptoe to place the helmet back in position.

'I just defeated a super-powerful baddie,' she retorted. 'Two of them, actually. I'm not going to end the tale by falling off a statue. There.'

Using the very tips of her fingers she pushed the helmet into position, and with a thin ringing sound it settled neatly into place. At once, there was a faint disturbance in the air. The trees surrounding the clearing sighed in a sudden warm wind. And, when Frankie Best hopped down from the plinth and rejoined her brother and grandfather, they turned to see a figure standing on the soft grass behind them. It was hazy and indistinct, almost like a trick of the early-evening light, but it took the vague shape of a tall, willowy woman.

'My thanks for returning the Talisman,' came a soft voice.

It was hard to tell where the sound came from – almost as if it was formed by the swishing of the trees and the wind in the grass.

'I chose my custodian well. And to you –' the figure seemed to turn to face Grandad – 'I offer my gratitude for your years of faithful service. There are other tasks ahead of you now.'

'Thanks, Ilvatar,' said Grandpa with a solemn bow.

'You're the spirit of light?' asked Joel excitedly. 'I have so many questions.'

'You have so many answers,' contradicted the spirit kindly. 'Your sister would not have completed her quest without her wise brother.'

Joel also bowed, flattered briefly into silence.

'And you, Custodian,' said Ilvatar, 'what did you learn?'

'Don't order the starfish soup,' shot back Frankie without thinking, and the leaves around the clearing shook gently in silvery laughter. 'But I also learned a load of other stuff.' She screwed up her face in thought. 'I suppose I learned – listen to your little brother, right? And choose friends who look out for you. And that help comes from the most unexpected places.'

Suddenly remembering the moment beneath the volcano when her phone had unexpectedly buzzed into life, she pulled the familiar shape from her pocket. The black screen, smashed during her attack on Slytely Good, reflected several different Frankies back at her in a collage of diamonds.

'And I guess I learned that I can choose which Frankie I want to be,' she said quietly, once again wondering what her school friends would make of all this and deciding, finally, that she didn't care.

When Frankie looked up, the figure of Ilvatar had gone. There was only the peaceful clearing, surrounded by the darkening trees and, here and there, the golden, glowing forms of the angel owls. Frankie Best sighed with satisfaction.

'This belongs to you now, I think,' said her grandfather from behind her. She turned to see that he had taken off his necklace with its metal star inside a circle – the symbol of the five Protections of Parallelia. She bent her head to allow the old man to fasten it around her neck. 'There,' he told her. 'There's lots more to tell you, but for now I think it's time to go home. Ready, Princess?'

She narrowed her eyes. 'Oy! I know it's been a week of Frankie rediscovery, but I still hate being called that, you know.'

'Well, you'd better get used to it, petal' the old man said, his face puckering up into a mischievous smile before he turned and began walking away towards the Mirror Door.

'What do you mean, Grandad?'

'Haven't you worked it out yet?' he asked her over his shoulder. 'Every five years, the ruler of Parallelia changes.'

'Oh!' Joel clapped a hand to his mouth in delight. 'I've just realized what's about to happen! Oh wow! This is the most brilliant and hilarious thing ever!'

'What?' Angel owls took flight in alarm as Frankie stamped her foot on the grass in frustration.

'Well, it's almost time for the leadership to move to Angel Woods, you see,' Grandad explained. 'The Forest Court will be convened right here. Ruled over, of course, by the new . . .'

'PRINCESS!' Joel was now rolling around on the grass, hooting with helpless laughter. 'You're going to be a princess! An actual . . . real-life . . . princess.'

Frankie Firebrand – Custodian of Angel Woods, leader of the Fellowship of the Bacon Roll and soon-to-be Princess of Parallelia – watched her brother with her hands planted on her hips as he thumped the ground with his fists in delight.

'YOU HAVE GOT,' said Frankie Best, **'TO BE ACTUALLY, FLIPPING WELL KIDDING ME.'**

THE END

Loved *Frankie Best Hates Quests*?

Of course you did! Then we strongly suggest you read *The Great Dream Robbery* – a hilarious, mind-bending adventure you won't want to wake up from!

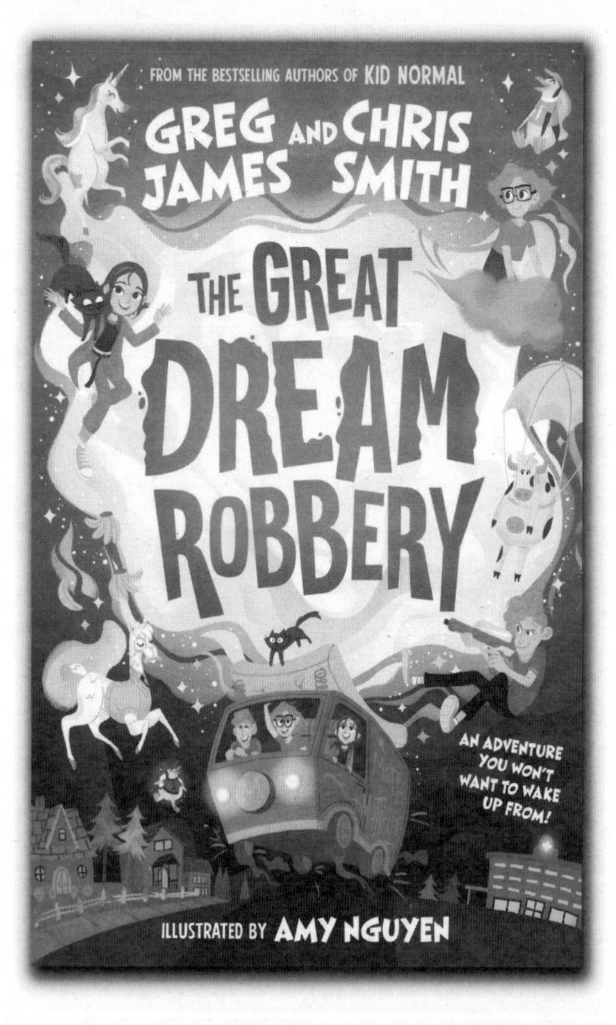

It's quiz time! Which *Frankie Best Hates Quests* character are you?

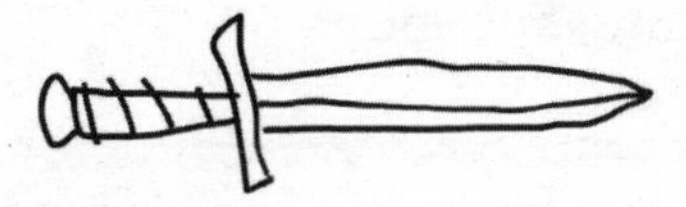

What's your ideal way to spend a Saturday?

A) On your phone catching up with friends and surfing the web

B) Playing Spingle's Quest

C) Stealing an artefact of great power

D) Chasing magical creatures up trees

E) Hunting down criminals

What is your favourite food?

A) Bacon rolls

B) Mumbai Madman snack pots

C) No time for food – too busy devising evil plans

D) Bethcar pears

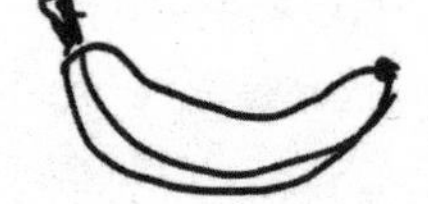

E) Anything but soup

If you were stranded on a desert island, what one luxury item would you take with you?

A) WiFi

B) Dusty old book of magical creatures

C) Ancient helmet

D) Woolly hat

E) Compass

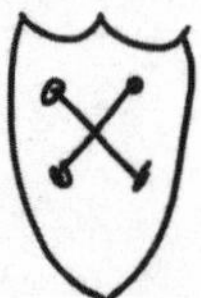

What would you say is your greatest strength?

A) Leadership (and rescuing grandads from certain doom)

B) Knowledge

C) Cunning

D) Friendship

E) Courage (unless faced with another bowl of starfish soup)

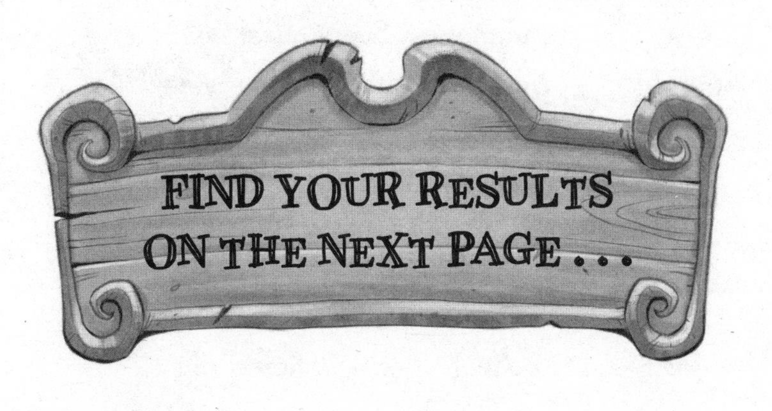

Mostly As: You're Frankie Best – A hero and great leader (when you can stay away from your phone).

Mostly Bs: You're Joel Best – An intrepid explorer, you love all things fantasy and are extremely useful in a quest situation.

Mostly Cs: You're Haggister – You're evil and cunning, you're obsessed with power and money! Every quest needs a villain and that's you!

Mostly Ds: You're Garyn – A loyal and kind friend with a never-ending supply of snack noodle pots and woolly hats.

Mostly Es: You're Justice – A fierce and honourable warrior, you are always on-hand to protect others. You also really really hate soup.

ACKNOWLEDGEMENTS

A huge THANK YOU VERY MUCH to the following:

All the writers and artists who inspired parts of Parallelia: Ursula K. Le Guin; Cressida Cowell; David and Leigh Eddings; Christopher Vogler; Tove Jansson; Jim Henson; Brian and Wendy Froud; S. Morgenstern; Shigeru Miyamoto; Steve Jackson and Ian Livingstone; Greg Follis and Roy Carter; Wil Huygen and Rien Poortvliet; the team behind the splendid Reader's Digest tome *Folklore Myths and Legends of Britain*; George R.R. Martin; C.S. Lewis – what is it with fantasy authors and initials? – and John Ronald Reuel *actual* Tolkien.

Stephanie Thwaites, (chaotic good) for being a level-twelve agent, archmage and all-round sorceress.

Editor extraordinaire Carmen McCullough – from me and Mrs Mumpish, the starfish soup is on the house next time you're at the Wandering Walrus.

Everyone at Puffin who's been so enthusiastic and kind about Frankie – especially copy-editing ninja Jane, wizard proofreader Pippa, PR paladins Chloe and James, and viking heroes Jan and Anita, who designed the book – it looks awesome, doesn't it?

Kenneth, for your mind-meltingly good illustrations – thanks for bringing Parallelia to life.

Jenny, who read the very first draft of what was then called *The Door to Parallelia* and thought of its new title. Thanks also to you and Lucas for letting me go and nerd out in a treehouse, and to West Lexham for building said-treehouse.

And finally, to all my teachers – especially Mrs Lawman, who gave me the entry form for a story competition and said, 'This is for you', and Mr Cotter who read us *The Hobbit*.